WEEKEND IN WOOLWICH

First published 2019

Copyright © L Anne Russell 2019

The right of L Anne Russell to be identified as the author of this work has been asserted in accordance with the Copyright, Designs & Patents Act 1988.

All rights reserved. No part of this book may be reproduced, stored in a retrieval system, or transmitted in any form or by any means, electronic, electrostatic, magnetic tape, mechanical, photocopying, recording or otherwise, without the written permission of the copyright holder.

This is a work of fiction. Names, characters, businesses, places, events and incidents are either the products of the author's imagination or used in a fictitious manner. Any resemblance to actual persons, living or dead, or actual events is purely coincidental and unintended.

Published under licence by Brown Dog Books and
The Self-Publishing Partnership, 7 Green Park Station, Bath BA1 1JB

www.selfpublishingpartnership.co.uk

ISBN printed book: 978-1-83952-032-7

Cover design by Andrew Prescott
Internal design by Andrew Easton

Printed and bound by CPI Group (UK) Ltd, Croydon, CR0 4YY

This book is printed on FSC certified paper

WEEKEND IN WOOLWICH

L ANNE RUSSELL

Covent Garden & Bath
1986–1992

I would like to especially thank two important individuals who have always been enthusiastic about my literary endeavours: Sister Teresa, Handsome Tom.

And Bruno... you may even enjoy this!

I would also like to thank the team at Self-Publishing Partnership for making my vision a reality, in particular: Douglas Walker, Frances Prior-Reeves, Andrew Prescott and Andrew Easton.

PART I

THE THERAPIST

HATFIELD

DECEMBER 1986–APRIL 1989

'There is nothing like the tyranny of a good English family'
Florence Nightingale

FRIDAY 5 DECEMBER 1986

On the day I thought that I would kill myself, I went to The Doctor. 'You've got to help me,' I said. 'I don't know what to do; I feel pretty stupid being here in the first place. It's not that I'm unintelligent or anything – I mean, why the hell can't I sort it out myself?'

She raised her eyebrows.

'I've put off coming to see you.'

'Yes?'

'I think I need to see a psychiatrist.'

'Do you need one?' she asked, with a look of surprised disbelief.

'Yes. I wouldn't have come otherwise. I've hit rock-bottom. I feel overwhelmed, worthless, inadequate. I can't explain why – I don't understand. Why should I feel like this? Things are going well; I'm happily married; I live a calm and ordered life – my studies are fine. Yet I feel complete despair.'

'How long have you felt like this?'

'I'm not sure – a couple of years, perhaps. I've felt worse recently, but don't know why that should be.'

'It might be a long wait before you can get treatment – months, a year even – even if you have private means.'

'A year?' I gasped.

'I can get you in quicker privately,' she said.

'Impossible. James wouldn't countenance that. He thinks that I'm potty anyway.'

'But you're married! Surely he could give you some support?'

'I try to live on my grant; I don't like to ask him for anything.' She started to shuffle her papers. 'It's going to be difficult.'

'But can I see someone?' I persisted. 'Anyone?'

'I'll have to say that you're a special case. Let me see ... first you will need to go to The Clinic for an assessment. They're very thorough about it; it's like an extended interview ... it can take two hours. Before they even agree to see you, you will have to fill in a long form. They will ask you all sorts of things: family relationships, present feelings, personal issues, what you think the problem is. You will need to complete it as honestly as you can. You might find it distressing; some people give up then, but if you can do it, you will probably be strong enough to cope with the treatment.'

'Strong enough?' I asked, 'I thought that they were supposed to help me. OK, I'll have to do it.'

'I'll write to The Clinic,' she replied. 'You should hear from them in a day or two.'

*

MONDAY 19 JANUARY 1987

I had asked for a male therapist, and so was surprised to meet a soberly dressed woman, not many years my senior. Her tiny, fourth-floor room was cheerless, painted a cold pale green, a permanently open window taking up one wall. There was a couch on the left, at its foot a bookcase with a trailing plant; over it a clip-framed photo of an amiable-looking old gent with a couple of chows. George Bernard Shaw, perhaps? At its head, her chair and desk. The only other decoration was a poster from the Picasso Museum. They've allocated her because of her artistic leanings, I concluded.

My first emotion on seeing her neutral expression was one of innate superiority. Who the hell did she think she was? After all, apart from feeling worthless now and again, things are pretty good. I'm married ... happily married ... to a handsome man. My work is going well; I'll get my PhD in a couple of years. I've lost loads of weight; I've got some lovely, colourful clothes: flowing skirts, layers of petticoats, Victorian blouses, glittery shawls. And her? *Her?* Fatter than me (I noted with satisfaction), no make-up, sensible shoes, all black outfit. I piqued myself on the figure I thought I cut: people often take me for an artist ... that's not so surprising. At least I have a nice expression; I smile. She doesn't even have a friendly face, a right old sourpuss. Not that it's hostile; more studied, blank....

'Hello,' she said, unsmilingly, as she drew back a chair. 'We won't begin our work today.'

What a swizz, I thought angrily. After all this time? Next week might be too late. And I thought that therapists were supposed to be caring; this seems pretty lax to me. Fancy calling it 'work'! How coy can you get?

'We just need to sort out how we'll conduct things. How do you feel about using the couch?'

'Ambivalent. How should I know? I have never tried it before, but I don't see why we can't sit around a table like civilised human beings,' I replied, a contemptuous note in my voice. 'It's all very well for you, but down there I won't be able to see your expressions.'

'Right!' she exclaimed. 'Eventually you will see why. I think we should try it. Two sessions a week – Tuesday and Thursday. We'll start a week on Tuesday.'

*

TUESDAY 27 JANUARY

I arrived twenty minutes early and went to the ground-floor waiting room – another bleak den – where I peered furtively at the other 'patients'. The young woman wailing into her handkerchief ... well it was clear why she was there, though if she repaired her make-up and combed her hair you might not think anything amiss. But the relentlessly cheerful young man, sitting between two older people? His parents perhaps ... two old friends? Why should he bring them with him? What will they do to him in there? Will he be in such a dreadful state thereafter? Is he 'Before' and she 'After'? Christ! I'm not looking forward to this. The Receptionist called out my name. I knocked at The Therapist's door. A calm voice: 'Come in.'

I had taken particular care with my clothes that day, though for all the notice she took, I felt that I shouldn't have bothered. I felt deflated.

'Good morning,' she said, her voice flat and face expressionless.

'Good morning.'

I took my shoes off, stretched out on the couch and waited. Several minutes passed. Silence. I stared at the photo of the benevolent gent, at the Picasso poster, at the titles of the volumes in the bookcase: Freud and Jung; some feminist tracts, and two imposters, The Pre-Raphaelite Tragedy and Wide Sargasso Sea.

When I realised that she wasn't going to make the first move, I remarked:

'Yes ... very funny! What are you playing at? What's going on? Is this a game, a ploy of some sort?'

No reply.

'You can hear me! What are you doing? You said that you would treat me – you said that we would work together. I thought that you would ask me about my background; we would talk about my past ... there'd be gentle questions – that sort of thing – and in talking whatever is bothering me would go away ... simply dissolve. I would feel cheerful again. I'd rather have unpleasant questions than this silence. What the hell do I do? I thought it would be like everyone's idea of therapy ... Richard Burton in Equus.'

And I started to laugh. Very clever, I thought. Very witty.

'But this? Why?' Then I had an idea: 'You're trying to humiliate me. You're pushing me to see how far I will go.'

At last she said:

'What is happening now is just as important as what has happened before. I can see that this stirs up feelings of anger. There's a suggestion that you think I'm not doing my job; I'm neglectful, unhelpful. An unkind, uncaring therapist.

Inadequate even. Yes?'

'No! No!' I interrupted. 'I'm sorry. I must have sounded terribly rude; that's not at all what I meant, but what do you expect? What's the form here? What do you want me to do?'

'Why should you do anything? Just be here, the rest is up to you. Here you please yourself. I'm not your keeper.'

'But if I don't do anything, I can't see how I will feel better. At least I should ask intelligent questions!'

'Aha! So you associate performance with reward.'

'Yes, I have felt like that for as long as I can remember.' And then we were properly off.

'When I was a little girl, no more than five or six years old, I had to earn my pocket money by dusting my parents' antiques. I did it a damned sight more thoroughly than my mother, and it took ages ... the house was stuffed with indescribable junk. All this rubbish piled up on every surface. My father would do a tour of inspection and run his finger over the most inaccessible spaces. He always brought it out triumphantly, covered in dust, and I didn't get my full quota because – he said – "I hadn't done it well enough". I had to help with the washing-up. My brother Mark never did a thing but he always got his pocket money. It was unfair, but I never got a real answer. My father would stare at me superciliously; my mother would retreat to the kitchen. If I asked my Grandma N – she was Czechoslovakian, with a Yorkshire accent; can you imagine? – she'd say: "But dahling, eet's becos hee's un boy". "So what?" I'd think, and I'd point out that he was three years younger than me. Well, that never got me anywhere; they just ignored me.

'I disliked Sundays: that was when the grandmas came. Mark and I would escape to the garage roof; a flat roof over the garage my father had made into a sunroof. We were often compelled to "bask in the sun" there, as my parents did. They loved it – I hated it. It was too hot, too boring; they hadn't heard of sunglasses or of suncream ... it was too bright to read; I always got burnt. Sorry,' I said. 'I'm digressing....

'Anyway on Sundays we'd go there to spy on the grandmas as they walked down Scutari Road. Grandma M was always the first; we could spot her a mile off, before we could see her properly. She was tall – bolt-upright posture – and would stride along confidently. We'd lob crab apples at her and duck below the parapet before she noticed us. We aimed short and missed. Grandma N would come waddling down twenty minutes later, dressed décolleté in yards of flowery finery. Even then I thought it unsuitable for someone of her age and dimensions. She wore clumsy platform shoes which made her look ludicrously off-balance. We used to shout out names in silly voices. She always spotted us.

'After we'd had lunch – everyone being excruciatingly polite through clenched teeth: "Would you be so kind as to pass ..." "Can I trouble you for..." "Not at all! Thank *you*, Mrs M", "No, *thank you*, Mrs N", "Might I venture" and so on – I had to put on some sort of entertainment, a demonstration of singing and dancing: "what I'd learned at class". I'd dress up in my mother's version of a beautiful dress: a vile, sugar-coloured, scratchy nylon/lace confection which made me, a plump child, look even plumper. I detested the whole charade; the clothes were bad enough, but singing was a private thing for me. I could sing in a choir, but not on my own. I was no soloist – I didn't have the voice. I thought I was a laughing stock.

'I felt exploited – I thought that they were treating me like a performing dog. Their rules were no performance, no reward; they implied that, because I was otherwise pretty useless, it was the least I could do ... I had to pay for my keep after all.'

'So that was humiliating?' she observed.

'Yes. I don't think you put it too strongly. If they had allowed me to choose my own dress, and do a reading rather than sing, it wouldn't have been so bad, but my overriding feeling was that it wasn't fair. My brother didn't have to do it, so why should I?'

'How old were you when he was born?'

'Three.'

'And before that, what sort of relationship did you have with your mother?'

'You know, I never thought about it much until I had to fill in that damned form! I suppose that it was good, though she did go on and on about my arrival: the dreadful nursing home, the difficult birth; the fact that she couldn't breastfeed, how "crabby" I was; on the other hand she claimed that something special had happened when I was born. But then there was a nasty story about how – at the nursing home, on reaching for her writing paper – she put her hand on a massive cockroach. When she told me that Mark's birth was easy, trouble-free, "a hoot", I began to feel like that cockroach.

'Before Mark appeared we seemed always to be having fun: going on trips to Leeds, having lunch in a big department store, going to the pictures, to the hairdresser's. Afterwards, all that stopped; it was the end of life as I knew it. Once I asked her: "Can't we leave it in its pram and go to Leeds?" I was furious when she wouldn't ... I couldn't see what pleasure it brought her.

'I am sure that I wasn't supposed to know about the pregnancy or the birth. I can't remember my parents preparing me for it. I noticed that she was short-tempered, and seemed to be getting fatter and fatter. I put it down to overeating ... She was always gobbling odd foods and being sick. It seemed stupid to me. Why bother? One day I was sent to Grandma N's. She told me that when I got home my little sister Angela would be there. How did she know? I asked her. Where was she coming from? "From under un gooseberry bush, un prezent from ze stork," she said. I thought that she'd gone gaga.

'When I went home, instead of the beautiful, blonde, be-ringleted little sister I had imagined, there was an ugly, bald, red, wrinkled, squalling monster. It must be said that Mark wasn't prepossessing. Later he got nappy rash; my mother was always powdering his bum.'

'What else did you notice?'

'What do you mean?'

'Well, you'd hoped for a sister,' The Therapist remarked, 'and you got a brother. You watched your mother changing his nappy. Surely you noticed he'd got a different sort of bum?'

'Of course I did,' I replied, laughing, a note of exasperation in my voice. 'Are you trying to pin some sort of Freudian complex on me? I just thought it looked funny; my parents were the ones who said that it was *rude!*'

'Your 50 minutes are up,' she announced.

'But we've only just got going!' I protested. 'And you're going to chuck me out?'

'It's not quite like that,' she laughed, 'but your time's up!'

Fuck it! I thought, I don't care. I'm going skiing next week, and won't be back for a while. But I smiled politely, put on my shoes and left.

*

TUESDAY 24 FEBRUARY

I went into the room smiling. Again her face was blank, impenetrable, and she was still wearing her black outfit. Of course! I thought. Colourful clothes upset hysterics! She thinks I'm a nutter.... Well, she's got another thing coming. I'm sane, horribly sane....

'You know,' I volunteered, 'there's a huge difference in the family photos before and after Mark's birth. Before, I smiled all the time – photos of me dressed like a Mabel Lucie Attwell child: chuckling, wheeling along one of those pipe-cleaner-leg dogs, laughing on Morecambe Pier. All the photos afterwards are grim, unsmiling. There's one of the family on Scarborough Beach. We're carefully grouped, but not touching: my mother looking anxious, my father cross, my brother squinting, me woebegone. There's another: Mark and me on a fairground horse, faces close together, showing our teeth, but we both look angry. He was a little bastard!'

'When did your father die?' she asked.

'Eight years ago, I think. Boxing Day 1978. I hated him; I thought that he was an ogre, a wicked old troll. He was always playing nasty tricks: jumping out from darkened doorways and frightening us. *He terrorised us*! I was so scared of him that if I woke up at night, I daren't go to the bathroom. He was a light sleeper and left his bedroom door open, you see, so if I switched on the landing light, he'd wake up and come storming out. If I crept across in the dark, he'd wake up anyway and ambush me. I couldn't help waking him; he went to bed so damned early. Abnormally early.'

'What time?'

'About nine. No wonder he was so bloody tired; he carried that massive bulk about all day.... Still, I suppose it's difficult to love someone who was always hitting you – who swore and threatened you constantly. When he died, my first thought was: "the Old Bastard's gone at last", but I also remembered that he was my father. If I had been the good and dutiful daughter, I would have cared about him. Wasn't it my fault? If I'd tried harder he might have cared for me. I might have been worth it. Perhaps it really was my fault? I wasn't good enough, useful enough; I wasn't slim or pretty; I wasn't as clever as my brother ... or so they said.

'I never wanted to think that I'd been born of them. It was such a disgusting thought. Our Headmaster's nickname was Ben; we called his wife – who was indescribably ugly – "Ben Hur".... ha-ha-ha! We used to go around saying that Paul, their son, had been created, not born. That was how I felt about my parents; I wanted to think that I'd sprung from the ground, like a goddess!' I laughed at the imagery, thinking, how clever I am! *And how conceited!*

'At the time I heard of Pater's death, I was living in a 1930s flat in Leeds, with Number One – my first husband. One morning he sprang out of bed at 5.15. A very odd thing for him to do; I was still asleep.... I realised that the phone had been ringing. He sat on the bed, put his arm around me, and said that he was dreadfully sorry, it was bad news; my mother had rung; my father had died suddenly – a massive heart attack. The hospital couldn't have saved him. He seemed to expect me to cry, but instead I stared at him stupidly.

'The funeral was at Dewsbury Parish Church. Somehow that was ironic; my parents were married there, and all those "good friends" who had never seen them since turned up. My mother asked the vicar to stay in the church with Grandma N – who couldn't walk very well – while the coffin was carried to the grave. She wouldn't stay behind, of course, so there was a scene while they found a wheelchair, and she was half-pushed, half-carried there by four strong men, lamenting, making dramatic gestures; my mother meanwhile making snide comments.'

I started to cry:

'But I felt so damned guilty; guilty that I wasn't sorry, that I didn't cry, that I couldn't do what any decent daughter would do; that I didn't do what was expected. I suspect that if my mother had been honest she would have left him long ago, but she always protested that she loved him. I couldn't believe that.'

'What made you think she didn't?'

'I know that you can't see into other people's relationships – they're so much more complicated than they appear – but the outer signs weren't good. They had spectacular shouting matches; it was like living on the edge of a volcano – being on a knife-edge. You never knew who or what would blow up next. She seemed bored, frustrated, resentful at having had children.

'She used to talk of the distastefulness of childbearing, how revolting it all was, how she felt like a "milch cow", how she deserved greater things. Picture of a happy family at breakfast: all of us sitting at the breakfast table; Mark and I ready for school, Pater in his suit and Totectors, ready for work – he was a glass engineer, you see; heavy things were often dropped in the mould shop – my mother perched on a stool in her dressing gown with a Mississippi on her head.'

'*A what?*' The Therapist interrupted.

'Oh, I said absently, 'a bit of rag wound into a turban. I suppose that she thought she looked like a Hollywood starlet. And she had some nasty habits! One that I particularly detested was the way she poured her tea into the saucer, and slurped at it, tipping it everywhere. She was in a hurry, she said, too busy to drink it out of the cup. It never saved time *and* it looked disgusting!

'My parents used to argue about "what marriage really meant". My father: "You don't bark yourself if you've got a dog to do it for you ... you don't run after a bus once you've caught it", and my mother litanising about the work, the drudgery, the cooking, the scrutting, and for what? For so little reward ... *for nothing...!*'

'Scrutting?'

'I'm sorry,' I said. 'I think that Mark and I invented that word. It means "general household tasks", "all the things a woman revels in": scrubbing, cleaning, washing up, dusting.'

'You sound contemptuous. Is it a derogatory word?'

'Oh yes,' I laughed. 'A "scrutting woman" is someone *really thick*, who scruts because that's all she is capable of doing. A "scrutter" is always female, but I wish that weren't the case.'

She laughed: 'We'll have to leave it there.'

*

THURSDAY 26 FEBRUARY

I walked in, said 'Hi!' and stretched out on the couch. 'I hated their fucking antiques!' I shouted. 'No wonder the young Soanes turned against their father. I detested their complaints, their professed penury, their greed and acquisitiveness. They couldn't do this, they couldn't do that, yet they ran an R Type Bentley which guzzled petrol at the rate of eleven miles to the bloody gallon! Every week they did the round of antique shops: Halifax, York, Hebden Bridge, so that they could buy more and more objects.

'I was fed up with it and reasoned to myself: "If they've got no money, why do they keep buying things? Why the greedy grabbing? Why not stay in, read, talk, communicate ... why not do something to improve their minds? But if they've got to go on buying, stop complaining. They can't have their cake and eat it."

'They worshipped that car: my mother pretending to be the Lady Mayoress, lapping up the status it conferred; my father lavishing care and attention on it, caressing the bonnet with his chamois leather. I once said to him: "You care more about that bloody heap of metal than you do about me," and do you know what he said? "Yes, I do. It's nicer-looking, a lot less trouble and it's cheaper to run. And don't bloody swear!" That really hurt.'

The Therapist made no comment.

'For Christ's sake, say something!' I shouted. I looked at the ceiling, the photo of George Bernard Shaw, the Picasso poster. Then I realised: How stupid of me! It's Freud; it's got nothing to do with Shaw! I examined my hands, counted my rings: nine plain silver bands.

'My mother even copied my rings,' I said, 'except that she wore vulgar great nuggets – horrible bulbous things – two or three to each finger. She might have tried something plain and tasteful. But she wouldn't have known anything about that.... She wouldn't let me choose my own clothes ... at school I wanted to be the Flowerperson, the mod, the trendsetter; I dreamed about little shirtwaisters with military buttons, bloomer dresses, floaty Indian kaftans; she insisted that I wear "pretty" nylon confections. When I went to the first grammar school dance in one of those ones, I felt foolish, babyish.

'Even now, twenty-five years on – she tries to foist her choice on me: "I saw something lovely, dear, the other day, and it'd look good on you." I groan inwardly. "A designer number." "I don't like designer numbers." "It was a skirt and top" – ignoring me – "the skirt in tiers; long and flowing." "I've just chucked out all my long skirts! I took a bag down to Oxfam because they conjured up visions of suburbia." "It was yellow and black." I try to end the debate: "Thank you, it's a nice thought, but I don't like to wear yellow and I detest yellow and black together. They're not my colours. Sorry but I'd rather you didn't choose my things." Sometimes I'd try to be more gentle; I'd say: "Remember Brighton? We looked at clothes and you were surprised that I could tell immediately if they were not for me. With things you liked, the proportions were wrong. If I don't like something, I won't wear it! It goes straight to Oxfam."

'But, again, that's grounds for guilt. I suppose that she is trying to prove her affection: "spending money means she cares more". It isn't necessary. I remember when I was studying for my first degree – in Manchester – she came over for one of her long weekends: Thursday to Tuesday. A great commotion on the stairs when she arrived; she came up banging some overstuffed plastic bags against each step. She handed them over: "For you, dear." Inside, some awful rubbish: clothes in nasty fabrics, nasty colours, big sizes; glitzy designer jewellery, the sort of stuff which she loves and I hate. But the least significant item – in her eyes – would usually be the best. Once, at the bottom of a bag an envelope containing two tiny gold charms: masks of Tragedy and Comedy. I've worn them in my left ear ever since.

'I'm thinking of what I said about the Old Man's Bentley. My parents were interested in "one-upmanship". Scutari Road: private, gas-lit, unmade for years and years, was a leafy cul-de-sac; they were one of the first couples to buy a plot and start building. It was immediately after the war and they couldn't easily get hold of wood and other materials, but their house was the biggest with an enormous garden. An enviable achievement, I suppose, for a smart young couple who had a car, a fridge, a telephone, all the trappings of success. Oh, and two status symbols – Mark and me.

'I started speaking early – I could read before I went to school, but I resented my mother broadcasting it up and down the street. She would tell everyone – and at great length – about how, when I was less than a year old, I'd recite nursery rhymes and fairy tales, word-perfect. At the junior school, though, the Headmistress said Anna is clever, but Mark is a genius. Not that she knew anything about it. I started off in the top form at the grammar school and was top in everything except Maths and Latin for which I got deplorably low grades. My parents went around trumpeting my achievements, but at home there were great scenes: "Just what had gone wrong? Why couldn't I work – really work – and pull my socks up? If I was so good at everything else, then I was just being lazy", and so on, and so on.

'The truth was that I had no aptitude for those subjects and didn't enjoy them; I would have never excelled there. Anyway, every night after my two hours' homework, my father insisted on a further two hours of "private tuition". I came to dread those lessons because all of his horrible traits – his bullying, his lack of sympathy – came out in them. The following year, my grades were worse; from being top in almost everything, I dropped dramatically to bottom in all except art. My conduct report was little short of scandalous.'

WEEKEND IN WOOLWICH

'What happened?' asked The Therapist.

'I don't know. I'm not sure. I didn't catch up again until the sixth form, but my A level grades could have been better if I hadn't spent so much time thinking about Stephan ... but that's another story....

'My feeling is that after I'd done so well in the first year, instead of getting the encouragement and praise I hoped for, I got a lot of criticism: "You're capable of doing better, coming top in nearly everything isn't good enough ... no, worse! It's failure. It shames us, but then you're good at disappointing people; you *like* letting us down". It wasn't like that, but I lost the will to work; I gave up.

'I sat over my homework dutifully, but most of the time I was dreaming about Stephan or what I would do if Eric Burdon or P J Proby sprang up from the pavement. I'd chew my pencil and stare into space. Suddenly I discovered it was easy and great fun to be "The Form Joker". I became popular with a large group of followers and acolytes; I could be relied on to carry out big dares. From being an outsider, I was suddenly accepted, and that felt nice, reassuring....'

'Surely,' The Therapist observed, 'it was a very effective way of punishing your parents?'

I laughed: 'It certainly put a stop to their bragging. After that there were one or two red faces and they were quieter; that was funny. It served them right, but at the same time I was stupid because I should have realised that I was working for myself, my own qualifications; I was letting myself down.'

'That's it,' said The Therapist. 'See you on Tuesday.'

TUESDAY 3 MARCH

I remarked: 'My mother had no right to read my diary. Some of the things I'd etched into the cover like "I love Wayne Fontana" or "Crispian St Peters *is* SEX!" were innocuous enough, but I objected to her prying on my thoughts and quoting them at me. I thought that she derived a prurient and salacious thrill from them. Do you think that's literary voyeurism? Occasionally, just to inflame her, I'd write something *really sensational:* "Spent the afternoon locked in Stephan's arms, had it again and again – now *I really am* a woman". It was untrue, of course, but I enjoyed writing it. It was worth it to see that look on her face ... I didn't tell you about Stephan ...'

To my embarrassment, I started crying.

She ignored me – or so it seemed – and I struggled to regain my composure.

'Sorry,' I said. 'I had no idea that that would happen.'

'You're talking about things that happened twenty-odd years ago.'

'Yes, but I thought that I had forgotten it.'

'Tell me about it.'

'It's a long story. One day when I was about sixteen, I looked out of my bedroom window. I had a big room at the front of the house with a large bay window overlooking the street. I noticed that new people had moved into the bungalow opposite. Their son was in the garden: tall, thin, blond hair, and

– best of all, I thought – a Union Jack T-shirt. I invited myself to tea and made it clear that I intended to go to a concert – Free and Deep Purple – at St George's Hall, Bradford. Very daring, considering that I had never been to a concert of any sort in my life.... I casually hinted that if he wanted a ticket, I would get him one. My parents agreed to allow me out and it was a great, great evening.

'Stephan – a few years older than me – picked me up and drove me there. I was overwhelmed – knocked out – by the sensational building ... I was amazed to find that people raved around the balconies while the band was on. It was a physical experience; we were bombarded by sound.

'I saw him again several times. One night as we were driving back from friends, he parked the car some distance from our road, turned to me and said: "We've got a problem." I didn't know what he meant. "The clutch?" I asked, jokingly. "The steering wheel? The fact that we're in the front seat?" "No," he sighed. "More serious ... much more serious." He broke off and thought for a few moments: "My parents don't want me to see you. They want us to finish." "Christ!" I thought, but I said: "Why?" "They say that you will distract me from my studies ... Anyway, my mother is ill." "That's a pretty wild thing to say. They might find that – contrary to expectations – that I might help you; our interests are similar. I'm sorry about your mother, but I don't see what that's got to do with it." I stopped and took a deep breath: "But how do you feel?" "I want to see you." "Then we must continue to meet. It's our life, not theirs. Perhaps we should try to discuss it with them?" But something in his expression made me think that wasn't the whole story. "Is anything else bothering you?" I blurted out. "I need to know." "They don't like your appearance," he said.

'I should explain,' I remarked – remembering The Therapist – 'that at that time I would sweep down Scutari Road in floor-length Edwardian skirts and black velvet opera cloaks. I wore inch-long multicoloured false eyelashes and "twiggies" daubed under my eyes in thick, black eyeliner. I thought that I looked gorgeous; my father said that I looked like a whore. He had a point; in photos of the time I'm so plastered with make-up that I look as though I'm wearing shades. Pretty startling at the lowest estimate! I protested to Stephan that his parents based their judgement on my appearance alone; let me speak to them – I might win them over. He agreed that they were being unfair; as for a meeting, he'd think about it. Thisbe's mysterious illness was, he said, epilepsy. As far as I could see she (literally) threw a fit whenever there was a danger that she might not get her own way. I thought her hysterical, manipulative.

'During my A levels, I met Stephan secretly. He'd drive up the road and around the corner; I would take a shortcut via the garden of a sympathetic neighbour, and meet him on the backstreet. But I hated that. Why should I hide? Later, I decided to get a job in Leeds rather than go to university.

'He was living in Leeds, you see, and had just started his second year at Leeds Poly. I managed to get an interview at The Yorkshire Post. It was a lovely day, and I felt so adult, so glamorous.... Stephan drove me there; I was offered the job immediately. We celebrated over lunch and I met his friends, who to my eyes seemed very mature and erudite. He had recently moved from his parents' and shared "156", a huge, damp, ramshackle Edwardian terraced house, with three others. 156 acquired quite a reputation and at one time, if you mentioned that number to anyone in Leeds, they knew exactly what you were referring to. When I first saw it, I exclaimed, "No one can possibly live here!" It was a mess, the street was rough. Stephan commandeered the best room and immediately set to, removing the layers of yellowing wallpaper, the pitted lino, installing a new carpet. He hung his pictures, arranged his books – alphabetically by author, of course! It was palatial; everyone else's room a doss-house by comparison. But again, I'm going off the point....

'When I started work I was determined to move to the city. I didn't know Leeds at all, and had no idea where to start looking – which areas were civilised and which weren't – so I went to an accommodation agency. They found me a garret in Roundhay; an odd place full of meticulously typed notices tacked with four drawing pins in prominent positions: "ABSOLUTELY *NO overnight visitors*", "No visitors *at all* after 11pm", "Baths between 5 and 6pm *only*" – which meant that, given work, it was difficult to have a bath at all.

'What a dump! It was depressing; my room had the vilest yellow rose-trellis wallpaper, but at least it was mine. I started to surreptitiously move my favourite objects from my parents': whenever I met Stephen I smuggled out one or two items which we deposited at his place. One day I was nonchalantly walking down Scutari Road with a bust of Richard Cobden under my arm. It was Parian porcelain and I had kept it because it looked like Stephan, right down to the long sideburns.

'Thisbe spotted me through her Venetian blinds – she had horrible little gimlet eyes – gave chase in her car, and cornered me. She forced me to admit that I was still seeing him, and insisted I get into her car. So, I got in and went back for the big meeting.'

'And where was Stephan?'

'He'd driven off.'

'He left you to face them alone?'

'Yes. At the time I felt that that was perfectly reasonable. Of course, the meeting was a disaster; Thisbe and Henry both at me, ranting that I'd never be any good, I'd drag Stephan down, ruin his life, make impossible demands; besides, why did I have to dress like that?'

'And what did you say?'

'I defended myself vociferously.'

She chuckled.

'Well, I wasn't going to take that lying down. I argued that, contrary to their assumptions, I might be the vital stimulus for ideas, thoughts and imagination. We had a similar taste in books, literature, film; we were never short of things to talk about. My appearance might be alarming to their eyes, but I might be "good for him". Anyway, why should it matter? It was my right to dress as I pleased. To make a positive statement was preferable to following the sheep, subscribing to the norm.'

'What did they say? By the way, you've only got a couple of minutes left.'

'Thanks! Not a lot. They didn't appreciate that their opposition only strengthened my resolve to go on seeing him. I wasn't going to allow them to beat me into submission. Now I think that if they and my parents hadn't been so difficult, then things might have finished much sooner.'

'Perhaps you were just a little bloody-minded?'

'I admit it,' I said. 'I was. It's funny, but I don't really mind that now.'

'That's it for today.'

*

SATURDAY 7 MARCH

A beautiful sunny day. James and I were in the garden, reinforcing the 'cat defences' and pruning the apple tree when the phone, somewhere indoors, started to ring.

'I'll get it!' he said – and shortly after – 'It's for you.'

I ran to pick it up. 'Not next week? ... for how long? ... it seems like a reasonable question ... well, I'm sorry to hear it ... what's wrong? Why can't you say? That's silly ... I know her quite well by now ... can't I even send her a card? OK, OK ... please just pass on my good wishes ... you'll ring me? Thanks.'

'What was all that about?' asked James.

'Therapist's ill. I don't know what's up with her, but there's some talk of "taking it easy ... complete rest". Christ! It would have to happen now.'

'No problem,' said James, his face brightening. 'Now, this

organisation I've heard of ... I mean, while she's away you could come to a "Weekend Workshop" ... give it a go, see what you think ... no obligation. You might even like it. Look at my friend Dave....'

'No,' I said emphatically. 'No! I have no great admiration for Dave.'

*

TUESDAY 4 AUGUST

I opened The Therapist's door.

'I trust you're recovered,' I said, battling to contain my resentment: *Why? Why? It's been a rotten five months ... shoved off onto other people ... James behaving oddly ... all sorts of things going on.*

'Fine, thanks,' she replied, impassive as ever. 'We were talking about Stephan and your move to Leeds.'

'Well,' I said, taken aback, 'it was unpleasant, traumatic. I'd told my mother about it a week before, but I didn't dare tell my father until that morning, when my possessions were safely packed into my car. Stephan had promised to help but, as usual, he never showed up. I had a mass of things, all in and out of boxes; at the other end, five rickety flights of stairs. It's a good job that I didn't have as many books as I have now.'

'Why didn't he help?' asked The Therapist.

'I don't know. He never really explained, and I couldn't talk to him about it. He couldn't make it, he said; there was something else on, something had come up. I was bitterly disappointed, but dared not tell my parents because they'd use it as ammunition. They found out, of course.

'The first night in my new quarters was bleak. A violent storm rattled the door and howled through the windows; it was cold and cheerless; I couldn't sleep. I found myself wondering if I had done the right thing. I had give up a "comfortable existence": large room in a detached house – food, clothes, and trips to antique shops gratis – but, as I fell asleep I can remember thinking: That's the material view. This is much more fundamental. Now at least I've got my freedom, my life, the right to choose.

'Mind you, I could have done without the rows. Memories of my parents arriving unexpected, unannounced; sitting side by side on my miserable bed, howling, begging me to come home. My father ranting about what a good home I'd given up, how other children would have "given their right arm"; I'd had everything, I was so ungrateful, a nasty little bitch. My mother in incoherent floods of tears, alternately screaming and cajoling. Neither attitude was likely to make me change my mind.'

'And after that?'

'It got worse. After The Yorkshire Post moved to Wellington Street, when I saw myself as the rising young executive, my father would phone me at work and accuse me of making my mother into an old woman, behaving like a whore: "after all, no man likes damaged goods".'

'He said that?'

'And worse! It was humiliating; more so when I realised that my trainer had inadvertently overheard all. But that was what helped. She took me to a café, ordered coffee, and told me that I couldn't allow them to treat me like that; I was an adult, a young adult. I had to stand up for my life, my rights....

'That night, we composed a letter; nothing too sensational, all quite calm and logical, but you can imagine its effect. I didn't stop seeing Stephan. Even though he went home every Sunday so that Thisbe could do his washing; even though I was left behind in Leeds; even though my parents knew, and took every opportunity to taunt me. Nasty messages left at work, cruel letters stating: "We told you so. You're nothing to him; you never will be. Why fool yourself? But you're a little fool anyway. Mark our words – no man likes damaged goods". So I stayed in Leeds.

'Unfortunately I had no idea how to meet people or make friends, so when I wasn't seeing Stephan – which was about 80% of the time – I spent long hours in my cheerless room, reading, writing, painting. At least – I told myself – I was learning, being productive, creative. And I was, if not attractive, interesting; I was improving my mind, consolidating future riches; one day someone would appreciate me. But I resented the secrecy. I made lots of futile attempts to force another big meeting. Several times I threatened: either tell your parents or I'm leaving.

'I had a couple of affairs during those years; one with a young man who was 6'7". Imagine! Isn't that funny? I'm only 4'11". We must have looked pretty odd, but you know what they say....'

'Oh?'

'I was living in a tiny terraced house in Horsforth, a crazy place which I shared with a crazier companion, Lynne. I was fond of her, but she had a knack of disappearing whenever she was most needed. I mean, she would put a note through my door: "*Reserve tonight. I've borrowed the boss's car. We'll go to The Intime*", a deeply sordid night club.

'I'd dress up, put on the Amazing Pink Conga Shoes, have a drink, then wait, and wait ... and she'd simply not turn up.

'Later, I'd ask, "Where were you?" and she'd say: "Oh, you should've gone out. I ran into a friend; I didn't think you'd mind." But I did. The point was that I'd promised to see her and I had nowhere else to go.

'When she emigrated to Australia, Matt, a civil engineer, moved in. One night The Landlord sent him over for me to interview, and advise if he might be a suitable tenant. He was tall, good-looking, personable, articulate, literate. Naturally, I didn't object! He would often knock at my door: "*You're in again! Come on! Let's go to the Folk Club on Poole Bank*" – that's just outside Leeds – and off we'd go in his Frogeye Sprite. As we were driving there, I noticed an even more handsome man in the car in front. I could see him fiddling with his rear-view mirror – apparently having a good look at me. Then Matt spotted him and yelled: "It's Pete! A great mate!" We were introduced. We went to some parties. One night I met him at his flat and inevitably....'

I broke off, hoping that The Therapist would help me.

'Inevitably?' she asked. 'Well?'

'I had it off with him,' I confessed. 'Not that I regretted it; it was most diverting, but I'd promised to see Stephan later that night. To my great surprise – he must have been drinking – he was unusually demonstrative. I hadn't intended anything to happen. Afterwards, I felt awful, cheap, a tart.'

'Why?'

'Use your imagination! Two men in the same night! *Two*! It's not something I go in for regularly. I suspected that Stephan knew, as in Blue Eyes, Black Hair....'

'Perhaps you're taking the conventional view?'

'OK, perhaps, but at the time I couldn't think further than the stereotypes. In any case I didn't consider it a pleasant thing to do.

'Finishing with Stephan was unpleasant. After so many years it was like losing a much-loved brother or a favourite relation. Part of me argued, yes, of course it's hard: he's been around so long that the relationship has become a comfortable habit. That doesn't mean to say that I love him. I'm uneasy because I've never been on my own before. How do I meet people? But I was fed up with the secrecy, the pretence, the humiliation of staying in my room at Christmas while he retreated to the bosom of his family.

'I felt compelled to do something positive, so I went to Edinburgh for a solitary two weeks, to think about it. I read all sorts of doleful Pre-Raphaelite stuff: Morte d'Arthur – heroine as beleaguered Queen – Keats, Dante. I stayed with Peggy – I'd met her years before when my parents replied to her holiday accommodation ad.

'She lived in a grim, early Victorian house on the Joppa seafront; a place enlivened by a collection of aged retainers: Aunt Ina, who loved her wee dram; Uncle Peter – who wasn't anyone's uncle as far as I could see – who was forever bellowing: "The cat's oot! *THE CAT'S OOT AGIN!*"; Jim whose surname I never mastered; a stowaway from the Outer Hebrides with such an impenetrably thick accent that you caught one word in five if you were lucky – and he was always muttering darkly about sheep stealing and people being murdered in their beds....

'Peggy gave me her best room; an eccentrically old-fashioned parlour bedecked with antimacassars, ashtrays on leather strips, overstuffed furniture, glass fairings, standard lamps with fringed shades. There was a large bay window overlooking the Firth of Forth, and I'd fall asleep watching the grey water and the intermittent flashing of the lighthouse....

'I wandered about the city examining the buildings, making notes, taking photos. It was cold and it rained constantly. Stephan had Peggy's address and phone number, but he never contacted me. I told myself: if he rings, then things might be different. If he makes a move, there might be a chance. Every day I'd come back longing for a letter, a telephone message, but there was nothing. On the last day I wrote: "Either we go to your parents when I get back and we make it clear that we're still meeting, or we forget it". To my amazement he agreed, but the meeting never took place because he always had good reason to postpone it: "he had a headache", "the car needed repairing", "he had an essay to finish". So I dismissed him.'

I started to cry.

'Dismissed? What an odd thing to say.'

'That was how it was. Ten days or so after I got back, we still hadn't visited his parents. I invited him to my place. When he walked in I was painting at my easel in the corner. Outwardly I was composed and collected; inside a mass of agitation. I kept my eyes on my work as I told him that I didn't want to go on; that I'd had enough, that he should vanish from my life. I showed no emotion, but I couldn't have done it if I hadn't been painting. He begged, pleaded, promised everything, but I refused to listen. At the time I was thinking: "If he *once* puts his arms around me, I'll take it all back; I'll forget that I said anything". He didn't; he just turned on his heel and left.'

'And then?'

'I congratulated myself on my courage and fortitude: "At last! I've done it! That will show him." But it wasn't so easy or so painless.... After a couple of weeks, when I had started to feel desperately lonely I rang him with a pretext for meeting: I'd just bought a facsimile edition of The Moxon Tennyson – the one with Pre-Raphaelite illustrations – perhaps he'd like to see it? Christ, how priggish!

'We met in some wretched Hartshead pub. Between drinks and pretending to show him the book, I begged, pleaded, grovelled, wept, but to no avail. I said all sorts of wild things: I wanted him back on any terms, it didn't really matter, I was sorry for all I'd said; I would always be his slave, his servant, if only he'd give me a second chance. It was too late, he said. He sent me away.'

'We'll have to continue next time.'

'Oh, fuck off!' I shouted. '*FUCK OFF!*'

WEEKEND IN WOOLWICH

*

THURSDAY 6 AUGUST

'You know what I'm struck by?' The Therapist asked, and I almost jumped with surprise, since she had spoken first. 'It's the contrast between the queenly dismissal of Stephan and the abject grovelling to get him back.'

'How do you explain it?'

'You might work that out,' she replied. 'Isn't there something of a contrast in your relationship with your parents: being, on the one hand, the clever daughter, praised, valued, top in everything, then rapidly descending to being spectacularly bad, the derided dunce. Somewhere there's a parallel.'

'Do you mean that I deliberately set up these situations?!' I exclaimed. 'You must think me odious! You must have a very low opinion of me.'

I thought a little: 'Mind you, my parents asked for it; equally it served Stephan right, but I'm not sure I want to talk about that now. I felt much more, finishing with him, than I did in finishing with Number One; my first husband, that is!'

'Number One? What was his name?'

'Charlie. Is it important?'

'Not especially, but you do have a marked tendency to give people nicknames. It could be that by doing that you're reducing them to a number, a handy formula, a figure of fun. You'll have to work it out. I contend that it's much easier to think about "Number One", "The Actor", "The Barrister", than it is to think about Charlie.'

'You mean that I'm distancing myself? If someone's "Number One" with a mania for doing sporty things, then – certainly – it's easier to cope with. That break-up wasn't anywhere near as traumatic as the one with Stephan, but there were some similarities.

'I'd been on the Victorian Society Anglo-American Summer School: three weeks of architectural history – London, Liverpool, Leeds and Manchester – 21 days with like-minded people, I told myself. I came home on the eve of our second anniversary, to the house he'd bought four weeks before. I'd scarcely seen the bloody place. I knew I had to tell him that the situation was untenable.

'He'd bought me a present; fortunately it wasn't anything personal such as jewellery, perfume or flowers – just six rotten dinner plates! As soon as I put down my case, I blurted out: "Charlie, I'm not happy; I want to leave." He looked shocked, but he poured himself a large Scotch and a glass of beer, drained them, switched on the telly, and slumped down in front of it.

'Then he told me that if I intended to go, I had better go tomorrow; he didn't want to discuss it or to see me again. And – by the way – I must never call him at work; he didn't want to hear anything from me. That night I shut myself in the spare room with my books and my favourite things....'

'Let me interrupt,' she said. 'It seems that you had everything planned.'

'I had ... I knew when we moved in that things couldn't continue. I'd known for some time. I confined my belongings to one room, ready for the quick getaway, when it came to that. In the morning I rang some friends, and asked them if I could stay – not for long; overnight, a week, however long it took me to find somewhere to live. I carried away what I could and came back a couple of weeks later to collect the rest. Then I divorced him. It was as simple as that.'

*

EARLY SEPTEMBER

Again, a gap in our communication; no word, no real news, just the same things as before: 'Not well ... no, no, we won't tell you what it is ... you're still her patient ... enjoy your summer ... come back later.'

In some ways, I didn't mind; I worked, I felt stronger, my thesis took shape; part of the time I was closeted in my study ... during the rest I was 'Expert Exhibition Organiser' ... 'Volunteer Chef to the Festival Club'.

St Albans wasn't bad that summer, the School given over to Festival Club and meeting place; innovatory productions of Shakespeare in the turf amphitheatre – geese waddling across the stage.

OK, so James was behaving in an embarrassing fashion ... that time at a party when he pinned one of the musicians in a corner, his eyes set and penetrative: 'Suppose I gave you a chance to change, to transform your life ... you'd take it, wouldn't you?' Musician meanwhile diffident and doubtful, but registering some interest; James continuing to push him; me saying: 'For God's sake, give it a rest! We're at a party, not a recruitment drive!' Then the blazing row on our doorstep....

Still, it wasn't such a bad summer.

*

THURSDAY 29 OCTOBER

I was between hanging pictures and mounting an exhibition and was wearing leather trousers and a wrap-around top. The Therapist looked surprised.

'Apologies,' I said. 'They're my most comfortable and practical clothes.'

'I didn't ask for an explanation.'

'But I thought that you gave me a funny look.'

'Should I have?'

'Well ... all sorts of things are passing through my mind. I see wearing trousers as something deeply disrespectful. I've never dared wear them in front of my parents; besides, I thought I was too short, my bum too big, my legs too fat; that I looked ridiculous. Trousers were banned in the early days at The Yorkshire Post; we only won concessions when trouser suits came in. Even then, we couldn't wear "loons"; trousers had to be part of a suit.

'So it now seems rude to visit you dressed like this. 'Before, I only ever wore them when I was camping with Stephan, so I think that there's some vague association with dossing, scruffiness ... moral laxity, even ... but then, some people think my normal clothes are strange, unacceptable, diametrically opposed to smart business wear. How many people go to work in layers and layers of net petticoats and bright colours? Still, I like these things; I defend my right to wear them *and* the right to wear trousers if I feel like it.'

'You're making a statement,' she observed.

'Naturally! Clothes are a statement. Are you implying that I'm attracting unwarranted attention?'

'Don't ask me: you're quite capable of answering that.'

'You remind me of the person in the Architectural Historians who said that if I continued to dress like this, then people would say that I am like Old Queen Anne. She wore the same style until she dropped dead. OK, it was fine when I was twenty, but fifteen years on, it was risible. I felt hurt, so I told him that it was none of his business, and I cared "this much" – and I jabbed my fingers in the air – "for what he and his boring friends thought...."

'But by wearing certain clothes,' I continued, 'you present a visual puzzle, a joke, a conundrum. People can't quite place you: who or what you are: nationality, job, social background. It's only when they take the trouble to talk that they start to pick up clues. There's always the risk that they might not bother; they might make assumptions and turn away. That's up to them. I comfort myself by saying that if they're not going to take the trouble, then they're probably not worth knowing.

'I also think that much of today's fashion – Lycra skirts, clingy tops, underwear as outerwear – leaves little to the imagination;

though it might be polite if some people would take the trouble to lose a little weight! Certain men have suggested that my style – layers and layers – is intriguing. It's like being given a massive Christmas present; when you take off the outer layer, you find a layer of tissue, then another, another, and another ... finally, many, many layers later, you get to the hidden gem *and* you've had all the fun of unwrapping it. The idea is faintly titillating, I suppose, like The Draughtsman's Contract. Draughtsman approaches older, wiser, more experienced woman – by no means unattractive – wrestles with elaborate outer casing to find "untold delights in her autumn garden"...'

I started laughing and I thought that I heard her laugh, too.

'But I want to talk about my skiing holiday,' I said, 'last February. I don't know...' I stared at the ceiling. 'I can't decide whether I enjoyed it or not. It had all the makings of a complete disaster. I didn't want to go in the first place.'

'Why not?'

'I suspect that Joe and Joani, the couple who invited us, only did so because they had no alternative; I'm James's wife, after all. James and Joe have known each other for years, but I was convinced that Joe and Joani didn't like me. But, you see, they liked James, so they couldn't avoid inviting me, too. Unfortunately, I didn't like them and I wasn't sure that I would enjoy skiing. I was worried about "trooping off in a gang" ... Joe and Joani, Dan and Mary. In ones or twos they're bearable, but in a group they're pretty hard to take; people behave differently in groups. James was determined to go and, out of loyalty, I felt compelled to. If I'd refused, he wouldn't have gone, and I would have deprived him of a holiday.

'I voiced some of my misgivings to Joe and Joani. I told them that I was in therapy. Not that I was crazy or anything – it was just that I was feeling miserable, fragile. And do you know what they did? They laughed. *They laughed at me!* Anyway, when we'd finally come to some sort of agreement, I booked a series of ski lessons on the dry slope at Hemel. I spent most of them on my bum, and emerged with some wonderful bruises, but I liked it; I liked it a lot, and soon I became quite proficient. I saw myself as the expert in a pink ski suit, whizzing down a black run..... But I suppose I should finish what I was saying before....

'The reason why I wouldn't want to dress in the conventionally smart "Next Ethos" is because it might look as though I'd sold out to suburban mores: "John Lewis Gold Card values!" ...'

The Therapist chuckled: 'I beg your pardon?'

'Good, isn't it? "John Lewis Gold Card values" are held by the sort of people who see the ideal theatrical evening in terms of entertainment only; something which caters for the lowest common denominator. They justify it by saying that "people like it"; "it gets bums on seats". Spurious, eh? Forget anything that might make you think or stretch you intellectually! After a hard day's work, all that right-minded people want to do is to be entertained, slump in front of the telly.... Shame on them! No wonder they lead such dull, tedious lives. No wonder they're such wretched bores!

'They're the sort of people who, if they go abroad, look for hamburger or pizza joints. When we were skiing, Joe and Joani spent the whole of one lunchtime crabbing that they couldn't even get French onion soup. Of course they couldn't: we were in Savoy! They'd got the wrong region. They're the sort of people who you know for years, but who you don't know at all. You know nothing about them; you can't get beyond the superficialities, the party small talk. Perhaps there's nothing to know; perhaps they can only talk in jokes and light matter. Bugger that! It's not interesting. I comfort myself by saying: "Well, they don't like me, but at least I am interesting. I am, after all, a woman of genius."

'They're the sort of people who buy a house, spend ages restoring it, knocking down walls, reinstating chimney pieces; hours and hours agonising over a Laura Ashley wallpaper and the *absolutely right* shade of pink for a sofa – from John Lewis, of course – endless faffing about. Then they'll ruin the general effect by scattering Joani's knitting all over the floor. What's the point of spending all that time and trouble if they're going to do that? Why bother? I'm told that they are clever people with responsible, high-powered jobs, yet they're dull, dull, dull ... devoid of ideas.'

'Well, they're not your favourite people,' she commented.

'Certainly not!' I confessed, smiling. 'I'm amazed to say that this is the first time I've dared to admit it.'

'How do you explain that?'

'I've not decided yet ... perhaps I should think aloud ... this probably sounds half-baked, but I suspect it's because I've got this sneaking suspicion that James isn't like me, he's like them. He admires them; he says they've done well. I suppose that's true if you're only talking about money. They've made a killing with the house: from a dump in Catford to a palace in Kentish Town – though why they should term that "Central London" is beyond me. Kentish Town is Kentish Town; it's not Westminster or the City. They've got two large cars, good jobs, loads of money, and now this baby's on the way, they've got the lot! But they're thick, thick, *thick*! They're empty, devoid of knowledge, of inner beauty. I keep thinking of O Lucky Man! – "If knowledge hangs around your neck like pearls instead of chains, you are a lucky man!" That's important.

'One day I was discussing this with James and he told me that if I didn't like them, then I didn't like him, because he was the same as they were. Impossible, I said; I refused to believe him. I reminded myself that he likes theatre, reading – though I privately admitted that in the four years that I've known him, he has only read one book, The Woman in White. He goes on and on about it ... twenty-minute monologues. I'm sick of The Woman in White – still, he's interested in the arts, he says.

'When we first met, he said something like: "So, you're an architectural historian? That must be really interesting. I'm really into architecture, you know." He contends – and I am sure this contains an implicit attack on me – that with his friends "what you see is what you get"; that I'm devious, people don't live like me, nor do they move in such circles. Perhaps it's a head-on clash of ideologies? But why does he value them so much more than he values me? Besides, I'm not devious!'

TUESDAY 12 JANUARY 1988

'Happy New Year,' I announced. I was wearing pink DayGlo trousers, a tight pink, yellow and orange stripey T-shirt, a blouse with a Van Dyck collar, and my black trainers. As usual, I was carrying my red plastic briefcase. I put it down carefully, next to the chair, then took off my shoes and stowed them under the couch, glancing surreptitiously at The Therapist. She was looking in my direction, though her expression was, as usual, blank.

'Are you amused?' I asked.

'What do you think?'

'I think you could give me some help for a change.'

'Well, late last year we were talking about clothes ...'

'And now!' I yelled. 'VOILÀ!'

'You've got to admit it. First you say you equate trousers with something subversive, though whatever they symbolise isn't borne out by their appearance; they look rather good. Now you come in wearing a clown suit!'

We both laughed.

'You asked for it,' I said. 'It's a joke. *A JOKE!* Make of it what you will. I like these, they make people smile in the same way this stupid briefcase does. One of my friends claims that it's the mark of a true yuppie. Imagine! I think I'm beginning to know something about myself, and one of the things I can be certain of is that I'm no yuppie! But I must ask you something: it seems you always stare when I put down my shoes and my case. Why?'

She ignored me.

'Well, I didn't really expect you to answer,' I said, 'but I suspect that you'd be happier if I came in, chucked my shoes onto the floor, and flung my case into the corner. That might be more "normal", instead of this obsession with order. I admit that I'm awkward. Sometimes I deliberately try to shock; in James's social circle, acceptable female party wear is a smart little black cocktail dress, or an extravagant off-the-shoulder number: the sort with a tight-boned bodice and massive bow wobbling on the buttocks. Perfectly charming on those 12-stone Amazons! I'd rather go to parties in "Rock Baroque".'

'What?'

'Well, you take an ordinary tiered skirt and enliven it with two petticoats: one of lace, the other of net; you hitch up the top layer asymmetrically to reveal those beneath. You wear a fussy blouse and a wide, elastic belt, so as to look tight-laced, you see. You put on dance shoes and coloured tights; you weave multicoloured ribbons and spray glitter into your hair.'

There was a long pause.

'Very impressive,' she said dryly.

'When I was at school,' I continued, by way of explanation, 'I was constantly reprimanded for wearing short skirts. I didn't consider them acceptable unless they were 12" above the knee. On me that's indecent! After one detention, I came in in an old skirt which flapped around my ankles. The Headmistress took a dim view of this and retaliated by giving me a double detention with extra homework. But I'd have done it again for the amusement value and the admiration it brought. People applauded me ... instant notoriety! You know, when I first came here one of my thoughts was that you'd say: "Sorry, I can't help you. If you get rid of him, you'll feel much better." Do you think that's what's wrong?'

'You'll have to do a lot of thinking about that,' she replied. 'I don't know. I can't tell you. It's your life; I'm not here to advise or judge.'

'James is always bandying about the accusation: "You think you're better than my friends." At first I'd turn to him horrified, and say, "No, NO! How can you say that? You must think me monstrous, arrogant." But the real problem is that I believe I am. If he says that now I reply: "Yes! Quite right. I know more than they do; I think more than they do. I've got different, higher values, a richer life: art, literature, culture ..." He'll make as if to hit me: "How dare you, you bitch! What gives you that right? How can one human being put themselves above another? You haven't a job, a car, or a house; they've made it; you haven't. You'd have gone under if I hadn't rescued you. I got there just in time. You were flogging off everything – soon there'd have been nothing left." "Rubbish," I'll interrupt. "Times were hard; you forget that when I went to university I was a mature student – I wasn't going to sponge off my parents as you did, or retreat to them when the going got tough."

'Yes, I was flogging things – my own things – but it was some feat to finish my first degree with a £50 overdraft. That was modest – most of my friends owed thousands – I lived frugally, but I know I've come out of university with more than you have. Less materially, but more of what really matters. Naturally that didn't go down very well!'

She remained silent.

'The latest thing is Joani's pregnancy.' My lip curled in contempt as I thought of it. 'What the hell will it turn out like with parents like them? *And* it was an accident, she says. Isn't that embarrassing? She claims to be a feminist yet she hasn't got her contraception sorted out: isn't that rather elementary? Even if it was an accident they've no need to keep broadcasting it. That child might carry around a neurosis all of its life: "the unwanted one", "the unwelcome one", "the one who spoiled things". Their conversation was tedious before; now it's even worse: weight gain, hormones, prams, pushchairs, the conjectural merits of breastfeeding. The changes in her body don't interest me, though I'm sure it's terribly exciting for her. I think she looks revolting ...'

'Really?'

'Frankly, yes.'

'But some people revel in that, wear clothes to display rather than conceal. You could argue that it's natural, beautiful, a celebration of their love, their successful marriage.'

'It depends on which magazine cover you've seen,' I commented, thinking of the recent pregnant Demi Moore one, wearing only body paint....

'OK, OK,' she replied. 'It might have been more convenient for them if it hadn't happened, or if it hadn't happened just then.'

'For me the tent dresses in pastel shades, the vast weight and waddling gait symbolises women's drudgery and subjugation. Why spend all that time getting a degree if all you intend to do afterwards is sink into a life of cooking, cleaning and washing up? Very clever! I'd rather stick my head in the microwave!'

'Do I detect a note of bitterness in all this?'

To my surprise, I started to cry....

'I was going to say "NO!" Perhaps I'm not so sure. When I first met James we had a long discussion about marriage, families, children. He made it clear that he didn't want to have a family; at first I agreed and I admired him for his honesty and integrity. I considered it unusual; I thought he'd got his life sorted out. Besides, I wasn't all that keen either, so that was that. I can see the way it alters your life; how you might have to curtail all cultural activities, forget spur of the moment decisions; how on Sunday, instead of lying in bed and reading the paper, you might have to get up and start scrutting.

'That sounds bitter, doesn't it? But I'm sure that there are many rewards: seeing that child develop; learn to speak, write, reason. But then I have this strong conviction that many people have children not because they desperately want them, or even because they've given it much thought, but because it's the convention – the done thing – or because they think it will cement a failing marriage. It doesn't, does it?'

'You still haven't answered my question.'

'I'm sorry. I don't dislike children; it's just that I hate to see people apparently having children as insurance against their own mortality. What's really difficult is that our first fairly casual agreement has become a condition of the marriage. Right now, I think I should discuss it with James. I might have revised my stance, but he won't hear of it, and I'm so upset that I can't begin to broach the subject.

'If I ever pluck up courage to speak he'll say: *"But you promised – you promised before we got married. Remember?"* and I'm so choked that I can't reply. How could I predict what I'd feel? It's not fair! It's not fair! I've been labelled "child-hater" by his friends; I've defended myself by claiming choice, the courage of my convictions. But I know that I'm on shaky ground. My feelings aren't quite so simple.

'There are certainly some aspects of pregnancy which I find disgusting, repellent ... the time we were invited to Joe and Joani's "Autumn Barbecue" ... it sounded nice: drinks on the terrace at 6pm, a meal in the garden ... a lovely garden with good plants, appealing colours. When we arrived Joani was *"Britannia Triumphant"* in voluminous sailcloth and I couldn't help feeling that if she hadn't stuffed herself so much, then she wouldn't be quite so huge. Why regard it as a licence to eat?

'While we were sitting on the lawn over the Bulgarian Cabernet Sauvignon, the sound of birdsong in the trees, she gave the full litany: cramps, backache, food obsessions, vomiting, how she was off sex. Worse, she was scratching the bump ... it made me feel sick.'

'Why? Did you equate it with public masturbation?'

'Not quite, but it seemed almost as bad. I thought it in poor taste. She was inviting people to feel: "Here, press. It's so interesting; you can feel it kick...." Worse, James's eyes widened and I could see that he was tempted. It felt like a betrayal. Why should he get so damned excited? I don't think I'm too bad but he doesn't like to touch me. Perhaps he finds me so fat, so ugly to look at, that he can't bear it.'

'I'm sorry to hear that, but we've run out of time.'

'Already?' I asked.

I marched out of the room and slammed the door as hard as I could.

*

THURSDAY 21 JANUARY

The Therapist said: 'You've implied that there's little contact between you and your husband. Physical contact, I mean.'

'I don't like to admit it,' I said, 'but it's true and I don't understand. When we met we were *always at it;* now he's just not interested. He claims that he's so tired, he feels so awful that he can barely drag himself around....

'At first I thought he was joking, especially when he said that *I wore him out, brought him to his knees, perhaps I thought it funny*? I'd point out that "doing it" was normal and natural; there was something wrong if he found it so debilitating.

'But I started wondering if he was punishing me by avoiding me, treating it as a system of rewards for good behaviour. I hope that things haven't got to that.... He has always blamed me: "You're not nice enough – not calm like my mother. I don't fancy you anymore". And I'd worry about my demeanour –

which isn't *so* bad – and my weight. I'm around eight stones – not exactly huge – I'm careful about my food; I exercise all the time. Now I'm beginning to think that it's his problem instead of mine.

'I'm fed up with his fucking "illness"! At first I thought that it was because he wasn't sleeping well; he's always snorting and grunting. Our old bed was soft and uncomfortable; I suggested that we get a new one. Now he complains that he can't sleep because it's like lying on a block of concrete. Later, when he was crabbing on about me being a vegetarian, he insisted that he lacked vitamins. That's ridiculous! I do all the cooking, and we eat good, varied, vegetarian food. On that regime he lost weight and his skin improved. "Not good enough," he said, "I'm missing something vital." Which is even sillier because he stuffs himself with meat at work anyway! You can't say I didn't try. I put him on multi-vitamins; I cooked things with plenty of iron – spinach and all that stuff.

'The next thing was: "I've got allergies", so we both went onto a Stone Age Diet: the one where contentious foods are reintroduced, very, very gradually, to see if they cause a reaction. None did, but I managed to curb my migraine. Stilton is bad for me, apparently, but I still love it. Then it was "dust and general pollution". I took the curtains down once a week and washed them. There was no difference, of course.

'He was worse when we went skiing last year. In desperation, I insisted that he go for psychiatric counselling; perhaps his symptoms were psychosomatic? He refused. Typical, eh? He was fine as he was, he said; *the real problem was me.* I'm not sure if it is quite as simple as that.

'Which reminds me ... the skiing holiday ... we discussed it over a bottle or two at Joe and Joani's, and finally came to an agreement. By that time I was enthusiastic, but James was having second thoughts.

'I agonised about other issues: I'd never flown before; I thought I'd be frightened. I wanted to buy a ski suit; James argued that since I wouldn't enjoy it, it would be a waste of money; far better to wait and see what happened. I was reduced to borrowing one from James's friend Mary, of Mary and Dan. She claimed that she was a size 10 or 12, and I remember thinking, "My God, I'll never get into that", but I could have fitted into it twice over. It looked huge, ludicrous, and people were amazed when, in the evening, in my black jazz trousers, I was transformed into someone half my apparent size.

'I didn't like flying ... the sensation of increasing acceleration, the gradual, torturous climb to "optimum cruising height". At 30,000 feet I forgot, ordered another drink and began to enjoy myself.

'Les Deux Alpes! We stayed in a chalet with sixteen others; each couple with their own little cosy suite, so it wasn't as incestuous as you might think. All meals, except for lunch, we took together around a massive table, the dining room the focus for all social occasions. Superficially, it was a great holiday. On the first morning, before formal ski lessons, we went all the way up Les Demoiselles and skied all the way home: my first time on real snow! I was slow, but I did it and I enjoyed it.

'By Tuesday Joe and Joani were complaining of aching

muscles and stiff joints; James said he couldn't straighten his legs, and I remember crying with laughter when he tried to climb the chalet stairs: "Oooh! AAARGH! It hurts!" All of them pointed out that I wasn't sporty and wouldn't enjoy it, but I was fitter than they were: I did, and I didn't ache! They resented that and were even more put out when – by the end of the week – I was doing the same runs as they were.'

'Why should that annoy them?' she asked.

'I think it made them feel diminished. They were at sea over my studies, my interests, my pursuits. This was one area in which they were superior; they'd been skiing three years, after all ... suddenly, they weren't.... I saw a good deal of hypocrisy that week. On the one hand they were furious about my enthusiasm, yet when it came to our third wedding anniversary – on the Thursday – out came the champagne and canapés, a card, presents. All very conventional and I couldn't decide if my feelings were unreasonable, or if they were really were two-faced. I'd picked up on the notion that the three of them – James, Joe and Joani – were against me. There were scraps about something and nothing....

'On the Chalet Girl's night off, we walked – with Moon Boots – to a "typical Savoyard restaurant". The way back was via a steep uphill slog over a long snowfield. The threesome were all much taller than me and strode on ahead, throwing out remarks such as: "Oh, we thought you were fit! Now who's behind, eh?"

'It may have been trivial but I decided henceforth to boycott their parties and never pretend to enjoy their company again.'

'If you follow that course, it will be difficult,' she interrupted.
'I know,' I replied. 'I'm not sure how I can break it to James.'

*

TUESDAY 2 FEBRUARY

'As you know, I don't weigh a great deal; I don't eat heroically: just salads, fruit, hardly any fatty or sweet things, yet I feel huge, gross, ugly. Sometimes I've deliberately starved and I've punished myself if I've dared to slip, yet when I finally went to buy a ski suit, the only one that fitted me was a child's. Isn't that funny?'

'It must be obvious by now that there's a great difference between reality and your perception of it: how you think you look, and how you do. It's in the mind, but it may also be that by forcing your weight below its natural level, you're trying to exert control over one area of your life. What I mean is that you can say: "Well, my life's pretty well out of control, but if I can control my weight, then it proves I can control something." Isn't that rather like something else we've discussed?'

I stared at the photo of Freud, wishing that she would change it.

'My tidiness!' I exclaimed. '"My life's a mess but my desk is tidy". But this raises other issues surely? When I first met James – 1983 – he said he needed ideas on décor; he had a nice house, but he hadn't got it properly sorted out; it needed *a different touch.* I was certainly struck by the dearth of pictures and decorative objects; the unimaginative arrangement of things. The second and third bedrooms – nicely proportioned rooms – were junk stores: wardrobes, dressing tables, chairs, all surplus to requirements, playing trains around the walls.

'He gave me carte blanche to sort it out. Naturally I did. I exiled his mum's "Doggie Calendar" and hung his degree certificate in 'my' (future?) study. I asked the Boy Scouts to cart off the spare furniture; they did but they weren't impressed! James begged me to live with him. I told him that before I did, I needed to have my own niche; I claimed the second bedroom as my study.

'I wanted a noticeboard; I've always had one, even in temporary places. I had one in my tiny hall of residence room in Manchester: a living collage, postcards from friends, souvenirs; cuttings of witty or ludicrous comments, quotes from newspapers; all my icons: Gance's Napoleon; Fitzcarraldo, Last Year at Marienbad; Nijinsky as the Golden Slave, the Boy Chatterton, Man Ray and Lee Miller's solarised photographs, de Beauvoir and Sartre at their half-century, and – of course – lots of photos of buildings.

'I think it's related to the need to put down roots, to feel at home. Even when I'm staying in an hotel I put my favourite postcards on the mantle and tastefully drape a scarf over a chair.

'James agonised for so long about the noticeboard that I became impatient: *the exact shade of the tiles? What glue to use? Should we or should we not strip the wallpaper?* So much buggering about.

'One day when he was out, I went into town, bought some cork tiles and slammed the whole lot up, sans plumb line or measurements. When he returned, it was done. "You fool!" he shouted. "It looks OK, but it won't last. How much time did you spend thinking about it or preparing? That's just your trouble: you're too impulsive!" But, of course, it's still there and it shows no signs of falling down.

'He spends too much time wickering, thinking about how to do something, staring into space, reading around it ... *it might be better if he just got on with the job!*'

'Wickering?'

'Sitting on his backside, gazing into space, twiddling his thumbs round and round and round and round.' I laughed.

'When I moved in with him, I hung my pictures, sorted out my books, rearranged the furniture as invited. *Now* he claims that I've taken over *his* house, stamped my personality on it. In a way I have, but I did it at his instigation, and I've made an improvement – in my eyes, anyway.'

The Therapist interrupted: 'You can't decide if you're a good influence – bringing order and beauty into his life – or whether you've invaded his home – whether you're a life-enriching force or a malignant cancer.'

'You have a point, although all of that business was rather traumatic. He asked me if I'd clear the cupboards; the furniture which hadn't gone to the Scouts was stuffed with random bits of string and wire, old Sunday supplements, discarded bedding and similar. So, I set to with a vengeance!

'I wish this hadn't happened, but I found many mementoes

of his ex, mostly – I noted smugly – in questionable taste. I found silver ingots inscribed "A", an identity bracelet ditto, cuddly toys ditto, jumpers ditto. Why did she have to put it on *everything*? I wouldn't have the confidence; I couldn't assume that "my boyfriend" would want to carry my initial. How could she take it for granted? How could she be so proprietorial?

'There were loads of letters, too. I didn't look at them, but he told me that they were of mind-numbing banality. So why bother keeping them? I suggested that he put them in the attic or throw them out, which eventually he did.

'Then there were the photographs, albums and albums; hundreds of images: views of glamorous and exotic locations with Aurelia's grinning visage; posing as a model, always dressed in cheap chic. At the time I said to myself: "I could never look like that. I could never be so thin, so glamorous." At the same time I'd think: "He claims that he didn't love her, that he doesn't love her, that she was a hard-hearted bitch, spiteful, emotionally and sexually cold; that he loves me."

'I would also reason: "There *is* something hard about her. Anyway, she's not so intelligent, she only got a 2.2, and he claims that she worked hard. If that's the best she could do, she should have given up." But the images bothered me. I felt inadequate, superfluous; it seemed that he hadn't been able to keep her – someone infinitely more attractive and desirable – so he'd settled for a poor second. There are superficial similarities: we've both got long dark hair, we're both small, short; both with a university arts education, both – ostensibly anyway – literate.

'Thank God there are fundamental differences: personality,

attitudes of mind, principles. She seems to me to be an unprincipled bitch with the personal code: "Tread on everyone on the way up ... sponge on your relations; fight for Grandma's clock against the terms of her legacy." I've got a low opinion of her; I find her aggressive personality unattractive. On our honeymoon, I asked James to get rid of the photographs, or at least hide them. I didn't want to live in someone else's shadow. He refused, we argued; I begged, I remonstrated; he said that it would make no difference.

'I pointed out that he'd married me on the rebound – or so it seemed. He was drawn to my appearance, my long hair, but whatever or whoever I was didn't really matter. Some of his claims – "I'm very interested in architecture, actually" – have since been disproved ... on holiday I drag round an unwilling pupil. I'm fed up with always having to lead.'

'You've strayed a long way from the original point, if you were making one,' The Therapist remarked.

'I'm sorry. What was it? Reality? Perception? Order? Tidiness? I suppose you can see order and tidiness as a defence mechanism; like Sasha in Good Morning, Midnight. She goes to Paris, buys new clothes, has a blonde cendré hairdo – a great success – and no one would ever know that she'd been in the deep, dark river, except that some scar always remains. By the same token, the outer signs are good. Our house is perfect, ordered, calm, nothing out of place. People envy us; people envy *me. But they don't see how I really feel.*

'Tidiness. I need to elaborate on that, I think,' I continued. 'It's also a reaction against the past. My parents were chaotic:

every available surface covered with a rash of ornaments and antiquities; important papers stuffed into obscure drawers, newspapers – and always The Daily Express! – spilling over furniture. I was infuriated ... whenever the life insurance man came to collect his subscription, as he did every Thursday, the vital document was missing. Once they had to prise it from the back of a drawer with a pair of scissors. I've never worked out how it got there in the first place. I felt embarrassed by them. How stupid! Why not keep it in the same place? Surely that would have been easier? So, my order might be a reaction to my parents' chaos, though it may have become more pronounced over the years.'

*

THURSDAY 22 SEPTEMBER

'What a shitty summer,' I remarked to The Therapist. 'A shame that you went missing again; I won't bother to ask. Well, anyway, there was a party at Ken and Paula's the other night. We were invited. And for the first time, I refused to go.'

'And?'

'James wasn't pleased, we argued. If I refused to go, I was refusing his love and affection; I was spoiling things, letting him down, being unreasonable, ruining our social life. But I couldn't stop thinking that when I went to his friends' parties I was held up for general ridicule: jibes about my clothes, my hair – "long hair is so passé" – my interests, my studies. After all, Art History is "so cool" it puts me "above other people".

'My enthusiastic manner is always attacked: "Why get so excited? Life's so boring!" I stuck to my original decision. He came back drunk and noisy at 4.30am; meanwhile, I'd had the most pleasant evening: reading, writing, thinking, listening to music, phoning my friends. But I also felt guilty.'

'Aren't we back to something which has come up before?' asked The Therapist.

'The need for individual space? I remember how worried I was when he first let me loose on his house. I tried to confine my possessions to the study but he resented me having "my room".'

'Why not? That seems pretty reasonable.'

'He argued that his three-bedroom house wasn't big enough. Shortly after, he invaded my study with his computer, his computer mags, his car mags, his hifi mags. He filled my filing cabinet with his junk; whenever I took refuge, he barged in because *there was something he had to retrieve; it really couldn't wait.* He said that I was too territorial; if I was going to behave like that, why bother to get married in the first place? The whole idea was to share our lives, and that I was being selfish.

'I reasoned that marriage didn't mean that we had to live on top of each other, it was healthier not to. I valued my space and would respect his. No, he said. Later he commented that he felt like a stranger in his own home. I begged for a little consideration.

'Sometimes, if he was in a good humour, he'd say that he

admired my order, my books, my study, my library, and that when he retired he'd start at A, and work his way through to Z. Like the Autodidact, eh? In a bad mood, he'd say: "You're such an arrogant bitch! You think you're more capable than me."

'The trouble is that I am!

'I think he felt safer before I started meeting people. When I transferred my studies to the Courtauld, I made new friends. I was drawn to Jeanetta immediately; she was a little older than me: late thirties, restrained in appearance and manner, like everyone's idea of a typical elegant Edwardian lady: very attractive, prematurely silver hair drawn back into a knot, long skirts, homespun shawls in sludgy colours, quiet voice, sympathetic manner. She seemed caring, sensitive, erudite, bookish.

'At first she and I met occasionally for lunch, then for dinner at The Dôme, Oxford Circus, then she came to see us at home. I knew little about her life, but I started to think of her as my best friend. We shared confidences, or rather I spilled mine out while she gave nothing away. I felt that I could tell her anything.

'When she first visited us at home I was in an agony of apprehension: would she like the food? Would she like the wine? The ambience? Would she get on with James? Would she find him boring? A turnip? A bozo? Suppose he launched into one of his deeply meaningful monologues – the sort filled with "wigwam platitudes"? Suppose he droned on about computers? She's an artist, I thought; in face of all her knowledge, I'm ignorant. I can't enthuse about my "favourite violinist". I'm not even sure how recently I learned that the "Head Honcho" was called "The Leader".

'I needn't have worried; she was the more nervous. James got on with her tremendously well; he rather fancied her, despite being alarmed by her "highbrow tastes". She found him attractive, charming; the evening was a great success. As the wine flowed, I learned that she was resolutely single; she'd never been married, but had had many proposals, all of which she'd rejected in favour of a solitary life in a ramshackle garret in Finchley.

'To me it seemed that she'd carved out her life without resort to compromise. She was currently involved with two men, each of whom knew about the other; she had lots of friends, all in separate groups. How does she do it? I wondered. I began to admire her.

'Anyway, the point of all this,' I said, remembering The Therapist, 'is that once, when James and I were arguing, he turned to me and said: "It's that friend of yours, Jeanetta, she's an unhealthy influence." I had no alternative but to admit that her image was attractive: lone female, committed to the life she really wants, living by the courage of her own convictions.'

'Clearly,' The Therapist remarked, 'she's important to you.'

'Certainly,' I agreed, 'I've never had a close female friend before. I tend to get on better with men, which is why – and please don't take this personally – I asked for a male therapist. I thought that I'd find it easier to talk to a man; up to now all my best friends have been men. I often find it difficult to form relationships with women.'

*

WEEKEND IN WOOLWICH

THURSDAY 26 JANUARY 1989

'Last night wasn't a success,' I remarked. 'I met Jeanetta at The Dôme. We started to discuss what people do with their lives, what directions they take – how choices are made. She launched into an attack, claiming that it was easy for me; I'd had choice, advantages. I replied calmly, saying, no, no, she'd got it all wrong. I knew early in life what I would like to do, but that didn't constitute an advantage. But she continued to protest and left in a temper.

'Surely I didn't have advantages?' I asked The Therapist. 'I remember how my future came to me, but it took me a long time to pursue it. I was about five years old and I was with my parents at Batley Museum, West Yorkshire. They were looking at an array of glass cases full of stuffed birds, specimens, curiosities; I was looking at the building and it was then that I suddenly realised that I wanted to be an architectural historian ... though I didn't have the words for it then.

'But advantages? No! I worked for ten years flogging advertising space; my mother and brother opposed my going to university. When I chucked in my job my mother's main concern was that I'd given up my flashy black and silver company car; the sort with go-faster stripes. I hit the University of Manchester in a beaten-up Fiat 127 with my grant and £25. That was all, I told Jeanetta. I had no private means; everything I've done I've done myself. She replied that I'd deliberately misunderstood her; my advantage was that I had always known what I wanted to do; others didn't. I'd had choice, others didn't.

Was she jealous?'

'Decide for yourself. Something significant,' she commented. 'You haven't told me anything much about your first marriage ... how did you meet him? How did you come to marry him?'

'This might be a long monologue,' I warned her. 'After I'd finished with Stephan, I felt dreadful; everything was so much harder than I'd anticipated. People didn't seek me out, so I stayed in and read. I was lonely; after Stephan had refused to take me back, I felt hurt and humiliated; even more so when I discovered that he'd been seeing someone for at least a year before we split up. Eventually I met this "paragon" and felt worse. She was, apparently, so stupid that it felt like an insult. Granted, she was tall, thin, blonde – all the attributes he sought in a woman – but her entire conversation revolved around the latest television programme.

'I couldn't imagine why he refused to see me again; I was at least – I thought – interesting. Now I think it was because I made him feel diminished. With Janey, there was no doubt that he was the more interesting, the more knowledgeable. There had been some unpleasant incidents. I'd kept running into him; the last time we'd met we went to his place where we drank a bottle of wine and – just like old times – got into bed together. Afterwards, he burst into tears and threw me out onto the street. That made me feel dirty, used, foolish.

'Stephan was living in another shared house, 34A: a massive, latter-day Arts and Crafts hulk, on which the three (male) friends had a shared mortgage. Charlie was a member of the triumvirate. I'd known him vaguely for years as "one of the friends". In my first years with Stephan, we'd often meet at Robert and Charlie's; Charlie and Robert lived with their parents, Toby and Amy, then. Their drive was always full of cars of assorted shapes and sizes: Toby and Amy's silver BMW, Robert's red Transit, Charlie's blue and white RS2000; Stephan's orange MGB GT, David's 'Family Car', Stuart's crappy pink Bedford and my white Hillman Imp. I was fond of Toby and Amy; they were warm people. I was an extra member of the family, and I felt comfortable with them; Robert was considerate, reliable.'

'Did you know Charlie well?'

'Scarcely at all; he was just "Bonks", "Robert's Kid Brother"; Robert was the one I talked to most and liked best.'

'Well, what happened?'

'November 76, a year after the break with Stephan and following a fling with a deranged actor, there was a party at 34A. I was surprised to receive an invitation, and because I was sure that I was over the emotional upheaval, I went along. Stephan appeared with Janey; I couldn't face him, I couldn't smile or attempt polite conversation. I fled upstairs. Charlie followed me and found me in tears. He said nice things; he was kind and affectionate. He commandeered a bottle of wine, we drank it and talked; I began to feel calmer. I knew that he liked me. By the time we went down to the party – hours later – we'd become a couple. We spent the rest of the evening together. I couldn't have driven home at four that morning, so I stayed with him.

'If I'm honest with myself, I knew immediately that we weren't on the same wavelength. He regarded theatre, dance, opera, country house visiting as "too highbrow"; his imagination was stretched to the limit by films like Death Wish II or King of Kung Fu. It reminded me of a wacky 70s postcard: "On waking, she realised that something was missing from the relationship ... HIS BRAIN!" But he was nice and it was easy, pleasant, uncomplicated, and I thought that I needed that after the seven angst-ridden years with Stephan.

'At first, I felt like a princess. We went out constantly: restaurants, pubs, discos, dances and parties, many, many parties. No one had treated me like that before; *I felt special.* Three months later – February 77 – in bed on Valentine's Day, he proposed. I felt valued; so I accepted. I knew that I wasn't in love, but I thought that, given time and kindness, I'd come to care deeply about him. But I also saw a marriage – any marriage – as a means of reconciliation with my parents. They'd always stressed the importance, the status of marriage and were bitterly disappointed and vindictive at my failure to – as they said – "net a man".

'No,' I went on, as The Therapist tried to interrupt, 'vindictive isn't too strong a word. They saw my relationship with Stephan not as so much experience, but as so much wasted time: I'd "thrown away the best years of my life"; "it had come to nothing". I pointed out that I'd loved him dearly, that there had been many good times as well as some bad ones. They argued that he should have "done the decent thing", and married me. They didn't seem concerned with my happiness, so much as with my "lack of respectability". Ha! I'd ruined my prospects, they said, since "no man likes damaged goods".

WEEKEND IN WOOLWICH

I reasoned: "I'm not damaged goods; I'm only 24 – scarcely an old hag". Unfortunately, though, something in me believed them; so, when someone – someone who knew about my past – accepted me, I thought that they would be delighted.

'We drove my parents over to his for introductions. Mine were anxious that we have a traditional white wedding; anything less would have been null and void, and would have reinforced my image as a "fallen woman taken out of charity". They made it clear that they wouldn't pay for the "Do" they "couldn't afford". The Bentley and their bloody antiques were more important, as usual. Fifteen people came to the ceremony and sixty turned up at the buffet, stuffed themselves at my expense, then thanked my father.

'Curiously, on the day, I felt happy, proud. The strain of the previous year had caused me to lose weight; the white dress looked well. I wore my hair loose, and carried a Victorian-style posy. Charlie was handsome in his morning suit and top hat. There's something seductive about dressing up in elaborate costumes and making public declarations. The mood of elation lasted through the honeymoon.

'When we got home, things were different. Charlie spent most of his time drinking with the boys at The Lewins – in Halifax, I think – or playing squash and football. I was expected to fit into the role of perfect wife; to have meals ready on time, irrespective of when he chose to turn up; to do all the cooking, cleaning, washing up, laundry, shopping, and work full-time. When he came home from his physical pursuits, he'd rush into the pot, piss copiously, then throw his sweaty kit into the bedroom for me to pick up. It would have been just as easy for him to put it into the linen basket.

'Suddenly we stopped going out because, he said, we couldn't afford to. He had still not managed to extricate himself from 34A's onerous mortgage; we were paying that, the endless bills for his RS2000, and our rent. Actually, I think that I was covering our rent.... Anyway, things stopped being fun, I stopped feeling special. I started to look shabby because there wasn't any money to replace worn-out clothes. He complained that I looked dowdy. Worse, there was no intellectual exchange.'

*

THURSDAY 2 FEBRUARY

'So,' I said, when I entered the room, 'you want to know what happened next?'

'As you wish.'

'The marriage proper had ceased a few weeks after the ceremony. One day, six months or so later, I was reading Madame Bovary in the black and purple back room of our flat; a room with a secret, safe feel and a cosy open fire. He was out, God knows where: at some low pub or playing football? Two passages struck me: the one in which Emma drives the point of her parasol into the turf and says over and over again: "Oh God, oh God, why did I get married?" The other, where she throws her lovingly preserved wedding bouquet into the fire and watches it burn. That so mirrored my own feelings that I took mine out of its layers of yellowing tissue and did the same; I knew then that I would leave, but did nothing for another eighteen months.

'Easter 1979: I joined the portentously titled Victorian Society study trip, "The Gothic Revival in South Devon", based at Exeter University. Comfortable rooms, Victorian buildings, rain-sodden gardens. I met The Barrister. Have I told you about him? I'd noticed him before at several similar events and concluded that he was a boring and crusty old bachelor. He was eight years older than me, his manner was stuffy, restrained; he had no clothes sense, but in conversation he was absolutely fascinating. Architecture was, for him, a passion which he pursued wildly, day and night. At the time I found that immensely seductive. He was well read, owned a huge library, took the most stunning architectural slides on his vintage Hasselblad. Initially I wrongly assumed that he saw me as young, frivolous, stupid and wacky. I hadn't been to university then, and my enthusiastic manner could have been interpreted as a desperate attempt to make an impression, get noticed. My clothes were even odder than they are now, but I told myself that I knew I was well read and serious, even if others didn't.

'On the second night of the trip we went out for a drink. It dawned on me that I was enjoying the conversation, and I rather liked him. He asked me to meet him early next day for a "private architectural tour of the university"; I decided he'd got style. Eccentric style, perhaps, but style none the less! That morning, it was raining, but he was waiting – as he said he would be – under my window.

'When I got home there was a letter: how much he'd enjoyed the weekend, especially our conversation; how I'd brightened up his time in Exeter; I was so full of ideas, so vivacious; could he perhaps come to Leeds, meet my husband, have a tour of the northern towns? I mentioned it to Charlie. "Fine," he said. "I don't mind, but it sounds pretty boring to me."

'On the evening The Barrister arrived, Charlie had gone missing; he'd "had to go out", "there was a team meeting" ... "something afoot". I'd made quite an effort; the table was carefully laid with Grandma N's best silver; I'd bought some good wine, cooked an excellent meal, lit the candles. I felt vulnerable. The Barrister was first off the train, as I'd expected, and was – predictably – strung about with cameras, cases, projection equipment, books, maps, the binos and a yellowing Army bag. The dinner was a great success and by the time Charlie appeared, the conversation was going so well that it seemed as if he was an intruder. He must have realised. Although he said nothing, he vanished for the rest of the weekend; which was odd....

'On the Saturday I drove The Barrister to Liverpool. On the Sunday we stayed in Leeds and visited Temple Newsam and Lotherton Hall; Lotherton enhanced by a wonderful exhibition of John Singer Sargent's swagger portraits. There was much intelligent conversation; I found myself wanting him and feeling guilty about it. After all, I was married, if disillusioned, so why was I looking at someone else? That was when I decided that I had to leave Charlie. Anything else would have been dishonest.

WEEKEND IN WOOLWICH

'I met The Barrister several times, once in a sordid hotel somewhere in Victoria. I had secretly hoped that the scene for the grand seduction would be The Ritz. It was obvious that he wasn't even remotely poor; all he ever spent money on was books and travel. So why did we have to stay in a bog-standard non-ensuite room with cardboard walls, cracked "pampas" sink and pink candlewick bedspread? Later, I discovered that he was mean, emotionally and financially; the one consolation was that he was bookish, intelligent, articulate.'

'What about his family? Did you meet them?' asked The Therapist.

'Ha! What a joke! In the short time we'd been together, he'd proposed several times, or at least he'd made various pronouncements – "I'll marry you, you know. I will!" – without stopping to ask how I might feel about it. It was somehow assumed, on his part, that when I went off to university my furniture and books would move to his house, and I'd follow after graduation.

'So, off we went for the introductions. His father was a civilised-looking, iron-haired bolt-upright no-nonsense gent in his seventies; his (much younger) stepmother, Romola – by contrast – rather fat, frivolous, blowsy, done up in an unsuitable purple pleaty Fortuny number with louche gilt jewellery. She was part Russian and had – to family admiration – gone off to university after having had the three Wyckeham children: first for her degree, then her MA, and then her PhD. This last she rammed down my throat in guttural tones. The fact that I hadn't yet studied didn't mean that I was stupid, but she concluded that I was, and overwhelmed any point I tried to make. It was not a comfortable evening; I felt on test, as though I were being weighed up, evaluated.

'The Barrister had gone on about her fabulous cooking, so I was surprised to find everything frozen, boil-in-the-bag, improperly cooked, inadequately drained: limp green beans swamped by tepid liquid, soggy carrots, bullet peas. The "pièce de résistance", an indeterminate greyish slime – "une specialité de la maison" was apparently potato purée. It was horrible! That, and being "taken into dinner", was laughable.

'We had "cocktails" – cheap sherry – in the reception room of their modest brick-built Queen Anne Revival semi; Romola firing merciless questions and eyeing me suspiciously, The Barrister doing nothing to help; Father keeping his head down over the sherry. When dinner was announced, Father stiffly offered his arm and, with great ceremony, conducted me to the shabby basement dining room.

'These lugubrious proceedings were lightened by the presence of a twenty-year-old apparently half-witted, but very entertaining, brother who had just got his "first real job", working in a joke shop near the British Museum. I suspected that they usually kept him out of sight "below decks". He and I spent dinner convulsed in vulgar cackles. Later, The Barrister pointed out that I had disappointed him; I hadn't been a credit, he had confidently expected "greater things" from me.

'Much later he came to visit me at my hall of residence in Manchester. I was looking forward to seeing him; I'd been at university two weeks. At first, on seeing the young, fresh-faced students, I'd felt old, out of place. By the end of the first seven days, though, most people had found their own friends and, given the attentions of a young admirer, I'd forgotten about my advanced years. The Barrister appeared to my readjusted vision beaten, old and weary. Worse, he'd had a disastrous military haircut. My new acquaintance were visibly surprised. I felt mortified and embarrassed.

'Our relationship finished that Christmas. His letters became less and less frequent, his phone calls increasingly cold; I noticed that he was evasive. I lodged my furniture in Grandma N's smelly garage, my books in a friend's attic. In November The Barrister had gone to Istanbul with the Victorian Society; I was later informed that he had "*fused together in a mosque*" with a beauteous vision in a pink Gucci mac and matching sandals. Who says that these "learned societies" aren't pickup joints? But I didn't know that when we arranged "Our first Christmas together".

'I had rented a ramshackle flat in Joppa, around the corner from Peggy's old family let. I drove to London in my beaten-up Fiat 127 to collect him. I'd travelled light, with the idea that "what you can't carry you don't need", and had expected to find The Barrister ready to set off. For most of that afternoon, though, he wandered 'twixt car and house putting in, item: torch, item: binos, item: walking boots – dirty – item: dubbin for said boots, item: volumes of Pevsner, item: projector, item: architectural slides, item: Hasselblad, and so on, and so on. It took ages and I became impatient; later, "to save time", he raced out to get a takeaway.

'In contrast with the polished manners I'd hitherto witnessed, he crammed the food into his mouth and wolfed it down.

'The holiday came as a shock: the passionate, all-consuming affair became one of indifference; all communication ceased. There were a few attempts to go out and explore the city together, but he behaved so badly that I went off alone. One night he confessed that he had met someone. At the end of the week I drove him back to London. I stopped to let him unload his junk, then reversed up the road and drove back to Manchester.

'What I wish I'd done was left him and all his sodding junk in Edinburgh. He deserved it, but I couldn't. After all, how else would he get it all home? That wasn't quite that. He cried when I left, phoned my friends, persuaded some of them to intercede, wrote to me, phoned me, but I refused to see him. Some of my friends claimed that I was heartless – pink Gucci mac and sandals was a temporary aberration – how could I be so mean? But they hadn't been on that holiday.'

*

THURSDAY 16 MARCH

'I don't know why I should want to speak of this,' I said, but I keep thinking of "The American Business" and it upsets me. Well, perhaps I do ... we're thinking of revisiting the States ... possibly late next year.

'In early 1983, just before I met James, I'd agreed to go on an all-expenses-paid Christmas trip to Texas with my mother, to my brother's. I hadn't seen Mark for six years, and I wanted to see him; he and I had been avid correspondents but I'd never had the money or the opportunity to visit. One problem: I was uneasy at my mother's largesse; I thought it might be used as a means of emotional blackmail.'

'Why?'

'It's been done before. When I first left my parents' I was very short of money. I'd had to set myself up, equip my flat; I had no savings. My parents' vision of a socially integrated person demanded that I run a car, which I did. My father took to ringing me at work, insisting that since I'd left a "perfectly good home" and was now "earning good money", I owed it to them to send a weekly cheque. After all, they'd looked after me for seventeen years with "no return on their investment"; it was my turn to reciprocate. I reasoned with them: sorry, I really don't have any money to spare. OK, I chose to leave when you might have preferred me to stay, but we've already discussed that. As for your "investment", I didn't ask to be born; you chose to have children, presumably for your own pleasure. You say that you have had nothing back ... nothing financial, certainly, but I'd hoped that there's been some reward. I'm not all bad.

'But you see,' I said to The Therapist, 'I suspected that they were right, that I had been a financial and emotional burden. I wasn't conventionally nice-looking, nor did I have the stereotypical feminine virtues of sweet, unquestioning submissiveness. Then I'd had this long relationship with an "unsuitable man", Stephan, rendering me "unfit for anything else". Mind you, I would have cheerfully married him, if he'd agreed to it, and the relationship might have been a great success: there might never have been anyone else.

'My father would point out: "You're a grave disappointment to us." Then my mother would chime in: "You're irresponsible. You've no idea what responsibility means; *you live in cloud cuckoo land* with all those books and pictures. Books never did anyone any good; you can't take them to bed, can you? I hope that you think that when you're in your cold and lonely room. Much good may it do you, dear. When I was a little older than you, dear ... only a little older – mark my words!" – raising her voice – "when I was not much older, *I had two children*." I'd retaliate: So, what does that prove? What's clever about that? Is it really so admirable? So enviable? I've seen enough of "family life" to put me off forever! Then my mother would yell: "Would you rather not have been born?"

'So, given all this on past hospitality, accepting money from my mother was fraught with danger. At its crudest, money equals power, but I allowed my feelings for my brother to overcome my scruples. "Look, it'll be nice," my mother argued, "you'll see Mark; you'll see something of America."

'I gave in. I did a lot of research, I secured the cheapest tickets. There were dozens of transatlantic calls: me to Mark, Mark to me, mother to Mark, Mark to mother. It was all very complicated. In the middle of all of this I met James. Our relationship seemed solid; he said he'd see me, he did; he promised to phone, he did. He sent letters, flowers, chocolates.

'He hadn't had a "real holiday" for a couple of years; naturally he wanted to come with me; he said he wanted to meet my mother and my brother. There seemed no good reason why he shouldn't, though I knew that they'd hit the roof if I dared to ask.

'You could argue that it was a reasonable request. I tried to explain to James that if it was up to me, then I'd want him to be there, with me, but I feared that his suggestion would not be well received. I realised that my mother and brother had expectations: it was "their treat" rather than mine; my mother was paying and would set the rules; the invitation was subject to their terms and conditions. It didn't matter to them if I derived pleasure from it or not. So, any personal request would be seen as unreasonable. One of my intended functions was, I think, to be escort to my mother, to entertain her and be there to deflect the continual caterwauling. I already knew that Mark's mysterious "new friend" would be coming, so I could have argued: if she can, why can't James? But I was unwilling to ask because I knew what the answers would be. I tried to convince myself that I'd have a glorious three weeks without James; if he was worth anything then he would wait for me. I would miss him, but before I knew it the holiday would be over and I'd be home. You can see that I had strong misgivings.'

'Why did you risk ringing your brother when you knew all this?'

'Because at root I was sure that James wouldn't wait; Mill Hill was nearer than Manchester or Texas, and he'd think "Stuff this!" and resume relations with his ex; the one that he *really wanted*.... Also, James couldn't understand why I was hesitating, and was starting to doubt my protestations of affection.'

'What happened?'

'One of the worst phone calls ever. Mark called me a whole selection of foul names: a whore, a tart, a bitch, and – lest I misunderstood – he spelled it out for me: "B-I-T-C-H". I tried to reason. I told him that I'd met someone, that it was serious; we got on well, I'd like them to meet. I pointed out to Mark that his "new friend" was coming, so it was reasonable for me to bring someone. Mark said that that was different. I accused him of taking my father as role model: dictating rigid rules, wagging his finger, treading on people. My mother phoned, wailing hysterically: "*Why do you always spoil things? Why are you always such a disappointment? You let me down all the time ... we were going to have a nice family time. You ungrateful bitch.*"

'My temper snapped: "OK!" I shouted. "If that's the way you feel, then I'm not coming," and I banged the phone down. Mark phoned back and piled on more abuse: I'd sacrificed him and our mother for some worthless upstart. That was that. I told him to forget it. Later, I had the unenviable task of cashing in my ticket and refunding my mother's money; I lost a lot of dosh as I forfeited the deposit but she *insisted* on having everything back.'

'And now?'

'I haven't spoken to either of them since; over five years already. My mother said: "From today, dear, you're dead to me." So why should I contact her? I can't bring myself to.'

'We'll have to stop there,' The Therapist said, 'but I'd like to pick up some points next time.'

*

WEEKEND IN WOOLWICH

THURSDAY 23 MARCH

After I'd settled myself on the couch, I gazed at the photo of Freud. There was a long silence. Then in her usual tones, The Therapist volunteered: 'It seems that you might have engineered The American Business. Think about it. If you're honest you'll admit that you had good reasons for not going.'

'OK, OK, I admit it. There were perfectly good reasons. I couldn't be certain of my role; I wasn't going there on equal terms. More than half an hour in my mother's company is a great strain.'

'Explain.'

'Well, there's no let-up. Constant yak-yak-yak; if there's nothing to say, she'll say something – anything! – to break the silence. Once we were in the Egyptian Gallery at the BM and I pointed out a statue of the jackal-headed god Anubis. She kept repeating: "Mr Nubis, Mr Nubis". "No", I explained, "it's Anubis: A-N-U-B-I-S." She protested, "No! No. It's a joke, dear, a joke."

'Why bother saying anything at all? What's the point? You can't ignore her voice. If only she'd adopt Salvator Rosa's motto: "Be silent unless what you have to say is better than silence". Admirable, eh? Whenever I've seen her I've had to plan her every move; decide where to go, what to do, choose and order her meals, provide learned comments, research; she reserves the right to decide what I think she terms "moral direction"! On the other hand, perhaps she's being too damned considerate....'

'How did you feel about meeting your brother again after so long?'

'Uneasy; it was a frightening prospect. When he moved to the States, he was married to Lisa, his first wife. I had the most marvellous letters: detailed, spirited descriptions of places they'd been, the buildings at the University of Texas; the many cultural events. When they separated, the letters became short and uninteresting. The present format is (1) the weather, (2) the crops, (3) associated work on the land, (4) eating and drinking – of which he does too much, (5) work on the vast new house and the figure-of-eight pond. I feared that Mark might be much changed, or – worse – a bore.

'We'd had arguments by post. He said that I'd changed. At the time he left, I was still the "stupid sister", the "inferior female", the one who was "merely clever"; he was the "genius", he'd been to university and had got a 2.1; I hadn't. I'd taken the "easy option" of a job; a glamorous sort of job, but still just a job; he'd studied, he was the "family brain". When, contrary to his predictions, I got in at university, his assumptions were challenged. Have I told you that my mother called me a fool for throwing in my career? Mark flatly predicted that I'd fail, fail miserably, I was deluding myself. Well, I didn't. I got a better degree than he did, then I put in for a PhD. He didn't like it; he had "the family PhD". Sometimes he'd ring and leave messages on my answerphone: "Since university, you've got too big for your boots. You need taking down a peg or two," then his voice would be drowned out by bar room noises.'

The Therapist interrupted: 'Do you think you're trying to prove yourself?'

'I've had many long conversations with Anton about that.

I've not really told you about him ... an old friend. We had an instant sympathy. He was similarly derided: the bespectacled family dunce; his sister was the golden child, the one who could do no wrong. At school he was ridiculed for his thick pebble glasses, in the way that I was ridiculed for being chubby and for still having plaits when all other "sensible children" had had their hair cut. He and I agreed that it was comforting to know that we'd succeeded when everyone else predicted we'd fail.'

'But why a PhD? Wasn't a first degree enough?'

'No,' I said. 'No. I loved the subject. I wanted to go on studying; I chose the topic because I felt inspired ... also to get a first degree wouldn't have been important enough; most students get a degree of one sort or another, even if it's an indifferent grade. The Barrister got a Third, and his intelligence isn't in question. I felt compelled to go one further; anything less than a First would have been a failure; anything short of a PhD seems insignificant.'

'Yes, I can understand that,' she replied.

'I think that there's another issue bound up in The American Business,' I said tentatively, 'but it's an historical issue, to do with my relationship with Mark. When he and I were living "at home", we hated one another and squabbled constantly. I saw him as a Brylcreem-bespattered twerp with NHS specs, who was always slorming on the floor.'

'What?'

'I mean rolling,' I said, 'or running around the garden with a pointed stick. On his first day at the grammar school, our parents insisted that I look after him. I hadn't had a similar consideration. My father could have easily driven me there on my first day three years before, but he'd said that I was "a big girl, too old", and I should make my own way. I'd never done anything on my own before, and I was unnerved. If I'd had to do that, why shouldn't Mark? But then there was a truce. We started walking there together, and having long conversations. One day I realised that I liked him.

'In 1974 he got a place at Imperial College, and moved to London. We kept in touch; at the end of each term, when he had to move his possessions to the parental home, I'd help.

'Generally, though, he'd phone on a Thursday night: "*Tomorrow's the weekend! Put your sleeping bag in the car and hit the M1!*" By 6pm I was on the motorway and three and a half hours later I'd be drawing up outside Southside. I think that he enjoyed those times as much as I did. We'd walk, tour the markets, visit exhibitions, drink, play music, have picnics, and spend hours in discussion. I loved Lisa, whom I thought of as "my little sister Angela" – the sister I never had.

'My parents accused me of using Mark as a meal ticket to "The Big City". It might have looked like that, but it wasn't; it wasn't at all. They pointed out that when he was in Yorkshire I hadn't taken much notice of him; now that he was living "somewhere exciting", I saw him "almost constantly". I argued that when Mark was at home he was young and not so interesting; now we had a great deal more in common.'

'Might you have visited him so much if he'd been studying in Loughborough or Coventry?'

'I don't know,' I replied, 'I honestly don't know. I liked to visit Mark, but it was also a treat to visit London; that didn't mean to say that I was using him. I made a point of paying for transport; I was acutely aware that I had an income and he hadn't, so I usually bought the meals, and paid museum admission charges.

'He and Lisa had his room; I'd have Lisa's. Mark was in Selkirk Hall, which I considered most enviable; his room on the top floor with a marvellous view over Prince's Gardens and the dome of the Royal Albert Hall. I thought of it as the heart of London: London as Museum Land; London as Seat of Learning. Lisa's room was in Keogh, overlooking the pink and white mews terraces. Some of our walks were wonderful: "The Hole in the Wall" – you leave Southside by the back door, go along the mews, through a triumphal arch, and into a narrow passage bordered by brick walls. There's a tiny opening, so small that you might easily miss it, leading into the gardens of Holy Trinity, Brompton. You can stop off there or wander about the Georgian squares until you emerge somewhere near Harrods.

'I remember my 23rd birthday. Mark had decided to stay in London that summer as he had a casual cleaning job at Southside. Selkirk had been given over to conferences, and he'd moved across the gardens to a grand Italianate residence in Phillimore Gardens. His fifth-floor room was isolated and cavernous; he'd advised me to ring the entryphone in blasts of five when I arrived. I did as instructed: no answer. I tried again: ditto, and again, ditto, and again, when suddenly his voice, with a ridiculously bogus accent boomed out: "Oo the 'ells that?"

That set the tone for the weekend. We stayed up late on the Friday night to see in my birthday. He gave me a marvellous present: a huge carrier bag full of extraordinary items from the Chinese supermarket – noodles, crackers, chopsticks, sake, green tea, rice of various types; chopstick rests in odd shapes, a brightly coloured fan, a fish-shaped penknife. I'd bought a couple of bottles of sparkling white wine which we drank rapidly, and ended the evening with some hilarity.'

'But,' the Therapist interrupted, 'it clearly makes you uneasy to accept anything from your family, in case they see it as unacceptable sponging.'

'That's right,' I replied.

*

THURSDAY 6 APRIL

'An odd thing,' I said. 'I can't tell how this has come about, but suddenly I'm feeling less desolate. There's much about myself that I still don't like: I'm a snob, priggish, arrogant, conceited, but there are some things that I do like: intelligence, bookishness, learning. My confidence seems to be growing. I'm glad that I'm different from James's friends. Damn it all! All this time and I've been trying to push myself into a mould I won't fit into. Why should I? What on earth have I been doing? What about my high-sounding principles? "To thine own self be true". I've given into emotional blackmail. I'm not prepared to do that now.'

I thought for a while.

'I really don't think that my family have been kind to me: blood relation as a means of control, words as abuse. They've played on my good nature. Some of the things they've said, I wouldn't stand for from anyone else. They got away with it because of "family loyalties". Another thing: when I first came here I claimed that my marriage was happy. I thought that it was. Now I'm not so sure. Is he a philistine? Does he value his friends more than he values me? Is he more comfortable in their milieu? I suspect that he might be. I don't know what's going on; he's been going to lots of mysterious meetings. He won't comment on them other than to say that someone at work introduced him, and that they just talk, have valuable discussions. I have no idea what they discuss, though he claims that it will alter our marriage. Why should it when he won't discuss it with me?'

There was a long silence, then she asked:

'Have you noticed?'

'Noticed what?'

'I might not be working for much longer; I might take quite a break.'

'What's wrong? Are you ill?' I asked with some concern.

'Nothing's wrong and I'm not ill.'

'My God!' I exclaimed, not bothering to conceal my mirth. 'Was it an accident? Full marks for observation! How should I have known? Whenever I see you, you're in black, you're always sitting down, and usually I'm so busy unlacing my shoes that I don't really look at you. I just didn't notice.'

'It wasn't an accident,' she said.

Then I realised why she had been away with such alarming regularity: illness, miscarriages, depression....

'Well, then, I should say congratulations,' I said.

'Thank you,' she replied, quietly. 'How do you feel about it?'

'What it's got to do with me? Surprised, I suppose. I'd categorised you as someone who'd decided to not have children, ever. Are you happy?'

'Yes. Tell me what you really think.'

'Surprised, but ambivalent. It has nothing to do with me. I don't feel pushed aside, rejected, supplanted. Not in the slightest!'

'Angry?'

'Not at all. But it occurs to me that all this time I've formed ideas and notions of your personality: what you are really like, what you are interested in; the sort of partner you have; your ideas, ideals and principles; the sort of place that you live in, and the order – or otherwise – that prevails. I think that I've made you into a sort of sister spirit, and endowed you with all of my emotions and reactions. Now I can see that you are not like that; far from feeling that I want to change you, I like you as you are.'

'That makes me think of what you were saying earlier. Perhaps you really are beginning to accept yourself, too, "warts and all".'

'I think that I can accept more about myself; perhaps I am becoming a little more tolerant of others.'

*

WEEKEND IN WOOLWICH

TUESDAY 11 APRIL

I went in wearing a new outfit: tight black leggings, bright pink ankle warmers, oversized pink artist's smock. Instead of the red plastic briefcase, discarded long since, a black leather backpack, today bulging ominously. I still wore my black beret: 'The true mark of an Existentialist,' I told her. I struggled to remove my backpack, took off my trainers, and stretched out comfortably.

'*Well!*' she exclaimed, with the suggestion of some amusement.

'Like it? I am fed up with looking like some country maiden; I don't feel like that. I was beginning to feel untidy, like Leonard Bast's wife in Howards End: strung about with shawls, beads, feather boas, things that caught and trailed; far from presenting a smart figure, she looked thoroughly unrespectable.

'I have thought a lot about clothes, matters of dress. I can see now that I might have looked like a dog's dinner.... I'm not surprised that I was cut at the Courtauld Fancy Dress Bash; my other gaffe was to be announced by my own name on the spectacular circular stair at Home House, instead of inventing something socially acceptable such as "La Belle Jardinière" or "La Bergère". Really, you know, I no longer feel grossly fat, ugly. In these clothes, I feel like a dancer.'

'You look like one. You should wear what you feel comfortable in. Why's that bag packed for a trip around the world?'

We both laughed.

'Ah yes. In some way I was hoping that you wouldn't notice lest you thought I was bragging. *But that's it!* It's my PhD: completed, written up, three bound copies: one for the Courtauld, one for Senate House, one for the examiners, plus photographs and microfilm. I didn't tell you that I submit it today.'

'I suggest that you wanted me to know. You didn't really *have* to bring it with you, did you?'

'It would have been possible not to, but it was far easier than taking the long journey home to pick it up later. Yes, of course I wanted you to know! It's six years of my life; hours and hours of research, days and days of the most ferocious concentration. I don't mind admitting that I'm rather proud of it. I feel that I have achieved something, although something in me always suggests that *I could do better*! All that I need to worry about now is the viva, and making the transition from student to professional art historian.'

'You won't need to worry,' she said. 'You'll do it. I know it from what I now know of you. Good luck!'

'Thank you,' I said. 'Thank you very much. Oh ... and another thing ... I might have got a job. There's a strong possibility. I was having lunch with Jeanetta, and she said, "I don't suppose you've heard about this," and handed me a sheet of A4 ... an internal advertisement for a job at The Institution: "Curatorial Responsibility for all Artistic or Historical matters; a collection of over 2,000 items". Modern isn't my strong point, though I could mug up on it. Anyway, I rang for an "informal chat", and it sounds most promising.'

WEEKEND IN WOOLWICH

'What does James think?'
'He's ambivalent,' I lied, recalling last night's altercation.
'Good luck,' she repeated.

*

TUESDAY 18 APRIL

Our last meeting. We spoke inconsequentially for a time.

'It's very strange,' I remarked. 'These months – years, even – during which I depended so much on you. You were so important, and now this meeting doesn't seem to matter. Perhaps it's because you revealed so little. We certainly had a rapport; we could communicate, we have things in common, but I don't know you. I once pointed out that I thought you were my clone: what I thought, you thought, what I felt, you felt; my artistic interests were yours. Now I can see that that's not so, and I'm delighted.

'I was worried that to "recover" might mean losing my personality, selling out my individuality. Far from it. We've spoken about some painful incidents, but some things were funny, too: my father chasing the gorgeous Roy up Scutari Road brandishing a sabre – "Yer've outstayed yer welcome, lad!" At the time it was a disaster, now it's merely ludicrous. I wonder how Roy felt about it. I never saw him again.

'Then there was the nickname my brother bestowed on my father: "The Oracle". He made a mobile spelling it out and hung it over The Old Man's half of the marital bed. Pater went nuts, but we all knew who had done it because it was spelled 'ORICLE' and Mark never could spell.

'Now I know that I am not to blame for my father passing up opportunities. He'd been offered a job in Greenford, Middlesex. Nearer to London, I thought, it might be good. At least I'd get close to "The Big City". But they didn't move "because of the children"; "the children were doing exams". You know what I thought of those, and I wasn't consulted.

'The real reason they didn't was my father's doubts, insecurities. It was easier to blame me and Mark.'

A short silence.

'We're close to time up,' she said.

'I wish you well. I hope that everything goes as planned.'

'Do you want to discuss anything else?'

I got up from the couch and for the first time looked her full in the face.

'Now I know why you wanted me to use the couch,' I replied. 'I had to work everything out for myself. If I'd faced you I might have picked up all sorts of clues and signals. Clever, very clever! I might have worked out all of the socially acceptable answers rather than the real ones. I might have played the conventionally polite role rather than sworn like a trooper when I felt like it.

'As for my feelings now ...' I laced up my trainers. 'I feel fine. Not quite able to believe that that's it, but rather looking forward to my freedom; freedom to get on with the rest of my life. And I feel confident that I won't have to come back.'

I unzipped the front pocket of my backpack and brought

out a small red parcel tied with a silver bow.

'It's not much,' I said, 'not much at all, but I wanted to say thank you. It has been a life-enriching experience.'

I stood up, pulled on my battered leather jacket and black beret. We shook hands.

'Thank you very much,' I said.

Then I turned on my heel and, without looking back, left the room.

*

PART II

LETTER TO STEVE

LONDON

APRIL – MAY 1992

LETTER 1 TO STEVE

London
Sunday 5 April 1992

Dear Steve

Here I am again in the New Look Café Bar, Covent Garden. You'd like it here: all yellow colour-washed walls hung about with scenes of glamorous people in exotic locations; dangling plants, Art Nouveau fittings, Art Deco lighting. I am at my favourite marble-topped table looking out over Wellington Street; a kir in front of me, Time Out and The Independent on my right.

I was surprised and delighted to receive your letter. I recognised your distinctive writing from that postcard you sent me years ago; I read it several times because I couldn't believe my eyes. How odd that we should have run into each other in the British Museum. It's difficult to believe that ten years have passed....

I put down my pen and started to think of some of the events which have led me here: the vicissitudes of my life and work; my early voyage of discovery in London, my precipitate move to Bloomsbury. It was here that I last met Anton; a long story.

I'd known him years ago when we were both in Manchester, 1979. I was a leading member of the Whitworth Arts Society, in my first term as a mature student. One evening there was a Private View at the City Art Gallery. I spotted this bloke in the crowd: a friendly face and lopsided smile, direct gaze, deep brown eyes, mole below the right one, slightly tubby but with an air of warmth, understanding. He came over. 'Hi! I'm Anton.' We exchanged some words about the pictures. I enjoyed talking to him, but there was something about the way in which he looked at me – the way he looked me up and down – which suggested that it wasn't my mind he was interested in. I was feeling old and bruised – I'd just emerged from all that business with Charlie, and a one-night stand was the last thing I wanted. So, when he asked me out, I gave him an old-fashioned look, turned on my heel and left.

Everywhere I went, though, I ran into him: among the stacks in the library, at lunch in the Postgraduate Centre, where I often gatecrashed, on account of my 'great age'; in the Union – his working habits and mine were similar. We began to talk, at first about informal things – films seen, places been – then about his work: the ethics of Business Management – and then about mine: the finer points of Neoclassicism – later about points of principle: personal integrity, following one's feelings, doing what one felt to be right, honesty. The conversations were long and intense and I didn't realise how much I enjoyed them or how fond I'd grown of him until he moved to Cambridge. Late February 1983, that was.

Suddenly, silence ... I wrote but he never replied, I phoned but he didn't return my calls. It might have been something to do with our last meetings. At the time I was in the throes of finishing with Chris, the publisher. One night I was alone and the phone rang: 'Hello,' said Anton. 'I'm ringing to see if you would like to join me for dinner tomorrow.' 'Dinner?' I wondered. 'That's odd. You've never asked me to dinner before.' 'February 14,' he continued. 'Valentine's Day.' 'My God!' I thought. 'A declaration of affection at last!' But still I hesitated. 'I'll pay,' he said, and I started to laugh: 'I didn't say anything because I was stunned, but yes – yes! Of course I'd love to come.' And we agreed to meet at the Old Postgrad.

I had five Dry Martinis – real ones – before we went to the Tapas Bar. He ordered a large carafe of white Rioja and we both got plastered. We reeled through Albert Square clinging to each other, then it was back to the Postgrad Disco for more drinks. We shared a cab home, and I was hurt and puzzled when he refused my offer of 'coffee', got out and fled into the night. Some days later he announced that he'd got a job – 'The PhD's nearly finished' – then he just disappeared.

Five months passed. In July there was a message: 'I'd love to see you again. Come to Cambridge.' This is it, girl! I thought. It's all going to happen.

*

It was a gloriously hot weekend.

When we met we threw our arms around each other. The first evening we walked to some pub on Jesus Green – me feeling beautiful, like a princess, in my long, white cheesecloth gown and green-fringed shawl; him attentive and charming. We sat on a wall above the Cam and got horribly drunk.

Later, back at his flat, he showed me my room; I remember

feeling disappointed: 'My room? But ... but ... *weren't we supposed to be spending the weekend together?*'

It was a lovely red and orange room with white walls, bright lights, an appliquéd bedspread, big squashy cushions and his collection of ethnic masks; the windows opening onto St John Street, the house martins screeching around the buildings. We opened another bottle and sat on the bed.

'I'm tired,' he announced, after the second glass. 'I'm going upstairs.'

I followed him. In bed he strained me close and kissed me passionately, but that was all.

'What's going on?' I asked. 'We've known each other a long time and I know that you like me.'

'That's the problem,' he said. 'We've known each other too long; I know you too well. You're too like me. I think of you as my soulmate, my sister, and it would be wrong – incestuous even – to fuck you.'

'Aren't you putting me on a pedestal? I know that we've got a lot in common: all that about attitudes of mind, books, learning ... all those long conversations. You know more about me than anyone. I can't see why that should be such a stumbling block. I've always liked you; I've regretted that I didn't go out with you when you asked me.'

'Well, you refused me,' he went on, drawing me closer. 'Anyway, you're cleverer, more cerebral, than me. You spend too much time analysing and weighing up. Nit-picking ... yes, nit-picking! I'm a charlatan, really, and I'd disappoint you. Besides, I don't find you attractive.'

'That's unkind! You know that I've just recovered from measles. I was ill for eight weeks. Eight whole weeks! I thought I was going to die.'

'That's not what I meant,' he reassured me, as he ran his hand along my thigh. 'It's not that you're bad-looking. Well, not exactly ... it's just that I like English Roses with peaches-and-cream complexions ... you ... well, you look too foreign, too gaunt, too much like a gypsy. You *look* eccentric, you wear funny clothes; you make people stare.'

What could I say? I didn't bother to defend myself.

'You sure know how to make a girl feel good!' I threw at him as I retreated to my room.

Then the following day, a lachrymose conversation in the Fellows' Garden at Magdalene. 'Very appropriate,' said Anton, 'Magdalene College! Isn't that good? Get it? *Maudlin,* you know!'

So, I went back to Manchester.

Then nothing for six years until Christmas Eve 1989, a card arrived.

'James. I don't believe it!' I exclaimed to my husband, concealing my delight with difficulty. 'I'd recognise that writing anywhere. It's Anton!'

Inside, a long letter explaining that he'd moved to London, thence Winchester and Bath; that he had a lovely bachelor pad 'because bachelor I am still'. His first PhD had been 'outdistanced by contemporary events', but he'd embarked on another, similar one. He enjoyed his studies: he was writing and lecturing. He was happy, he said; he loved Bath: *You know it of course. The city has an aura of enchantment. It's so nice to wander about the streets, admiring the architecture, its form and symmetry, watching the effects of light on the beautiful stone.*

'Yes!' I thought. 'He's finally found his niche.'

So, that July we went to Bath. I'd not dared to suggest that we visit Anton – James would be furious – but on our last day I casually mentioned that he lived in Monmouth Street.

We went to his address, and it was exactly as I had imagined: a modest late Georgian town house; Bath stone, beautifully set masonry, austere Doric portico onto the street, graceful cast-iron area railings. There were two doorbells. The maisonette, I thought, sounded too grand, too established, so I rang the bell of the flat:

'We're looking for Anton.'

'Oh?'

The voice sounded unfamiliar through the crackling system.

'Do you know him?'

'You've found him. Who's that?

'Anna ... Anna, and James,' I added, as an afterthought.

'Anna? Anna from Manchester?'

'Yes!'

'Good God!' he exclaimed. 'I'm coming straight down.'

He flung the door open and threw his arms around me. He looked just the same. We went for a drink at La Vendange, Margaret's Buildings, where we sat in the rear courtyard, in the winter strewn with rubbish and the wreckage of better times, but now full of climbing plants, sunlight, and our witty conversation. We returned home late. Then no news and when

I wrote, the letter came back marked 'Gone Away'.

I had another drink.

It was here, in The New Look, that I also told Sarah about James's loyalty to 'The Place', a sensitive subject which she was researching. We had never met before and the prospect of inviting her to my tiny flat was too intrusive, too personal. I'd suggested neutral ground ... somewhere that I knew, somewhere that I felt safe.

We recognised each other immediately. Her: friendly expression, tanned, long, dark crinkly hair, bright red tartan suit and a voluminous black hooded cloak. Me: friendly, pale, long, red plait with silver bow, baggy trousers and artist's smock, battered leather jacket, black beret. We ordered wine, coffee. But I felt awkward and at first it was difficult to talk about issues which I'd tried to forget.

'How shall we start?' asked Sarah. 'Do you mind if I take notes or would that put you off? Warn me if there are things you'd rather not talk about at all. It was very recent and you must still be feeling rather strange.'

'I'm OK,' I replied. 'It might help if I tell you the lot ... I don't really mind.' And I picked up my glass and gulped my wine.

'How did he become a member? Did he know about it before or was it sudden?'

'Through a friend of his, a senior colleague he liked and respected. Someone who – on the face of it – had everything: good looks, charm, a pleasant manner, ready wit, success at work and with women. This colleague, Dave, had gone to a

"Weekend Workshop" and came back insisting that it was the best thing that had ever happened to him. He went on and on, apparently, bragging about how it had transformed his life, solved his problems ... suddenly he was communicating, *really communicating,* with people. His retarded daughter had "progressed immeasurably" It had "regenerated his relationships"; I think those were his words.'

Sarah began to scribble furiously.

'Quite a claim! What did James do?'

'He spent a lot of time out, then went on and on about an "Introductory Evening". I set it aside, wasn't interested. When I "came to" – October 1990 – we were far apart anyway and I assumed that it was some sort of mutual admiration society for him and his boring friends. The invitation looked innocuous enough, if a little too flash, too calculated, too pushy: "We offer you the golden opportunity" ... that sort of thing. I didn't know what it was about, and I wasn't anxious to find out. I just wasn't interested.'

'Did you ever discuss it with him?'

'In a way ... but we'd been having problems. He hated my cultural interests and arty friends; I despised his dull values and philistine acquaintance. By Christmas that year things had got to such a pitch that I'd almost decided to move; I'd found a tiny studio in Bloomsbury, high up, in a respectable block. I've always liked living at the top of buildings. Just as I was about to exchange contracts, James persuaded me to pull out.'

'How?'

'I'm not sure. I can't quite remember. I've tried so many times to reconstruct the arguments ... he was very persuasive. He apologised for being jealous of my studies, my PhD, my success at work. He admitted that he'd felt ignorant, overwhelmed by my knowledge. After The Place he'd realised that he had "been dragging a dead body around for 30 years"; now he had come to life and wanted something of whatever it was that I had. He got down on his knees, cried, howled, *begged* me to stay. He apologised for all that he'd done. I gave in. I felt too tired, too weak to put up any resistance....

'Then he said an odd thing: he forgave me for upsetting him.'

'He forgave you for his problems? That's ridiculous!'

'Quite,' I agreed. 'I know it sounds odd; I never did work it out. Still, he apologised for railing at me, for not understanding things which he should have understood....'

I took another sip at my wine and looked out at Wellington Street. The business of my PhD was a painful episode.

I explained to Sarah:

'August 88, or shortly thereafter, I wanted to hold the party to end all parties. After all, it was the culmination of six years' hard labour – my independent research – my life's work! I wanted to commandeer the local wine bar and do it *in style* ... I wanted to get someone to do the catering, so that I'd have nothing to worry about. I would simply arrive and *enjoy!* I'd never had a party *just for me* – not even a birthday party – and I wanted one. All celebrations had stopped at my parents' when my brother hurled tomato ketchup all over the carpet. I saw this as the one to make up for all past disappointments. James insisted that if I was going to do this, then I invite all his friends – the same people who had sneered at my work and ridiculed my values. No friends, he said, no party. So, of course I refused.'

'That's very sad,' she said sympathetically. 'Let me get you another drink. Did you celebrate at all?'

'Furtively, with one or two close friends. Drinks in wine bars, lunches in cafés, that sort of thing.'

'But when we spoke on the phone I thought you said that there'd been some improvement in your relationship.'

'At first, there was,' I admitted. 'After James went to the "Weekend Workshop", there was a remarkable change. I remember telling some of my friends that he was a new man ... different, livelier. He'd previously been apathetic, bovine, "placid" – he called it – about life in general. Indifferent, I'd say! His former attitude was "bored", "not interested". Before The Place if we'd disagreed, instead of discussing, meeting it head on, he'd retreat into silence. It was infuriating; it was impossible to break through. I accused him of being a tyrant – silence *is* a form of tyranny, after all! Afterwards he was – by his own account – fired up, dynamic, hyperactive, prepared to talk. The only problem was that sometimes I couldn't follow his reasoning. He said a lot of words which had no meaning, but I remember thinking at least he's talking ... something's better than nothing.'

Sarah put down her pencil and looked at my thoughtfully: 'Did he look odd? Did he seem odd?'

'He had a funny look about the eyes. I put it down to the late nights that the workshop demanded. It seemed ridiculous to me ... why couldn't he stay in London, get a room in the hotel? He could well afford to. Instead, he'd come rolling in at 5am with stories of how they'd been locked in discussion until 3am and how productive the meeting had been. Then he would get up at 6.30am to go to the next session. His eyes were set, glazed, as if he were looking over my shoulder. Later, when I became fed up with it all, I called him a zombie, a soucriant. "Typical of you," he said, "to use a word no one else has ever heard of".

I laughed.

'But then I couldn't help but notice that some of his expressions were strange. I knew the meaning of the words, but they were meaningless in the way in which he used them. All the time I had to watch what I said. Certain words seemed to act as "buzzwords", and set him off ... I asked him to "change the tape".'

'What did you make of it?' she asked. 'You must have had some suspicions.'

'Naturally ... it all sounded so dubious. Before he'd signed up for the "Weekend Workshop" I'd tried to dissuade him, arguing that if his confidence was so battered, and he felt so bad about himself, then he should sign up for psychotherapy. Or at least consider it. He said that that was only for "nutters", people like me. What I couldn't accept was that if psychotherapy can take years – upwards of twenty if you believe Woody Allen! – then how could a mere weekend make such a difference? It wasn't possible, I claimed, unless it was brainwashing.'

'Do you think it was?'

'I'll come back to that,' I said. 'Let me tell you the rest of the story. He accused me of passing up a golden opportunity. When we went to the States – October 1990 – a holiday I'd been eagerly anticipating for the past eighteen months, we spent all the time bickering. It was *horrible* ... I didn't want to go to a sodding "Introductory Evening", but he went on and on about it: it was "such a small thing to ask, and the benefits would be great".

'I held out for almost six months – until February 91, I suppose – but by then he had done another two mysterious courses and some voluntary work. His tactics were always the same. First he would say: "I want to put a proposition to you. I think you're a great person, so let me invite you to seize the opportunity to enrich your life." What a load of eyewash, eh? "How would you feel if your problems were solved and your migraines disappeared? You'd be a fool to close your eyes, wouldn't you?"

'I'd be sceptical. "Thanks," I'd say, "for your concern. If you're talking about The Place, I'm not interested. I can't see how it could cure my migraines. Anyway, I like my life as it is". He'd continue: "Then you're bigoted, blinkered. You are too stupid to understand. I am trying to help you! You could be great; you could be perfect."

'Then a significant look would spread across his face: "We could transform our marriage". Ha! What a joke!

'I'd say something like: "You've forgotten all the psychoanalysis I went through ... I am OK as I am now, I don't want changing or transforming." "Fine," he'd reply, then the subject would be dropped for a few days. Soon he would start again: "I've got a business proposition to put to you...." "Oh yes?" I'd say, suspiciously, and he'd go on: "It's not what you think it is, not at all ... Petronia needs some cash for her studies, so she's going to hold a party" – long pause – "she's charging £5 admission." "Business proposition!" I'd scoff. "That's stupid! Why didn't you just ask me?" "I'm sorry. I should've done but I thought you'd just dismiss it." "You could have tried." "You'll like everyone. They're really friendly and open."'

'Were they?' asked Sarah.

'Yes, very. They *gushed;* they were so friendly that I thought I would *puke!* I didn't like it, not at all ... no, not at all. I knew nothing about them and I didn't think we had anything in common, so why were they so anxious to *force* themselves on me? They kept trying to touch me, to intrude upon my space. You know that there's a generally accepted distance people stand apart; they had their noses in my face! Their entire conversation revolved around The Place and the good it has done them. It was tedious – I really didn't want to know. I had agreed to go to a party, not a recruitment drive.

'Their argument was along the lines of: "You're OK but you could be so much better..... So, first you have to do The Place ... then you pay us a large sum of money."

'I should say,' I added, 'that Petronia's "studies" turned out to be a slot on The Place's Advanced Programme.'

'What happened next?'

'My memory is a bit hazy here,' I said as I picked up my glass. 'I can't remember quite when it was ... March 91, I suppose ... loads of people rang me at home praising The Place and claiming that *they had got all the answers.* To what? I wondered; a spurious phrase to say the least. I was fed up with James's new friends, and insisted that since I was the one most likely to be in when the phone rang, then we get an answerphone. If he considered our relationship to be worth the odd fifty quid, that is.

'About this time his language became more extravagant, full of jargon and meaningless expressions. His arguments sounded lucid enough, but if you analysed them they didn't add up. You could agree with each sentence but the piece as a whole didn't make sense; something was wrong, but I couldn't work out what it was. Then there were the invitations: dozens and dozens of them. Eventually I agreed to go to an "Introductory Evening" because I thought that it might shut him up. For a time, at least.'

'So, you did one of those? I'm surprised! What was it like? Sarah asked.

'Busy,' I said. 'Swarming with people. There must have been about 400 guests. At first I thought it brisk, efficient, friendly. We were met at reception where someone took our names, wrote out badges, gave us coffee. Everyone was friendly – overfriendly – "we were the best people that they had ever met". I noticed that The Leader's reasoning sounded logical enough, but I couldn't make head or tail of his arguments. Like James's, they didn't add up. I wish I could remember the words, but I can't.

'Another thing that struck me: the organisers and stewards were immaculately presented: designer clothes, expensive jewellery, seductive perfumes. They were perfect, too perfect.

I think that the message you were supposed to get was: "You, too, can be like me: young, happy, successful, attractive. I've got the lot".'

'Yes,' said Sarah. 'They're good at that sort of thing,' and she made another note in her book. 'Go on.'

'Well, The Organiser came onstage primping and preening, obviously very pleased with herself. She asked what experience people had had of The Place: "Hands up! Hands up, now!" And loads of hands – including mine, I'm ashamed to say – shot up. How stupid I was! It's very seductive being in a crowd ... I explained that I'd almost left James, then he'd been on a "Weekend Workshop" and had changed so spectacularly that I'd decided to stay ... the marriage had resumed in all senses of the word. The Organiser remarked that we didn't look like a couple on the brink of divorce. I was thanked and everybody clapped wildly.'

'Wasn't that rather heady?'

'Yes,' I admitted, 'but I can say – in my defence – that you get a high from confession and disclosure, especially in front of a crowd. It's good for the ego to feel that everyone loves you. After that we were invited to join the Workshop in April.'

'And?'

'I agreed to go on condition to reserve my right to leave if I found that it wasn't for me.'

'That sounds reasonable enough.'

'Yes,' I said. 'That's what I thought. I supposed by agreeing that I had put an end to the arguments, or at least I would get some peace until April. I was stupid to think that! No sooner

WEEKEND IN WOOLWICH

had I agreed than James dished out more and more invitations. I couldn't see the point. *And* he began to pester my friends. Not long after that I went to a party with him and one of my office colleagues. I got up to buy the drinks; by the time I got back James had cornered her and launched into a long monologue about his new beliefs. She'd agreed to go to an "Introductory Evening". She might have done so out of politeness; it might not have been something she that really wanted to do. So I felt bound to go, too. I was worried.'

'Was that the same sort of evening as the other one?'

'Sort of – but not so well organised and not so successful.'

A long silence.

'After that things became extremely difficult,' I added. 'James woke me at all hours – 2am, 4am, 5am – to extol the virtues of The Place. He became very good at confrontation, haranguing, shouting me down. About two weeks before the workshop, I received the Information Pack – a very chic production job on glossy art paper ... black and white images of Greek temples in bright sunlight, people of all nations embracing; handsome, muscular, Aryan young men in tennis whites; The Founder in a thoughtful pose ... "Mr Werner as Laurence Sterne" ... that sort of thing. It was peppered with quotes from Socrates, Sartre, Nietzsche, all manipulated or edited to make a different point from the one originally intended.

'There were numerous forms to complete in which you had to promise that you wouldn't eat until the first meal break – at six that evening! – you wouldn't take any medication, or leave the room for *whatever reason.* They emphasised that.'

WEDNESDAY 15 APRIL
THE NEW LOOK CAFÉ BAR

The Waiter in white shirt, black trousers, black braces, fetching little white apron, took up his post outside the window. I've heard all of his smooth sales pitch before: 'Good Evening, Sir, Madam! How about a delicious little snack? A hot chocolate? A nice little glass of chilled white wine? Pre-Theatre Dinner? Yes, yes, of course! You'll be out long before 7.30.' The couple look nonplussed but they follow him into the bar; which is what I did once....

April 1991: a year ago, already ... a sunny weekend. The Weekend Workshop was held in a large Brompton hotel; the smart venue conferring instant respectability. On the noticeboard it was billed as 'The Meeting' with no mention of The Place, and no clues as to its purpose. The delegates were shown into a reception area where, before I'd had a chance to hang up my jacket or get coffee, I was pounced on by Nick – the organiser who'd kept ringing me – who was exactly as I had imagined: dark-haired, good-looking, friendly, brimming with confidence. 'Hi, here I am!' he shouted, extending his hand and flashing a brilliant smile. 'Good to meet you, after all this time! It's great you're here ... but to business. Now, about this migraine of yours ... is it a problem?'

'It will be fine so long as I take my tablets.'

'Tablets?' he asked. 'You know that's out of bounds unless

it's strictly necessary.... It's all in the mind anyway.'

'It is strictly necessary,' I said, 'if I start to get the symptoms.'

'What are these tablets, anyway?' he asked, eyeing me suspiciously.

'Nothing special: Migraleve, that's all.'

Miriam, a senior member of the group – The Organiser of the first Introductory Evening – came over. As before, she looked poised and immaculate but her friendly expression had hardened to one of watchful hostility.

'So you're having trouble with our friend?' she interrupted. 'May I see the tablets?'

I got them out of my bag and held them up, out of her reach.

'We must insist you don't take these, and if you get an attack you don't leave. You have to promise that. It's not too much to ask.'

'But that's up to me,' I protested. 'It's got nothing to do with you or The Place. You're being unreasonable. If I don't take these when I need to I might pass out or be sick, or both. I'm not prepared to do that.'

'You'd be surprised at what goes on in that room,' said Miriam. 'At the end of the weekend we're all one big happy family.'

'So what? I don't see why I should follow like a sheep.'

'In that case,' Miriam retorted, 'you're not fit to do The Place. *If you elect to get it*' – and she nodded significantly – 'you must promise to do the whole weekend.'

'You haven't given me a fair hearing. There are two things I need to point out. It's not likely that I will get an attack because

I see this as work. I only ever get them when I relax – on Sunday mornings, for instance. Anyway, James has paid my fees and *insists* that it will improve my life. If I let you turn me away at the door, I won't have kept my part of the bargain. You have to let me in, otherwise he will accuse me of avoiding the issue!'

An aggressive male Supervisor joined us.

'Your attitude's quite wrong!' said Miriam. 'You say you see this as work. That suggests you're doing a task rather than coming along voluntarily.'

'That's true. I promised James I'd attend but I told him that I reserved my right to leave if I found that it wasn't for me.'

'You're misguided,' Male Supervisor interrupted. 'You don't understand what The Place is. How can you? You know nothing about it – we've been doing this for 25 years and you've got to trust us. The reason we insist that you attend the whole weekend, whatever you think or feel, is because leaving The Place halfway through is like having an operation and walking out before the surgeon has finished – with all your entrails hanging out! You can't do that, can you? That would be stupid and dangerous. Anyway, if you – as you say – reserve your right to leave, you're not bringing to The Place the level of commitment we demand. Your husband is a shining example – he knows the rules!'

'How do you expect me to commit myself to something when I don't know anything about it? I wouldn't sign a contract without reading the small print. Besides, it's silly to talk about operations – if you are going into psychotherapy, say, the doors are always open and you can leave whenever you want; even in the middle of a session.... Very few people do, but there has to be an element of choice.'

'Let me put something else to you,' The Supervisor went on. 'Do you have children?'

'No, but I don't see what that's got to do with it.'

'Well, pretend you do.... If you were a mother with a child, would you let that child starve to death?'

'Of course not!' I exclaimed. But before I could say anything else, Miriam cut in:

'But you might be ill, lose your job ... have an accident ... become disabled. We can't see into the future. How can you say that? You might have a big enough job looking after yourself.'

She exchanged smug glances with The Supervisor.

'I would cross those bridges when I came to them, but I still don't understand what you are trying to say.'

'We're asking you to bring that sort of commitment to The Place.'

'That's ridiculous,' I protested. 'I don't see how I can. I know nothing about it; I'm here to find out.'

'But I'm asking you to stand for it,' said The Supervisor.

'Can you stand for it?' echoed Miriam.

'Can you?' asked Nick.

I gave in: 'I don't know what "stand for it" means. It's not part of my vocabulary, but I am prepared to give it a try.'

They smiled approvingly and we all shook hands.

'Welcome to The Place!' they exclaimed.

Suddenly there was a great deal of activity: a last-minute rush as people pushed their way into the room. 8.59am already, and Miriam and The Supervisor were looking uneasy. I went in.

I looked up from my double espresso.

Outside, The Waiter and an attractive blonde female, whom I thought I recognised, were locked in an angry discussion. He looked sunk and less confident than usual; she determined to carry her point; I pretended to read the paper, but watched furtively over the top of the page. Later, I wrote a note: *This is rather presumptuous, but here's my phone number.* I pushed it into his hand and fled into the gathering dusk.

*

LETTER 9 TO STEVE

London
Monday 20 April 1992

Dear Steve

Greetings from The Coffee Gallery, Museum Street! It looks marvellous here this morning ... a delightful place – yellow and white walls, scrubbed pine floor, green tin tables and horribly uncomfortable chairs. My espresso is served in a heavy Italian cup decorated with thick blue lines and splodgily painted fruit and flowers. All around me ... glittering jewellery and vivid watercolours by a young artist who lives nearby. This place has become the regular haunt of artists, writers, musicians, refugees from the Round Reading Room at the BM. 'Did you find them or did they find you?' I asked Italian Owner. 'They found me,' he grinned. Francis Bacon has visited, as has David Hockney; Howard Hodgkin regularly commandeers a pavement table....

*This morning the light was so beautiful that I went on a tour of little-known London gardens: St George's, Handel Street – an eighteenth century burial ground – is the most hidden in London; so secret that I am sure I'm the **only** person who has **ever** found it. An irregular space bounded by high walls and traversed by serpentine paths. In the centre a life-sized terracotta statue of Euterpe – The Muse of Instrumental Music – who once, with Apollo and companions, adorned the exterior of C Fitzroy Doll's vanished Apollo and the Muses, Torrington Place. She was so stunning that I had to photograph her.*

To answer your letter received this morning (for which much thanks):

***My phone number:** I, too, owe you an apology, if that's the correct word. When we met again I didn't give you my home number, thus removing any possibility that you could easily call me. Our meeting unnerved me. I feared the way that the evening might end; I wasn't quite sure what my feelings were – or are, for that matter – about you. I found you attractive years ago but you had just embarked on a new relationship and so had I. I don't know what your present circumstances are; I imagine that you are married; I suspect that something has gone wrong. Forgive me for asking, but are you happy? Somehow I think not, otherwise why would you write?*

Time spent at The New Look: *Yes, it's true that I spend a great deal of time there. It's on my way home and now that I don't have to dash back to Hatfield, I've got many more hours in a day. I go there to read, write letters, write for my own entertainment. I know the staff so it's become a second home. They're my friends. It's comfortable and safe – they throw out anyone who pesters me – and they don't mind if I go in and spread out my newspapers.*

Brighton *– and my jolly seaside ocean-liner-postmodern hotel – was great! Wildness? Joie de vivre? You must realise by now that I am occasionally given to exaggerating for dramatic effect. The wildest thing that I did was to visit the Palace Pier by night, not 'to take photographs' – as I claimed – but, in reality, to have a drink (perhaps that had something to do with the failure of the photos?) and to look in on the karaoke evening at Horatio's Offshore Bar....*

You might wonder about what I see in Brighton. It's an elegant and slightly raffish Georgian resort: miles and miles of white stucco ranged along the seafront – Kemp Town to Hove; then there's the Pavilion and its association with the Prince Regent's racy exploits. Brighton makes me think of 1960s youth culture, Quadrophenia. You know the film: the romance of youth, summer, the beach, the 'lost decade'.... I know that it's an unduly romantic view. Still, I've carried around a conviction that Brighton is somewhere where 'things happen', where it's always summer.

Hove *–* ***gentrified Hove:*** *Ah yes! You wouldn't have understood that reference because I'm not sure that I've ever told you that old story. In 1976 I took six weeks off work and used my*

WEEKEND IN WOOLWICH

brother's 'London Residence' – his lodgings at Imperial College – as a base for my 'Grand Tour of the South'. I went to West Wycombe to study the work of the Dashwoods and the history of the Hell Fire Club. That was my story, anyway. I bumped into Robert, an actor: handsome, charming, intelligent, entertaining, but – as I later discovered when I found him smashing up his flat around his own ears – completely deranged.

The following day I'd arranged to go to Brighton to stay with a friend in Hove. Robert pursued me; I'd never been pursued before, and to an impressionable 23-year-old it was romantic, flattering. All we did was go to the King and Queen – 1930s Tudoresque extravaganza all done out with banners, stained glass, tapestries, bogus portraits – where we both got plastered, but at the time it seemed terribly important and meaningful.

Calm in my life: *I can't imagine why all my activities should make you feel old; it seems to be that you're also frantically busy. Yes, of course I need calm. Mine comes from sitting in cafés, bars and café-bars, writing. Writing as therapy....*

On writing: *Yes, I write, I write. Don't worry about the 'respective imbalance in our files'. You say that you 'don't write'. You do; you've written more to me in a short time than anyone else ever has. Re my (lengthy) letters: I've probably got more free time and privacy than you; for me writing's easier than picking up the phone. Warn me if (a) you can't decipher my writing, (b) can't stand my habit of scribbling on both sides of the paper, or (c) find all of this tiresome.*

Slightly Bizarre Meeting: *You must be referring to the 'Family Support Group' for families and friends of victims of* *shady organisations. I was at first taken for a victim because of my 'alarmingly New Age appearance'. Their words, not mine! I shouldn't have worn my head band! I didn't know that black and silver are 'hippie colours'. The reason I went was that I felt if my experiences with The Place might help others, then some good might come of it....*

'More coffee?' Italian Owner broke in. I put down my pen and stared at the counter as I waited for it to arrive.

The Place ... The Place.... The meeting room was massive, square, featureless. Four hundred people were already sitting on low chairs arranged around a high dais. People looked smaller, diminished; perhaps it had been done to put them in an inferior position? There were no windows; the bays were covered with curtains and bunched-up blinds of 'tasteful corporate type'. It was gloomy and chilly. Young and vital male and female 'Runners' crouched in the aisles, each clutching a microphone trailing yards of flex. You were not allowed to choose your own seat; one was allocated for you. Friends were forbidden to sit together or to make eye contact as that was deemed distracting and could – the organisers claimed – prevent The Place from happening. Oddly, no one yet knew what The Place was or what was supposed to happen. There were exactly enough seats for the people present; not one too few or too many. I objected to my place at the back; I wanted a full view of the stage. After some confusion, I was given a seat in the front row next to a friendly-looking male student-type with long, crinkly hair caught into a ponytail, single gold earring; scruffy sheepskin jacket.

Male Supervisor's dais was empty except for a blackboard bearing the legend 'REMEMBER, YOU and YOU ALONE are RESPONSIBLE FOR YOUR WELFARE', a low coffee table and a high X-shaped throne chair. Shortly after nine he bounded on. I'd earlier noticed his suave appearance, the stylised perfection of his attire. His suit was expensive: well cut with knife-edge creases; his shoes gleamed. He was poised, chic, not a hair out of place. *Very impressive,* I thought. *What are they up to?* We had all been 'advised', ordered even, to wear loose-fitting, comfortable clothes; most people were therefore in jeans and trainers and by contrast looked rather shabby.

The Supervisor glanced around the room and started to harangue the audience: 'Well, was I late? Was I? We said that we'd start at nine and we have! You can rely on our word. We promised you The Place and you'll get The Place, but to *get it* you have to make and keep – *and I stress keep* – certain promises.'

It quickly became obvious that the only way to speak was to put your hand up, summon a Runner and conduct your argument by microphone. All conversations were terminated with The Supervisor's 'Thank you' or 'I got it'. In the meantime, our views and misgivings were exposed to the audience and to The Supervisor's practised scrutiny. 'Where are you all from?' he asked. 'Yes? Yes? YES?'

A chorus of replies: 'Paris, Ghana, America, Australia, Rome, London....'

'You see,' he said, 'people come from all over the world. We're a worldwide organisation with experience of working in many different countries. This *proves* we know what we are doing. What do you all do? Don't all shout at once, use the microphone!'

A forest of hands: 'I'm an architect', 'an engineer', 'a secretary', 'a doctor', 'a teacher', 'a nurse', 'a temp'.

'But so what?' he said, contemptuously. 'These are just handy tags! What does that prove? What is it really worth?' He delivered a monologue on how little these things meant in the 'Grand Scheme of Life'. True, we might have achieved some professional standing, but so what? *He's deliberately undermining everyone's confidence,* I thought.

'Some people say it's not warm enough here,' he went on. 'Hands up all those who feel hot, cold, just right. I said, "Hands up!" Don't just shout or nod; if you've got anything to say, put your hand up and say it into the microphone.'

A flurry in the audience; the majority vote was that it was just, but only just, comfortable.

'You see, I've proved that it's only a matter of perception.'

Many people asked well-considered and relevant questions which were met with studied indifference.

A hand in the audience: 'Your refusal to let people eat could surely result in a lowering of blood sugar. It could be dangerous for some of us.'

'The Place doesn't *refuse* to let you eat. We *suggest* that you do things this way because there's a lot to do each day. If we broke off for meals, then we'd never get through it. Anyway, did you come here to improve your life or to eat? Do you want jam on it? Or butter and jam? Ha ha!' He surveyed the audience, as if asking for applause. 'You can't have it both ways. Some of you could do with losing a little weight anyway.'

'Why don't you just hold a longer course?' asked the woman.

'No,' said The Supervisor, looking shocked. 'Absolutely not! We've been doing this for 25 years and find it more effective if it takes place *over a weekend*. We don't allow you to leave the room because The Place *could happen at any time*. You might go for a coffee. It might happen at *that very instant* and you'd have missed it. You'd have wasted your time and money. We're experienced in this and we know what we're doing. You're only novices.'

The woman, now embarrassed, but unconvinced, sat down: 'I see, thank you. But it would be a waste of my bloody time and money, not yours,' she muttered.

I finished my espresso. 'Would you like anything to eat?' asked Italian Owner.

LETTER 9 TO STEVE (CONTINUED)

The Existentialist: Since you ask, I'll tell you a little about him. He's a connoisseur, a collector. The order, the perfection of this café reminds me of his flat. I'd invited myself around to watch Fitzcarraldo, a film which he claimed was too worthy and serious for him, though it seemed odd that he had it on video. His flat is atop some solid yellow stock brick chambers, close to Nollekens' house. You know Nollekens – that unsavoury eighteenth century sculptor of great talent and huge parsimony? If someone rang his doorbell, he never answered the first time lest it be a runaway and he'd have wasted a candle! Anyway, The Existentialist's flat was as ordered as I had expected, but decorated with a good deal more imagination and flair, indicating, perhaps, a greater sensibility than I had supposed.

The sitting room was hard-edged High Tech with stark white walls, slate grey blinds, aggressive chrome and black leather furniture, and banks of books disposed on either side of the chimney piece; spotlights were trained on single beautiful objects, artfully arranged. The three Gaudier-Brzeskas hung over the Eileen Gray sofa; other works by scions of the Bloomsbury Group or the Slade School were stacked neatly against the walls. There was a striking silver object next to the British Museum replica Athlete – a three-legged thing which I took to be an alternative design for the Festival of Britain Skylon. Much later, I realised that it was a Philippe Starck lemon-squeezer, to be found in all the best Kensington and Chelsea homes, along with built-in food processors, cafetières, ruffle blinds, rag-rolled walls, splatter-painted sconces, bidets....

The Existentialist's kitchen was white and silver and as hard as the sitting room: bright, gleaming, equipped with gadgetry, the freezer crammed with microwave meals for one. Not much cooking goes on here, I thought.

The dining room was a complete contrast: crookedly hung William Morris wallpaper, thick, dusty-looking curtains, stodgy mahogany furniture. Pictures were crammed floor to ceiling in subject-related groups and vignettes: Baxter prints and silk samplers of the Crystal Palace; satirical etchings of the Brighton

WEEKEND IN WOOLWICH

Pavilion and the Prince Regent's risqué pursuits; some of The Existentialist's own indifferent life studies. **And** *he goes to the Slade! The Summer School, that is! The table was covered with a V&A monogrammed silk damask cloth. Numerous clocks ticked away tensely and struck indiscriminately. An infrared burglar alarm winked intermittently from its perch over the door....*

'A refill?' Italian Owner asked.

But my thoughts had returned to The Place and the moment when I stood up to speak. I seized a microphone:

'You claim that we and we alone are responsible for our own welfare. It is chalked up on your blackboard for all to see. I don't see how you can reconcile that with the removal of so much personal freedom.'

'We do this for a good reason,' replied The Supervisor. 'We know more than you do. Remember that.'

At that moment a Runner brought him a steaming cup of coffee and placed it reverently on the low table. The Supervisor ignored it ostentatiously.

'What good reason?' I asked, the microphone in my hand and the steady tone of my voice increasing my confidence.

'We've been conducting The Place for many years now and in many different countries. We know it works well.'

'You keep saying that. I don't know you. Why should I trust you?'

'How long have you been in this room?' he interrupted.

'Twenty minutes.'

'Then you don't know as much as we do.'

'But you haven't answered my question. You can't make all these rules on the one hand, and on the other claim that I'm responsible for my own welfare. It doesn't make sense.'

'Trust us. This is The Place. Wait and see.'

There was some talk of separating the 'doing' from 'the being', but no indication of why we should want to do this, or what good it might bring us. I sat down uneasily. The Supervisor sipped his coffee, a disgusted look on his face.

'But this is stone-cold!' he exclaimed.

What do you expect? I thought. *You've been ignoring it for the last ten minutes!*

He snapped his fingers. Another steaming cup arrived instantaneously in the hands of a cowering acolyte.

The Supervisor suddenly asked: 'Is there anyone who's here under pressure?'

Many hands shot up.

'One at a time, please!' he shouted. 'One at a time! Speak into the microphone. If you've anything worth saying, stand up and say it in front of your friends. Don't sit down until we've finished speaking.'

Or until he decides to release you, I thought.

Soon I was the only one on my feet.

'So what's your problem?' he asked.

The friendly-looking, crinkly haired Student on my right had started to mutter: 'Bitch ... neurotic, stupid bitch ... paranoid bitch.'

I struggled to ignore him.

'You asked if anyone was under pressure to come here. I am.'

'Oh well, *you would say that*,' The Supervisor sneered. 'We always get one troublemaker in the audience. *Pray explain!*'

'James, my husband, went to several introductory evenings, liked what he saw, and enthused about it. People kept ringing up and talking to me about The Place. I didn't want to come here. I know who I am and I like my life as it is, but James argued that the least I could do was to accept his offer. I agreed, with certain conditions.'

'So why did he want you to do this? Why do you think he wanted you to do this?'

The Student waved his hand in the air.

'I've explained,' I continued. 'He said he found it beneficial and he insisted that I would, too. I wasn't convinced; I needed to know more about it. He wouldn't – or was it couldn't? – tell me *anything* about it; what it does, how it works. Neither will you. He refused to tell me how it happened, or how – as he says – he "got it". That doesn't inspire confidence. We'd been having problems,' I admitted. 'Perhaps he felt it would help. I thought I'd give him the benefit of the doubt.'

'Everyone else, what do you think?!' yelled The Supervisor.

'I've not finished!' I shouted before anyone could interrupt. 'There are other ways of looking at it. Perhaps he doesn't like me as I am, and wants to change me. He might be jealous or bear me a grudge. He might want to put me through an unpleasant and humiliating experience. He might want to "teach me a lesson". How should I know?'

'No, NO!' The Student chimed in.

'*I'm speaking to her!*' bellowed The Supervisor. 'SPEAK

INTO THE MICROPHONE!'

The Student grabbed a microphone and bawled: 'It's probably because he loves you and wants to show you happiness – a way to improve your life. Some people' – glancing at me – 'aren't half neurotic. NO! PARANOID! That's it!' He looked at The Supervisor as if he'd said something immeasurably clever, and several people started to clap.

'But what really happened?' continued The Supervisor.

'What do you mean?'

'What I say', he persisted. 'What really happened?'

'Well, James went on and on; he kept inviting me to introductory evenings and parties. I gave in; I agreed in order to keep the peace. I thought I could try it.'

'We've already been through that,' he glowered. 'But you might as well explain to our friends. *You know the answer.* Is that the right attitude to bring to The Place? Come on.... *Come on ... come on ... is it? Well, is it?'*

'Stupid bitch. Fool! Idiot!' muttered The Student.

'Yes,' I said. 'Yes. I have already told you that I reserve the right to make my own decisions.'

'Some people don't know what's good for them,' The Supervisor shouted. 'How *dare* you call your husband's care and concern pressure? Now, what really happened?'

'It might not seem like pressure to you. I insist that it was. It was: "Look, I've done this and I know what I'm doing; if you really care about me, then you must follow suit. You owe it to me.... I rescued you in Manchester and brought you to Hatfield. If you don't do this – this one little thing for me – then you won't have tried; you'll have slammed the door shut on our marriage. And you'll regret it!" Then he'd change tack: "But anyway, you could be a star. You'd love the weekend. It's great fun." Then there were the phone calls, people pestering me at work....'

'You call *that* pressure?' The Supervisor snorted. 'You're raving! I think my friend in the audience is right.'

And right on cue, The Student yelled: 'Idiot! Halfwit!'

'What really happened? Tell me, what really happened?' The Supervisor persisted.

'I've told you. That's all I've got to say.'

'No, what happened? EVERYONE!' he shouted, throwing the question to the floor. 'What really happened?'

Some stirring in the audience; for the first time The Student looked nonplussed. *He's not been briefed on this, I thought. You're not supposed to challenge The Supervisor.*

'I'll tell you what happened' – The Supervisor went on – 'since everyone's being so stupid. *Yes, stupid!* Not one single person's using their brain! I'll tell you: he talked and you listened. That's it! That's all! Have you at last got that into your stupid head? He talked and you listened. *Your partner has a great deal to put up with.* He's consideration itself; you're a pain in the arse!'

'No!' I retaliated, ignoring the insult. 'I don't agree. You are reducing a difficult, an unpleasant situation to a meaningless formula. You've oversimplified it, removed the emotional blackmail.'

'You're wrong,' The Supervisor insisted. 'Quite wrong! Everyone else. Come on – *have you no ideas?*'

A wild round of applause.

Was that clever? Are they mad? Is this group hysteria?

'I'm not going to stand here all day listening to this crap,' I said. 'I'm off. I'm out of this.'

I stepped forward, shoved the microphone into The Supervisor's hand, gathered my belongings and pushed my way out of the room, past a stony-faced Miriam and a grim-looking Nick, who made vigorous attempts to stop me.

'Goodbye!' I shouted, as I slammed the door.

Several people applauded.

But I didn't want to go home.

*

LETTER 13 TO STEVE

London
Monday 27 April 1992

God knows where your promised letter is, *but thanks anyway for the postcard. Today I'm at* ***The Bargritte, Covent Garden,*** *which is – as you might expect – Magritte-inspired. Do you know that the big Magritte exhibition opens soon? I'll be first at the Hayward. The bar here is adorned with (replica) 'Ceci n'est pas une pipe' [Ha, ha! Joke! Got you there! It's a* ***picture*** *of a pipe!], the 'Clouds Napoleon' death mask and – of course! – 'Time Transfixed'; I'm not sure about the rag-rolled walls. There are chrome and plastic 'granite' tables, squashy chintz sofas, plaited* *plastic chairs of the 'New Look' type. I am sitting on the balcony; one side overlooks St Paul's portico and the entertainers; the other, the southern half of the Piazza. There's no one here, but the balcony of the Punch & Judy (next door) is heaving....*

Crazy Mime Artist, *a skilled crowd manipulator, has just arrived; people are beginning to gather around the Piazza. Mr Rainbow and Mr Diabolo – 'I throw this up as far as the roof. NO FURTHER!' – are lurking behind the church columns, with Bogus Knife Thrower and Cycle Stripper. I can hear the strains of the Sigma String Quartet; Tom, my favourite, leading.* **The Arrival of the Queen of Sheba** *and Ravel's* **Bolero** *mix uneasily with The Bargritte tape: Van Morrison and Lou Reed.*

An odd thing happened today: *This time, Flat 103 has really flipped. As I went past his door early this morning I noticed, projecting from the letter box, a single, carefully arranged black leather glove, palm outwards, a playing card resting in it. It was a No. 7 with a curious central device. Is this a surreal trip? Did he see the Wildenstein show? Is he aware of Max Klinger? Perhaps it's the missing glove? The end of the quest, the Sanc Grael? It might be a performance ... he's certainly gone over the top. If he progresses like this he might get an Arts Council award! Or be nominated for the Turner Prize....*

Which reminds me, *I was invited to an Installation, a grandly titled 'Multi Media Arts Festival' on London's lost rivers: The Effra, Fleet, Wandle and Walbrook. It sounded worthy, exciting, stimulating. I was rather taken aback to find a tin shack, plonked uncomfortably close to a beautiful Wren City Church. The shack was strewn about with old coats, rubble, shredded phone* *directories; a pickaxe stuck in a mirror, a tape running with sloshing-watery-gumboot sounds, and a voice-over – a Professor of Psychiatry from a Leading London Institution, I was told – litanising about stress, hysteria, hydrotherapy; the good which would come from regenerating the lost rivers, and so on, and so on. Outside a poet type huddled on a folding chair; sock hat, aggressive 20-eyelet Doc Martens, vague manner. He claimed that The Professor wanders about the City streets distributing a calling card thus:*

> *LISTEN*
> *You are Walking*
> *on the*
> *River Walbrook*
> *LISTEN*

No wonder that so many psychiatrists have a bad name. Would you go to him for treatment? If you needed it, that is?

Later, I went to a Poetry Reading: *angst-ridden poet with tortured expression; arm crooked behind head, book held in the air, agonised stance, rocking from foot to foot – no shoes – kept running his tongue over his lips. 'Quiet at the back, please! QUIET!' A performance so ludicrous that it was hilarious; everyone else treating it with great reverence. But we're talking about art here, and you can't laugh at art, can you? Or can you? But enough of this. I still haven't answered all your questions.*

Photos that might surprise me: *Thanks for the thought. I am sure that I would be surprised. I don't want to explain my* *contradictory feelings to you or to myself, but please, no photos of 'idyllic family life'. I couldn't stand that right now. I think that I am in a far more sensitive state than I had supposed. The oddest things set me off ... tonight there had been a mix-up at The New Look and my favourite table hadn't been reserved. I burst into tears. Wasn't that stupid?*

Meeting in the British Museum: *Do you mean that I literally refused to go away, or did you just keep thinking of me? That meeting was a surprise for me also; we really talked. Not many people do. Herewith, by way of contrast, an accurate rendering of a recent exchange with The Existentialist:*

Me: 'I've not seen you for ages. What have you been doing?'

E (vaguely): 'This and that.'

Me: 'Where have you been?'

E (shifting uneasily from foot to foot): 'Here and there.'

Me: 'There's a lot on at the moment. Have you been to any good exhibitions?'

E (long pause while he took his specs off and polished them carefully): 'Not really.'

Me: 'Have you bought any new pictures? Any Bloomsbury?'

E (avoiding my eyes): 'The usual sort of stuff.'

Perhaps I'm being nasty; he's usually a little more interesting, but I can't imagine why he is so guarded. Once he asked me to explain what I meant by existentialism; I rambled on about 'a pessimistic philosophy put about by Sartre, with Simone de Beauvoir as its High Priestess' ... 'Man is alone in the world, abandoned by everybody, even by God'. He looked at me oddly.

Improper Suggestion: *Glad that you agree. I hope that you* *can come to London soon. I'd like to talk to you.*

Work: *Yes, of course I was joking when I said that I would chuck it all in and defect to the other side of the bar. I love my job and I feel a sense of responsibility for the collection and for 'my artists'. The 'grave incident' I mentioned was that Bernard, my boss, listened in to a sensitive phone call. I was summoning 'my troops' to prevent him flogging off certain important artworks, which he has no right to do. An uneasy truce reigns now.*

Don't take my opening sentence as so much whingeing. *I admit that I'm feeling a little depressed today. I've been rereading Anaïs Nin; I'd pictured her as muse to and supporter of starving artists, sacrificing all she owned to the greater good of her – and Henry's and Artaud's – art ... wonderful stories about her pawning everything she owned to buy Henry a typewriter. What people never mention is that she was – initially at least – the indulged and spoilt wife of a rich banker, from whom she scrounged in order to hang around in cafés and bars, and act out the life of a demi-mondaine.*

But no, I thought, as I put down my pen and took another sip at my cold white wine....

There was a tumultuous cheering in the Piazza. Mr Diabolo had just performed his star turn: throwing the giant yo-yo up to the level of St Paul's pediment, whisking a cloth from beneath a crockery-laden table, and catching it nonchalantly on the way down....

I'm upset because of everything that's happened.

WEEKEND IN WOOLWICH

*

As soon as I had pushed my way out of The Place, I rang Jeanetta – James's next intended victim – then James. His work number was engaged, so I left a message at home: this happened, that happened.... I'm not doing it and I'll be in the St Albans Pizza Joint later. That would have to do; *he wouldn't dare cause a scene there.*

The St Albans Pizza Joint had quarry-tiled floors, white walls, posters of the Rietveld chair and Mediterranean scenes, loud music and café clatter; cutlery, crockery, conversation. I secured my favourite table, facing the ponytailed chef who – for the benefit of the female customers – was vigorously pounding the dough, shaping it, hurling it about, catching it, and twiddling it on the end of his little finger. I ordered a drink.

Perhaps I'm overreacting, I thought. James mightn't be angry; I gave it a try, I explained why I didn't want to go through with The Place; my reasons are good, logical ones. He's reasonable – or is he? – and he should be open to different points of view, especially if I have a convincing argument. I'll refund the money; no question of that. A shame as I can ill afford it.... How could he object?

Suddenly he stormed in: angry, white-faced and red-eyed. 'You bitch!' he bawled across the room. Several diners put down their cutlery and stared. He blundered against the table, grabbed a chair and sat down heavily:

'How do you think I feel? I'm *fucking* disappointed. I gave you the chance to change your life, to sort yourself out, make a real contribution to our relationship instead of all this arty-farty stuff you're obsessed with, and what do you do? Make a fool of me! Refuse to **stand for** The Place. Pull the rug from under my feet. Let me down in front of my friends ... disappoint me! I should've listened to Joe and Joani. They're right – you're a washout! Stupid! Neurotic! I thought I could at least rely on you. I thought you cared about our marriage. Well, that's it. It was in your hands; you could've transformed it ... but I was fooling myself.'

'I do care,' I said, as I struggled to stay calm, 'but I told you that I had to make up my own mind. I had to investigate, then decide. I had a struggle to get into the meeting room, and then I was there an hour and a half. I gave it a fair trial, but I couldn't agree with them.'

Then I forgot myself: 'It was all jargon,' I said. 'Utter nonsense! All this talk about how you could "source" people later. What the hell's that supposed to mean?'

He leaned across the table: 'Sourcing? They talked about sourcing so soon?'

'I'm still none the wiser.'

'You would be if you'd been prepared to trust them, and me. *ME!*'

'There was also a great deal about empowerment,' I went on, 'which means nothing to me. Look, I'm fed up with all this. I know who I am and what I want to do, and I don't want to do this!'

'Well, then,' he retorted, 'you're foolish ... ridiculous, stupid ... a stupid bitch! And you're unreasonable. Fucking unreasonable! All you care about is exhibitions, galleries, museums, books. I'm sick of it. Sick, sick, SICK! No one lives like that! No one normal! You never look at anything else. You're narrow-minded. Well just remember – and I hope that you remember it on your deathbed – you've only deprived yourself. You've cut off your nose to spite your face. Fucking typical! You'd have enjoyed it!'

I banged my glass down hard: 'I'm sick of all this, too! People *do* live like me. Your philistine friends don't, but they know bugger all about anything. Well, that's their loss, not mine.'

'I should've taken more notice of them. They told me you were a bitch. I shouldn't have married you!'

'*You bastard!*' I yelled.

Chef dropped his dough and looked at me curiously.

'What is The Place anyway?' I demanded. 'Brainwashing?'

'Do I look as though I've been brainwashed?'

'Yes! You're dead behind the eyes unless you're talking about The Place. You never used to be like that.'

The man at the adjoining table gave up all pretence of eating and strained his ears. I lowered my voice: 'You sound like a man brainwashed ... all those catchwords, handy phrases which brook no opposition, one-word solutions to world problems....'

He shattered his glass against the table.

'YOU COW! FUCKING COW!' he yelled. 'I fucking well haven't been. I can still fucking think!'

Hold on, hold on, I thought, but instead I shouted: 'NO! YOU BLOODY WELL CAN'T!'

That night was the first that I'd really been unnerved.

The artistes in the Piazza were beginning to get on my nerves. I'll go to The Dôme, I thought, just around the corner. A change of scene.

*

The Dôme, Wellington Street, Covent Garden: marble-topped tables, pitted floorboards, and ochre-stained nicotine walls plastered with tatty theatrical posters and peeling Fin de Siècle advertisements; the legend Dôme-Dôme-Dôme-Dôme stencilled around the frieze; a buzz of conversation and distorted music. I secured my favourite spot, close to the bar with a view over the street.

James and I had argued until 4.30am the following morning. Insults were traded back and forth – why hadn't he listened – hadn't people always said – you, you – well, you're insensitive, uncaring, bovine – I'd cost him too much – 'Cost you too much? I've always been very careful.' 'Very funny.' – and so on. Occasionally the debate died down – at 11pm when I tried to go to sleep – but it was resumed at 1am – when I was shaken awake – 2.30am, 3am. At 4am he tried a new strategy – reason, argument, then rantings, ravings, threats. I needed peace.

Some days later I decamped to the British Library – to begin an article on John Carr of York (Architect), I said, but the real reason was to find out more about The Place.

The microfiche bibliography confirmed my worst fears. It was, I learned, a 'Self Religion', founded in California, the summer of 1967 as 'The Way' – associations of Flowerpower, Love and Hippiedom – closed down pending government investigation, amid horror stories of psychiatric disturbances, personality changes, broken relationships, lost jobs, suicides; later relaunched under a different name. Its latest manifestation – The Place – incorporated elements of Scientology and Eastern Mysticism in a New Age packaging. *Christ! So, it is a cult; I was right.*

I read further: 'great understanding of group psychology ... manipulation of crowd behaviour using mind control techniques ... public, cathartic disclosure followed by reward ... applause implies acceptance, love ... subversives eliminated at the beginning or discouraged by humiliation.... Supervisor trained in techniques of contempt ... "Plants" sometimes used in the audience.' *So that was what The Student was up to!* The more I read, the more alarmed I became. James must have gone through the conversion ceremony: a scene of mayhem, people fainting, crying, screaming, raving, vomiting, in order to 'rise again regenerated'.

That explained his behaviour; converts were expected to go out, spread the word, and bring in new recruits. I congratulated myself on my narrow escape, but I couldn't help but feel guilty. Why had he sought this in the first place? Had I unwittingly driven him to it?

Back at work I rang Psychology and contacted the Chaplain, a charming man who – by anyone's estimate – could talk the hind legs off a donkey. *At least he and James might thrash it out on theological grounds; James might reconsider his new beliefs; he might even start to doubt them.* I booked a series of appointments, for him and for me.

No, I mustn't keep dwelling on this, I mused as I drank my

kir. I'll give myself a nervous breakdown. I'll go out, forget it. But instead I started thinking about Anton.

*

Anton, you've run circles around me, but I've never really worked out what's going on!

July 1991, just before I left James, I took a short holiday in Bath. It will be nice, I thought, whatever happens. I might not see Anton, but if I do it will be a bonus. In the afternoon I wandered in a desultory fashion around likely addresses: the Royal Crescent, Great Pulteney Street, the Circus ... a solitary dinner, then I called Directories for new numbers. There was only one. My hands were shaking as I dialled:

'Hello ... is that Anton?'

'Yes.'

'Anton who was in Manchester?'

'Yes.'

'And who was doing a PhD?'

'Yes. YES! Who is this?' the voice demanded.

I could hear domestic noises in the background. Was there someone there? Perhaps he was married? There was a possibility, surely ... or it might just be the telly. I took a deep breath:

'Anton, it didn't sound at all like you ... it's Anna.'

'Anna! You've run me to ground again! Where are you?'

'Here, in Bath.'

'What brings you here?'

WEEKEND IN WOOLWICH

'A sort of holiday.... I'm relaxing, but I'll explain more if we meet. It's complicated....'

'I'm sure it is! What about tonight? Is it too late?'

'Not at all. Where?'

'Outside The Rummer, near The Old Empire. You know Bath, don't you?'

'I'll be there in five minutes.'

'See you there, then,' he laughed as he put the phone down.

Once again it was as if no time had passed. I described my circumstances, he told me about Jenni; she was important to him and had helped him through some of the bleaker days. 'You'd like her, I think,' he volunteered. 'But I'd value your opinion. I'm a bit isolated down here; I never talk to anyone with brains. As for Jenni, well ... I don't want you to be polite or considerate, just because we're friends. I want you to be honest. Don't worry about hurting my feelings. I just have to know....'

I looked him full in the face and saw the doubt in his eyes.

We met the following day at The Podium, a jolly, postmodern development near the Pulteney Bridge, the arcade distinguished by billiard ball capitals, disproportionate columns, truncated cornices, many of the shops full of hideous and useless glittering rubbish: *'Have nothing in your houses that you do not know to be useful, or believe to be beautiful'*. Jenni was gazing at the window of the Christmas Shop, an enraptured expression on her face. I was disappointed. She was pleasant-looking; a friendly enough manner but her comments were banal and the talk tedious. She had little to say for herself. Perhaps she was cripplingly shy? Her intelligence was not apparent; Anton looked bored and he drank too much. The following day I retreated to the Assembly Rooms and the Museum of Costume, then I went home.

But when I moved to Bloomsbury a month later, my first answerphone message was from him: 'Anna. Hi! It's me. I just wanted to make sure I was the first to ring and wish you well in your new home. I hope that everything's straight now, most of all I hope you know what you're doing. I hope that you won't be lonely. I lived in London for two years and met no one; it was a tough nut to crack. And do you know what I did? I spent most of the time alone, wandering from pub to pub ... drinking, too much drinking.... So, beware! Perhaps it will be different for you? You're so much more sociable than I am.'

Then the long phone calls – one or two hours at a stretch, two or three a week ... every subject, every personal issue held up for scrutiny, no stone unturned. One day, around three weeks ago, a different kind of conversation:

'Look, I promised to come to London, ages ago. Is it still on?'

'Of course it is, but you're not noted for keeping promises.'

'I'll keep this one.'

'That's marvellous.'

'I'm arriving about 11.30am. Where shall we meet?'

'What about The New Look Café Bar, Covent Garden? I'll be on the top floor near the balcony. You won't be very late, will you? Because if you are' – and I thought of the time when I'd waited two hours sans newspaper or notebook – 'I'll be very tempted to abandon ship, and you will have to seek me out.'

'Of course I won't,' he said reassuringly. But he couldn't help himself. By the time he walked in, I'd read three newspapers and written as many letters, but I was so delighted to see him that I forgot to be annoyed.

'Oh, I'm not late, am I?' he asked nonchalantly, fumbling at his watch, as he looked around absent-mindedly.... 'So this is your hang-out. Nice place! You look like a Parisian intellectual.'

I started laughing: 'You're impossible! *You know you're late* – by at least an hour and a half! What happened?'

'I had to dump my bags at the hotel, then I walked in the wrong direction and ended up somewhere in Camden.'

'That was pretty stupid. What's wrong with using an A-Z?'

'I'm sorry. Really I am. Am I forgiven?' And he flashed one of his irresistible smiles.

'I suppose so,' I smiled, 'but this does cast doubt on your protestations of affection.'

His hand closed around mine on the marble-topped table.

'Do I make you very unhappy?'

'Yes,' I replied. 'I'm extremely unhappy with things as they are now. Just seeing you is difficult; all sorts of stuff gets stirred up ... I start thinking of our conversations ... like those in Bath when we wandered about the streets, locked in debate. We talked about everything; I felt privileged, special, but that was before you introduced me to Jenni. I don't know why she bothers me so much. Perhaps it's because I expected someone different, more interesting ... an intellectual, for God's sake!'

'But she's important to me,' he interrupted.

'So you say,' I snapped. 'I know that I'm being priggish, but you did ask for my opinion. Anyway, admit that you're bored. Why associate with people you find tedious? You say that you can't talk to her, that you don't share interests or attitudes of mind. You tell me that you're fed up. Christ!' I exclaimed. 'If that's not bad enough you claim that you don't even enjoy fucking her.'

He looked away as he refilled our glasses.

'Yes,' he replied reluctantly. 'All that you say is true, but you don't understand. I really don't like to run her down, but I've never made friends easily. It was impossible to meet people in London; it's almost as bad in Bath. It's OK for you.'

'What do you mean? I could argue that it's much harder for a lone woman to branch out ... I know people who won't wander into a bar alone, as I do. You have to make the effort. You can't *expect* people to seek you out. It doesn't happen like that. It's probably as difficult for me as it is for you.'

'What I mean is that you're lucky. Your job offers the greater social opportunities. It wasn't like that for me. I found London, "The Big City", difficult.'

'I don't understand that. You're talkative, sociable. I've only been here eight months and I've already met dozens of people. Though,' I laughed, 'I did make a determined effort to rebuild my shattered social life.'

'You've done well. You're better at it than I am. No, when I moved to Bath I was lonely and depressed. I didn't know anyone; I didn't belong to a group or organisation. Then I met Jenni.'

'How?'

'A guitar class or something,' he said vaguely. 'I don't really remember. Anyway, it was straightforward and easy; she was sweet and loving. She accepted me as I am.'

'So do I, Anton,' I reminded him. 'I'm a little worried about some of your values, but I like your personality.'

'That's not the same. You're just a friend. With Jenni it's different. I don't have to think.'

'You think that's a recommendation?'

'Can't you see? You set too much store by intellectual pursuits. That's as bad in its own way. No, with Jenni, it was easy, and now I think that when I'm with her I'm in the presence of goodness. *She is a good woman!* Besides, I'm getting older. You've been married a couple of times *and you've blown it.* You've had two bites of the cherry....'

'That's cruel!' I exclaimed. 'There were perfectly good reasons why neither relationship was tenable. I value my honesty more than a flawless façade.'

'Sorry,' Anton said, 'I shouldn't have said that, but you've been married and I've not. What I mean is that I'd like to settle down with someone. It doesn't have to be an all-consuming passion – just someone I can rub along with – but I'd like to have children.'

'But Anton, things aren't quite so simple! Don't you see that an unsatisfactory relationship is no shield against loneliness? I know from my own experience that it is possible to be with someone and still be lonely. Marriage number one ... Charlie was a nice chap, but he was only interested in the football pitch and the locker room. I might have been able to "rub along" with him

– if I'd ignored my interests and enthusiasms – but we spoke a different language. I wanted real conversation with a like-minded person; wide-sweeping discussions, art, culture, literature.

'He was pleasant enough, a lovely man even, but in the end it was intolerable. There was no common ground. Neither of us understood anything about the other; we couldn't communicate. It was a head-on clash. I had to leave ... to stay would have been to live a lie, and I couldn't have done that. By the same token you might find that you marry Jenni, have children, then discover that it's impossible.'

'I don't think that I'll marry her,' he replied. 'If I'd intended to get married, I'd have done so before now. I'm 35 ... 35! At least I've resisted it, and that's more than I can say for you! And then I don't want to hurt her. I think that what will happen is that when she begins her literature course in Swansea....'

'Literature course?' I shouted. 'You're joking! She knows fuck all about literature. That's pretty rich for someone who's never heard of Laurence Sterne.' I started to laugh as I poured myself another drink.

The Waiter was hovering at my elbow.

Anton must look prosperous, I thought. I'm not usually given this treatment. Either that or he's eavesdropping.

The Waiter tugged at my plait surreptitiously. 'Thanks for the Birthday Card,' he whispered, 'though it was quite different from what I'd have expected. All those naked, nubile bodies!'

'But it was Matisse!' I tittered. 'And very tasteful.'

'When you've quite finished!' Anton interrupted. 'You're so horrible about people. No ... when Jenni begins her course things will come to a natural end. She won't want to come to Bath every weekend and I can't afford to visit her much, so we'll drift apart.'

'You delude yourself!' I exclaimed. 'I'm biased, but I'm not convinced that Jenni is as clueless or as innocent as you claim. She has certainly found ways of insinuating herself into your life, of making herself indispensable. She's proofread your thesis; she even does your washing and shopping. You should be ashamed of yourself! What's wrong with proofreading your own stuff – I did mine – and with doing all your own domestic chores?'

Perhaps she really loves him? Don't be so damned uncharitable! I thought. She looks like a nice, considerate person.

But I went on: 'It's all very suburban and comfortable. I mean, you're a nice catch for her: ten years older, good-looking, about to get a PhD, excellent prospects ... with all this effort invested she won't allow you to vanish. No, she'll hang on; she'll return to Bath every weekend. Mark my words! Anyway, what are you playing at? Are you hoping that she will drift off, thus absolving yourself from all responsibility?'

'You need another drink,' he interrupted.

'Look,' I put in. 'It's easy for you to go on; it's become a comfortable habit. Shame on you! You've taken the coward's way out.'

'I suppose I have. You're right, but I have this nagging feeling that Jenni's the best I can get.'

'Surely not?' I breathed. I leaned across the table and seized his hand: 'Where do I fit into all of this?'

He pulled me towards him: 'Oh, you're important to me ... no less important; more important. You are my sister, my soulmate, my conscience. You stab at my mind now and again to keep me on a straight moral path. You are so much more highly principled than I am, but we've been through all this before and things have gone on too long; far too long. I've known you twelve years! Twelve whole years, and that's a long time! Too long!'

'That's ridiculous! I suspect that you find me intimidating.'

'Well, you are pretty alarming. You got your PhD before me, yet you started it long after.'

'So what? That was the way things worked out. Besides, an important – if obscure – eighteenth century architect is unlikely to get "overtaken by contemporary events". You know that the failure – inverted commas – of your first topic wasn't your fault. You got a job while you were completing; I know that it's impossible to both research and write up while you're working.'

'Whatever you say, it's your fault. You shouldn't have refused me.'

'Refused?'

'When we first met.'

'Anton,' I protested, 'that was a long time ago. A lot has happened since then. What did you expect? I had come to Manchester on the heels of a failed marriage. I felt – on seeing all the fresh young faces in the hall of residence – old, fat and ugly. I felt guilty over the break-up; I hadn't formally started proceedings, my life was in turmoil. I had even more hang-ups. I suspected that you wanted an evening's entertainment; I didn't. I wanted something more permanent. Why hold that against me now?'

'The point is that you rejected me.'

'I didn't reject *you;* I rejected *a one-night stand.* I know you now, and I care about you very much now.'

'I don't think you're being realistic. I am much shallower than you are; I don't have your strength or convictions. You'd be bored with me in a short time – it wouldn't take long – then I would have lost my friend as well.'

'Surely not? I have been your friend for years; I've sought you out when no one knew where you were. Does that suggest boredom or inconsistency? I've written, I've rarely received replies. I don't know why I bother.'

Then I had an idea: 'Look,' I suggested, 'why don't you come to London? There's a lot going on here; you'd easily get a job. You admit that you don't enjoy the "village folk" atmosphere of Bath. I could introduce you to a whole new social circle: artists, writers, musicians, all sorts of interesting people. We could have fun.'

'I'm sure we could, but you don't understand: you thrive in London, in the artistic/cosmopolitan atmosphere, and I'm more suited to the out-of-town backwaters. I'm a big fish in a small pond and I'd rather keep it that way. I hate to admit it.'

'Christ!' I exclaimed. 'Among the net curtains....'

'Anyway,' he went on, 'you're my spiritual girlfriend. What more do you want? You're one of the most important people in my life.'

'I'm sick of that role, the confidante, the shoulder to cry on; it's not enough. You get all the benefits: the long conversations, the free therapy, the ideas, the praise, but you give very little. There's no real commitment, for instance.'

'That's not fair,' said Anton. 'You've had help from me, too. Emotional help. I'm not the mean cad you make me out to be.'

I thought for a moment. How easy it would have been to shout, 'Oh yes you are!' and slam out, but he had a point. 'I don't deny it, but at the moment it feels as if I'm doing all the giving. I know that you like me. Sometimes I feel there's more to it than that, so I don't understand.'

'Our relationship is nice like this,' he protested. 'We're friends, very good friends. We meet, we flirt a little, we tell stories, swop ideas. What I really want is a lifelong friendship,' he laughed, 'of the Sartre and Beauvoir type.'

'Yes, very funny, but what you don't know is that their relationship was as much sexual as it was intellectual. At first, anyway,' I added as an afterthought. 'What I mean is that Sartre had all sorts of other liaisons, but Beauvoir was always the most important. If we entered into that sort of arrangement, I would want to be the most important. I wouldn't play second fiddle to anyone. Anyway, I've got serious reservations about Beauvoir; she diminished her talent for the greater good of Sartre ... she didn't receive the credit she deserved; she inspired many of his ideas and edited much of his work – a lot of his writing wouldn't have been possible without her. It wasn't quite the equal partnership you might assume. In any case, I don't find Sartre a turn-on!'

Anton was beginning to look uneasy.

'There's something in our relationship,' he commented, 'but I don't know what it is: a meeting of like minds or a fuelling of equal neuroses? I confide in you more than in anyone; I suspect the same is true of you.'

'Yes. Yes, it is.'

Though, as I said it, I had the thought that Steve already knew and understood a lot.

'Well, you know more about my hopes, fears, anxieties, than anyone else,' said Anton. 'Just think about it – it might turn out to be a stoking of equal miseries. I suspect that if we embarked on a closer relationship it would be everything; all-consuming, passionate – for a short time – then it would just fizzle out. I'd have lost everything. One person might destroy the other. You're too much of a woman for me.'

And he started laughing.

'I warn you, Anton,' I said, 'if things stay as they are I'll find it difficult to stand by dispassionately in the role of "old friend" while you marry Jenni; things have gone beyond that. You might risk losing the friendship anyway. But the other alternative might turn into something much more interesting.'

'Have you any idea of the emotions which might be unleashed if we went to bed together? It would be impossible; I couldn't handle it.'

'Of course I've considered it. I think what I thought in 1983: you're a coward. You shy away from any form of commitment.'

'Anyway,' said Anton, 'it isn't realistic. You live in London and I live in Bath. That's the way it is.'

'So what? It doesn't have to be that way. It's not such a very great distance: an hour or so by train. You're just using distance as an excuse. If it were my last chance of happiness, I'd be tempted to seize it.'

'Not many women would say that.'

'Well, I have.'

*

LETTER 18 TO STEVE

London
Tuesday 12 May 1992

Steve, dear Steve

It was a lovely surprise to get your message and I'm only sorry that my answerphone – rather than I – took the call.

I'm looking forward to seeing you; by my reckoning that should be sometime during the week of 1 June. It was good to hear your voice again; I'd almost forgotten how much I like it.

When you phoned I was at The Theatre seeing a seriously wacky pair of plays concerning an actor's nightmare – actor who thinks that he's a Chartered Accountant performs assorted panic-stricken soliloquies from Shakespeare, Beckett, Coward – and an identity crisis. I laughed so much I feared that I'd be forcibly ejected. I will never think about the invention of banana bread in quite the same light again, in as far as anyone ever thinks about it, that is....

WEEKEND IN WOOLWICH

Today I'm in yet another hangout: Truckles, close to the BM. I've got a terrible weakness for this sort of place: sawdust-strewn floor, artfully stacked boxes of wine – Can you explain why they don't use the place marked 'Cellar'? – guttering candles in wax-spattered bottles, arcane agricultural instruments on the walls. It's so dark that I can barely see the page, let alone what I'm writing. Is this deliberate style or are they taking economy too far? I suppose I should politely wait for your next letter before unleashing another flood of words, but 'TO HELL WITH IT!' I want to talk to you now, so I'm writing:

I've been to some excellent things recently: in particular, the George Bernard Shaw exhibition at the NPG. The funniest thing was a 1930 film of GBS at Malvern; his vanity, egotism and smugness must have been intolerable. Rarely have I seen anyone quite so self-satisfied. Rough sample comments (GBS meanwhile strutting and preening in front of the camera): 'You know (PAUSE) it takes me twenty minuoootes (PAUSE) to get my hair up like this in the morning (PAUSE) ... and this adds greatly (LONG PAUSE) to my reputation as a playwright.' And: 'I always talk spontaneously. The fact that I've said it about 500,000 times before has nothing to do with it. It always comes off with that air.' On the naming of the 'Shaw Festival (bridling): 'a very excellent name, in my opinion'. Why was I the only person laughing? Do I have an odd sense of humour, or is there something wrong with everyone else?

Another funny thing: remember the angst-ridden poet I commented on? In today's Sunday Times he's described as 'the lipsticked visionary of the New Nineties'. Well! It's probably just as well that when I went to his last Poetry Reading/Private View I didn't know that the artist – inspired by him, apparently – teaches wrestling to support her art. The juxtaposition of the poet and the wrestler might have coloured my view of the evening! As it was – in my ignorance – I found both of them quite amazing!

*A rather embarrassing thing happened on Monday. I was invited to lunch by my friends at The Museum; soon I realised that the fourth member of the party, an Army surgeon, **was intended for me!** Various vulgar comments were bandied about … 'He has a keen eye and a steady hand'. He was, as it happens, a philistine bore, completely buttoned up, extremely conventional; chauvinistic, overweight, unattractive. Unfortunately he'd invited himself to that evening's lecture which I'd have otherwise enjoyed. Everything got off to a poor start with Army Surgeon and I locked in a heated dispute over some point of principle; a protracted argument which rumbled on all night over dinner. It ended with him accusing me of having 'impossibly high moral standards'. If that's true, I take it as a compliment, but the evening was not a conspicuous success.*

Since you ask, I'm unlikely to see The Existentialist again unless I run into him at some Bloomsbury PV. One night I met him at The New Look. I was fifteen minutes early and he was fifteen minutes late. I was happily installed at my favourite table with a kir and my newspapers, when I caught his owlish gaze outside. The Waiter had collared him and was giving him the sales pitch! He came in, sat down, and swallowed seven tumblers of 'house red' in quick succession. Conversation was difficult and the atmosphere strained; I suspected that he was deliberately being intransigent;

that he'd asked me out in order to make a point, teach me a lesson. I suppose I've got myself to blame: I shouldn't have sent him Sartre's celebrated line 'Hell is other people'. He'd already claimed that he was 'monstrously unsociable'; that didn't excuse my sending it on a postcard of a Wyndham Lewis work, especially as there were such marked similarities: Wyndham Lewis hiding his phone – Existentialist ditto, Wyndham Lewis studiously ignoring all callers – Existentialist ditto. Anyway, I digress....

At the end of the evening we stood talking ... or rather, I made frantic attempts at conversation ... on the corner of Coptic Street and Great Russell Street. This quickly accelerated into a full-scale dispute, Existentialist claiming that he valued his privacy, his personal space above all, that I came perilously close to intruding on it. I protested feebly. It would have been serious if it hadn't been so ludicrous. I've only ever seen him once every two or three weeks. Intrusion? That's crazy! It ended with him shouting: 'Well, I'm not going to stand here discussing it on a windy street corner. I warned you that I'm a bastard. GOODNIGHT!' At which he turned on his heel and stamped off; I'd have never thought him capable of such a display, such loss of self-control!

***To answer you: Imbalance in our Files....** You've already mentioned this a couple of times. I warned you that I write; I write a lot. I don't expect quite so many letters from you. I often write in cafés, bars, café-bars, by way of holding a conversation. I write as I feel, rather than exchange letter for letter.*

***Re: Anton....** I don't think that I've told you anything about him. It's a long story, best reserved for when we meet. He's never been a boyfriend, but I've known him a long time.*

At the same table for hours; time for a change of scene. Besides, the drunken mobile-toting yuppies at the next table were having a boring conversation of the sort I couldn't ignore.

I summoned The Waiter, paid my bill and crossed the road to The Theatre. Perhaps I could get a ticket for the evening performance of Whistler which was, according to Time Out, an imaginative if pedestrian production, barely redeemed by the white on black sets, Japonesque decorations and Aesthetic costumes.

I'd met The Actor two years previously when I'd been struck by his extraordinary resemblance to Beardsley: thin, skeletally thin; white skin, arresting face; high cheekbones, sharp nose, floppy dark hair parted in the middle. He won't remember me, I thought. How can I be so vain? He must see dozens of people.

But after the performance, which was all that I'd feared, he caught my eye, hailed me, and we retreated to The New Look with Marie, his opposite number.

'Whatever happened to your husband?' Marie asked. 'It was really bizarre; you were such good supporters of The Arts Centre, at every new production, always in the front row. Then one day you didn't turn up and I never saw you again; you just disappeared. James came in to remove your name from the mailing list – so we knew that something had happened – then he vanished as well and never came back. It was so mysterious; no one heard from you, there were no explanations or clues. And, you see, it was such a contrast from before; we thought that you were a happy and devoted couple. We didn't think that anything was wrong.'

'It must have looked strange,' I admitted, as I refilled our glasses. 'Things are never quite as they seem, are they? We might have looked happy, but there were problems, big problems. I moved because there was no alternative, then I tried to forget it all. I felt too fragile to think about it.'

And I told them about The Place and its effect upon James, his transformation from 'a placid person' – his words – into an aggressive and unreasonable monster. All this time The Actor was looking at me intently, and asking questions in a kind and sympathetic manner. As we finished the bottle, Marie looked at her watch – 'Good heavens! It's eleven already, and I've got to get home to Luton!' – gathered her belongings and dashed out.

'Another drink?' The Actor suggested. 'But let's go somewhere quieter.'

We went to The Crusting Pipe and sat close together. Later, we walked up Neal Street and Montague Street.

'But why are you still so sane?' he asked as he took my hand. 'After what you've been through, you shouldn't be like this ... cold, calm, collected.'

'Cold!' I exclaimed.

'You know what I mean. I deal with people all the time in the "day job"; I've seen them in similar situations and they've been destroyed, in pieces. A nervous breakdown at least. How do you do it? What's the secret?'

'Well, it might have something to do with psychotherapy, though I wouldn't normally admit to it. Nearly six years ago, when things were pretty grim, I signed up for it. There was no real alternative; I had to do it. At the time I blamed myself for all the woes of the marriage; it wasn't quite so simple. Going into therapy gave me a means of survival, a different way of looking at things. I couldn't have done it without the strength it gave me.'

'Did it really make such a difference?'

'Yes. No one was more surprised than I was. I emerged feeling stronger with the redoubled conviction that I *was* sane, with greater confidence in myself and my own ideas, whatever James or his philistine friends might think. Of course he said that I was "nastier, more difficult, aggressive". What he really meant was that I was more assertive. He accused me of "going over the top" all the time.'

'In what respect?'

'Certain subjects were taboo. At polite middle-class dinner parties with his odious friends, I wasn't supposed to mention anything about my work or enthusiasms; nothing about the arts. That left me with very little, so I always broke the rules.... once I got into some argument – I forget what it was about – but I defended my views and came home with black and blue shins ... where he'd kicked me under cover of the Laura Ashley tablecloth! Eventually I stopped referring to my work; he was always deriding it.'

'Deriding it? Why?'

'I can't be sure.... He often declared that I'd never get my PhD – it had gone on too long. It hadn't; he just didn't understand anything about it. When I did, I think he felt insecure.'

The Actor put his arm around me.

We crossed Russell Square, and greeted The Night Porter at

my block. I unlocked my door. Why is it, I thought, that when I mention that I live at Russell Court, people say, 'It's alright for some!'? So, OK, it's right in the centre of town, with a chichi WC1 postcode. The estate agents call it a studio, a pied-à-terre; they go on and on about the stylish 'ocean liner' block. It's a room, ten feet square! No kitchen, tiny bathroom, marble walls. Pretentious in such a small place, surely? All night I hear my neighbours playing music, having baths, washing up, and worse! There is absolutely no need for anyone to be jealous.

The Actor looked around. Impressed, I thought.

'You've loads of books,' he remarked. 'A private library. But that portrait? Who is it?'

The item in question hung over my sofa bed. I opened a bottle of Black Tower – 'bought for the quirky bottle,' I told him – as I explained:

'It was done by the retired Art Therapist at Tooting. One day, someone came to my office, showed me photos of Helmut's work, and I agreed to give him an exhibition. I am not sure what it was about this picture, but I found her face haunting and I had to keep going back to look at her. When I'd done that for the fourth time, I knew that I had to buy her. It's good technically; what paint there is is laid on with brio and panache.

'At the PV – Private View – someone chalked onto the frame "Face of Despair". That might be true, but I think that she's also a "Face of Hope". Perhaps that's why I like her – something to do with a journey from dark to light, emerging from the dim, dark tunnel? I can identify with that. I don't know her name, I'll never know it; she was one of Helmut's patients. Later Helmut told me that when she first came to him she was "finished, burnt out"; through art she made a complete recovery and went on to do great things. Unfortunately she looks rather formidable, Wagnerian....'

The Actor raised his eyebrows. 'No! She's beautiful, striking, but also rather ugly. An interesting face. I can see why you bought her. What about the landscapes? They're unusual.'

'Grateful Artist Syndrome: an Italian artist who specialises in etching and aquatint. As you can see, they are small editions, five or six plates per image. I gave her an exhibition, too: "Fields in the Sun"; that's where "Campo di Grano" came from. She gave me "Villa Doria Pamphili" to thank me for the time and trouble I'd put in.'

'And the posters? Why those? The buildings are a bit obscure to say the least.'

I smiled at the memory:

'They came to me from a friend in Manchester. They relate to exhibitions on "my architect", my PhD topic. I've carried them around ever since.'

'You've made this place really nice,' he commented.

'Thanks,' I said.

He sat on my decaying sofa bed; I sat – as usual – on my squashy ethnic cushion.

'This is ridiculous!' he exclaimed. 'I'm not going to lord it here if you're on the floor,' and he slid down beside me, his leg pressed unnecessarily hard against mine.

'So ...' he said. 'James was jealous when you got your PhD. What happened when you got your job? It must have been quite a blow to him.'

'Things got worse,' I said wearily. 'He sneered at my CV – I thought it impressive – he claimed that I wouldn't stand a chance at interview. Of course, the interview was great! I liked them; they liked me. When they offered me the job he insisted that I decline because, he said, I wouldn't be able to cope – I'd be unreasonable – I'd make his life hell. Things were, he said, difficult anyway, and I was *only* temping and writing.... *Only!* Just imagine what I'd be like in a nine-to-five environment, mixing with other people, hearing their problems, commuting every day? No! I'd make his life intolerable.'

'But you coped?'

'Yes,' I smirked. 'Rather well! That was the real problem. I loved the job, revelled in it, but that only made him worse.'

'Perhaps that's why he joined The Place? He must have felt diminished.'

'Yes, I think so,' I agreed, sadly.

The Actor moved closer and put his arm around my shoulders. 'I've discovered one chink in your armour,' he said.

'Oh? What's that?'

'You invited me back tonight. First you ply me with drink, then you offer me your worthy Nicaraguan coffee ... from Oxfam!'

'So what? What's wrong with that? I'm polite; I've enjoyed our conversation.'

'I'm sure you have, but I think it suggests you're lonely, in need of company; you're searching for something ... or someone. It's unusual for a woman to invite a man back.'

'Unusual? It might have been twenty years ago; I'm surprised at you. Think whatever you like; it's up to you. In my circles it's perfectly usual....'

'Artistic, Bohemian ones?'

'If you insist,' I laughed. 'But I don't think of myself as a demi-mondaine.'

He looked, away, sipped his coffee, changed the subject. 'The split?' he asked. 'How did you organise it? What happened?'

'In the end I abandoned ship. Outwardly James was charming, pleasant, personable; people thought him all sweet reasonableness; underneath he was monstrous, recalcitrant, intractable, *foul!* I had persuaded him to go to some counselling sessions; afterwards, The Counsellor would ring and ask: "Just what is the problem? He seems fine, very pleasant to me. You're sure it's not you? Have you tried talking, *really talking*, to him?" This was all very galling; I'd talked, reasoned, argued, the lot, at great personal cost, often until late at night or early the next morning. I'd left articles criticising The Place lying around the house in an attempt to plant the seeds of doubt in his mind.... I'd taken him to all sorts of people, so that he could discuss it, get it out of his system. I didn't realise, until we had joint sessions, that he'd lied his way through the single ones. Even then he'd tell them the most extraordinary tales; it was all I could do to hold onto my own sanity. I felt so alone and isolated. It's beyond the experience of most counsellors; it's difficult to get anyone to understand. James was a consummate actor ... and a liar.'

'What did you do about your house?'

'Christ, that was unpleasant! By the time I realised I had to move, James had lost his job. That left me with a problem. How could I leave when he had no income? Several people suggested that I was ditching him in his hour of need, that I'd pulled out when the going got tough. So I decided to take only those things I'd owned before we got married. I jettisoned the house, the car, the telly, the video. In the end, they weren't important. One August Bank Holiday weekend he'd arranged to go camping with his foul friends. The removal firm were on standby; as soon as he drove off down the road, they drove up the other end with the boxes. I spent the next twenty-four hours packing. Sometime,' I remarked ruefully, 'I'll have to weed out those bloody books. Anyway, the following day, they came back to collect me and my effects, so off we went....'

'So, when he returned you'd already gone!' You make it sound so easy.'

'Well, it wasn't,' I replied, but by then it was becoming difficult to disengage my eyes from The Actor's penetrative stare. He pulled me closer; he pressed his lips against my neck. *'Oooh!'* I thought, but I replied calmly:

'Three weeks earlier I'd tried to persuade my employers to loan me a flat – they had dozens of vacant ones – to give me time to think, to look around, sort out my feelings. I needed some peace. They refused. It was – they said – "a dangerous precedent". I decided that since I had to move I would go somewhere I wanted to be. For me, London's The City and Westminster, not Balham or the last stop on the Northern line. I've always loved Bloomsbury; my Grandma M told me stories of her glamorous life there in the 1920s. When I was eleven, I discovered the Bloomsbury Group and decided that they must have been intolerably pretentious and tremendously interesting. So, the area already had a special atmosphere, romantic overtones. Then, of course, there's the BM a mere stone's throw away.

'I went to an estate agent and explained that I had to find somewhere quickly. This place had just come onto the market ... vacant possession, recently refurbished. I decided that it would do; I thought it was within my means. My offer was accepted; my solicitor was conscientious and pushed things through quickly. We ended up exchanging and completing the same day; I had the phone installed while they were at it ... the day before I moved! It was a tense time all round.'

'Moves are never good,' he commented. 'Yours must have been dreadful.'

'Yes!' I exclaimed. 'A complete nightmare. The removal men took ages to load up; instead of the two strong men I expected there was only one, his skinny wife and three young boys aged seven to fourteen – summer holiday slave labour. The handyman I'd booked for twelve on the nail to put up the bookshelves and wall lights appeared an hour early, just as we arrived. Everyone met in the middle. You can imagine the chaos; questions fired from all directions as they dragged their filthy, rust-covered trolley over my new ochre carpets: "Where do I put this, Missis?" "Where do I put that?" the handyman meanwhile anxious to get on. The bookshelves, which should have been first off the van, were last! It was only afterwards when everyone had gone and I was sitting amidst the wreckage, I began to wonder if I'd done the right thing.'

'Why didn't you take anything from the house? You were entitled to, surely?'

'Misplaced pride, female guilt, I suppose. In the end I've got to live with myself and come to terms with my own feelings. "*The Existentialist's search for reconciling responsibility for others with personal happiness*" – sorry ... half-remembered Sartre! I couldn't bear to think that people might jump to all sorts of unpleasant conclusions. You know the sort of thing: "This – er – woman rescued by this charming young man when she was broke and studying. She ditched him when it suited her, and took him to the cleaners". I decided I'd rather just disappear. I thought that some people might assume that I'd run off with a younger man; there was no one. I bolted into a void.'

The Actor looked at me thoughtfully: 'You're very conscious of what people think, aren't you? I don't see why it should matter so much. Why does it?'

'I suppose that my judgement might have been coloured by past events. All sorts of awful things happened at the time of the move. My best friend Jeanetta, my mother and my brother all pointed out how lucky I'd been to have had such a good-looking man ... and such a charming one, too.... As if that were all that really matters! When I moved I phoned my brother to let him know that I'd gone back to my maiden name, and to explain some of the circumstances: "*I don't bloody want to know!*" he shouted. "*It's none of my business!*" and he slammed the phone down.'

'What about now? How do you feel? Do you feel you're in flight, on the run?'

'I did at first. I had no idea how I'd feel about being in London at last, after all the years dreaming about it and tracing its streets with my finger on the map. I didn't know anyone here, but it's not like that now. I've arrived, I belong here, I live in Bloomsbury and Covent Garden.'

'How did you do that? How did you establish yourself?'

'The first thing was to feel at home. After I'd sorted out my books and hung my pictures, I took a couple of weeks off work and played at being a tourist. For as long as I can remember, I've gone about saying I know London; I tried to forget all that, to see it with new eyes. That way, I might discover more. Each night I studied The London Encyclopaedia; each day I strode off purposefully with The Michelin Green Guide. I constructed a series of walks: Lost Gardens – St George's, Brunswick Square and Coram's Fields, The Phoenix off Shaftesbury Avenue; Brompton and Belgravia; Piccadilly and Park Lane; Leicester Square and Soho. Then my favourite: Bloomsbury and Covent Garden.'

'That's all very well but it sounds pretty solitary. What about people? How did you go about meeting them?'

'It was much easier than I thought,' I said. 'I know people at work, but they're not really my sort of people. I'd imagined that Jeanetta, my best friend, would introduce me to "London Society"; I changed my mind after I discovered that she had, apparently, jumped into bed with James, soon after our split.... One day I discovered Covent Garden. I listened to the musicians, visited the cafés and bars – sometimes armed with papers, sometimes with a notebook, sometimes with writing paper.

'One night I was sauntering past The New Look, when The Waiter sprang out onto the pavement and asked me to come in for a drink. Currying for business, you see. When I'd walked past for the third time, I felt I could refuse no longer. The New Look became my hang-out.

'You know how it is. You go to the same places, you recognise familiar faces. After a short time it's natural to greet them and exchange pleasantries. You get people's first names; eventually you have a conversation and find that you have some things in common. The café becomes your club and the staff and customers, your friends. Or acquaintances, at least.'

'And Jay? Jay at The Theatre? How did you meet him?'

'I'd been given a free ticket to see a one-woman show based on the life of Emma Hamilton, Nelson's mistress. I arrived early and made for the bar. The barman was very striking: he had a nice demeanour and friendly expression; very tall, very thin – long, crinkly red hair flopping onto a pale freckled face; odd clothes – patchwork trousers, bright red jacket bristling with buckles. As soon as I saw him I thought of The Boy Chatterton ... a beautiful, doomed youth. Anyway, I liked him; we started talking.

'He explained that he was a student in his final year of Cultural Studies, bar work was just a sideline. I knew that he was at least twenty years younger than me, so I was surprised and flattered when – at the end of the evening – he scribbled his phone number onto a crumpled piece of paper and pushed it into my hand.'

'That's not my style, but some men do that,' The Actor

commented. 'Go on.'

'One night, a couple of weeks later, I was feeling forlorn so I rang him. After all, why not? "Hi! It's Anna, remember me?" and we arranged to meet at The Theatre. After that we went for a drink and now The Theatre's on my regular circuit and Jay is one of my dearest friends.'

Friend? I thought, as I remembered our single night of wild, unbridled passion ... my shrieks that might have aroused the entire building.... What a fool I've been!

'But,' I exclaimed, remembering The Actor. 'All this so far has been about me, and I've talked for far too long, as usual. Tell me about you; you know lots about me already. I would like to know about you. "Chinks in my armour" ... where are the chinks in yours?'

'I'm full of chinks. I'm one big chick with a tiny piece of armour!'

'But seriously,' I protested, 'how is it that you are not involved with anyone? When did you finish with Marie? Have you had any relationships since? How do you feel about them? Is it all too traumatic?'

'All that finished six years ago. She's getting married soon and it's been difficult for her fiancé as he knows all about our shared past. We still work together, you see. I've been out with other people since but I haven't had a relationship. Not exactly.'

'But why not?'

'At the back of my mind there's the lingering feeling that they're not really worth the bother. People make demands, have expectations, get hurt, get upset, and for what? Not a lot.

Then there's my work; I have two jobs, you see. My day job is in a centre for the mentally/physically disabled; my real job is acting, being an actor. And then there's all the reading and rehearsing, so I don't have much spare time.'

'Could you make acting full-time?'

'I couldn't survive on that. There aren't enough jobs to go round unless you've got the right contacts; you need to know people who know people. At least by doing this I can choose the parts I want and do what I feel to be right. In some ways, working at The Centre is good; it's advantageous, stimulating, and I live in. In a space smaller than this, remarkably,' and he looked round at my four walls and tiny bay window as if he could barely believe it.

I noticed that he was looking faintly uneasy.

'What is it?' I asked. 'Am I keeping you?'

'No, but I won't be able to ring you as much as you might want, and it worries me – especially now when I think I've found the other chink in your armour.'

'What's that?'

'Your change of persona.'

'Really?'

'Well, when we were in the café talking, it seemed to me that you were exuberant, enthusiastic, loud even.'

'Loud? Good God!' I broke in, dismayed. 'How awful. I'd no idea.'

'But that's how you first appeared. Now you're quite different: quieter, more reserved, shyer than I'd thought, more serious, more thoughtful. Much nicer. Why?'

'I suppose that the loud persona is so much bombast. There's been much fine talk about meeting people, the business of getting to know people; despite what I said, I don't find it easy. People like Marie who don't really know me at all seem to think that the "vivacity" – or whatever you call it – is me. It's as if they expect me to be "the life and soul of the party". Perhaps it's a defence mechanism? I cover the hurt and pain with a mask of hilarity; I become the clown, the joker. I'm quite sure that in all my favourite hangouts I'm seen as a wacky character with eccentricities of dress and manner ... a caricature rather than a real person.'

'How is it I've seen another side of you?' asked The Actor.

'We've talked, we've discussed personal issues. I feel more at ease. It may be that I have recognised something of me in you. That makes it easier. Perhaps I can afford to relax, to drop my guard?'

He turned to me and looked me full in the face: 'Next time we meet, we don't have to start at the beginning, do we? I want to start here.' He kissed my neck gently and slid his hand under my T-shirt.

'Did you see your husband after you moved?' he asked nonchalantly.

'A couple of times,' I said as I struggled to regain my composure, 'but I didn't want to. After the first time we almost separated, Christmas 1990, we booked a series of events – cinema, theatre, music, lots of Prom concerts – to celebrate our reconciliation. As usual, he had no idea about what he wanted to hear or see, I was his "artistic director".... Naturally, I booked all of my favourites: Monteverdi, Zieleński, Handel, Stravinsky, Borodin. He doesn't go for any of them. When I moved out he refused to give up his tickets; I refused to give up mine. At each concert he'd bring a grubby little brown paper bag full of objects "I'd forgotten"; things which I'd deliberately left behind. So we sat there, side by side, in grim silence.'

'How awful!'

'The worst one was The Last Night of the Proms – all heavily symbolic: the end of the summer, the end of the relationship, joyous celebration tinged with regret ... but I was damned if I was going to miss Prince Igor! When I got home that evening I wept, but I also knew that I'd done the right thing and there was no turning back.'

'How do you feel now? Do you regret it?'

'Not at all. No, not at all.'

I opened another bottle and poured two glasses. He downed his quickly, sat back and stared at me fixedly. 'I'm puzzled,' he said. 'What do you want from this evening?'

'That's a funny question,' I remarked. 'What do you mean? We've talked, we've had a drink. As for "what do I want", I'm not quite sure I understand ... I don't know.'

'Do you want me to kiss you?' His arms were around me.

'Certainly,' I said, 'but what then? I'm not into one-night stands; I don't want you to disappear into the night. But anyway, I feel awkward....'

'So do I,' he said, but his mouth was already on mine. I closed my eyes. 'Do you know,' he said, as he drew back and gazed at me tenderly, 'that you have already told me more in the past minute than you have all night? I know you crave love and affection, but I fear that whatever I've got to offer isn't enough. I'm not reliable; I might let you down. I'm undependable. I'm horribly undependable. What then?'

I started to think of Steve – all the letter-writing, his visit in another few weeks – what did I really think about him? But The Actor's body was strained against mine. I didn't resist ... I couldn't resist ... we tore off our clothes....

....afterwards he said: 'But you're beautiful. Your body is slender, your skin is soft. It was wonderful, but we shouldn't have done it. It's your fault; you tempted me. *You ... you devil! You made me want you.*'

'But why are you so cross?' I asked. 'I thought that you enjoyed it.'

'I did,' he said, 'but I want to love you for what you are and not just for the pleasure of fucking you. *You shouldn't have given in so easily; I'm not just a knob!*'

'That's ridiculous! You wanted me; I wanted you. Why shouldn't we have done it?'

'Because!' he shouted, 'it confuses all the issues! We've done it now. That's it! That's all I've got to offer. You wanted my body ... well, you jolly well got it!'

'But....' I protested.

It was no use. He pulled on his clothes and blundered out of the room. 'I told you I was undependable!' he yelled as he banged the door to.

'Idiot,' I thought. 'Pompous idiot!' But I couldn't decide if it was him or me.

WEEKEND IN WOOLWICH

The following morning, a tiny slip of paper dropped through my letter box. A note from my neighbour, perhaps? She couldn't have heard that angry exchange surely? Though I might have been talking too loudly.

Then I had an unpleasant thought ... could it have been ... was it the ecstatic groaning? *Oh God!* I smoothed it out.

There was only one word on it – *from him!* - in large black capitals:

TART

*

LETTER 21 TO STEVE

London
Saturday 23 May 1992

Dearest

I think that this writing, which grips me like a disease, is becoming an obsession, so please forgive me. Clarissa Harlowe to Robert Lovelace? A Cyrano complex? Please advise!

Today I'm in The Crusting Pipe, which is similar to Truckles: sawdust-strewn floor, guttering candles, a general tenebroso air. Here, though, there are tables in the Lower Piazza from which I can spy on the young and personable musicians of the Sigma String Quartet. Today I feel a little sorry for myself as I have the remains of a heavy cold, the legacy of that 'date' with The Army Surgeon. I knew no good would come of it.

Excuse gleeful reference to **Liverpool.** *Ever since I went there with The Barrister – 1979 – I have never been able to think of it in quite the same light. It was – I told myself then – an architectural/photographic trip; we were on friendly terms, nothing more. We examined and recorded Cockerell's Branch Bank of England and Thomas Harrison of Chester's magnificent Liverpool Lyceum – easily the best building in Liverpool – then we went on to the Anglican Cathedral; another of my personal favourites. It was one of those rare occasions: a beautiful day and the tower was open. At the top, with the whole of Liverpool spread out beneath us, he lunged at me and took me in his arms.... I was torn between admiring his style – the way to an Art Historian's heart? – and feeling faintly embarrassed.*

I don't know why I should tell you this now, but since I seem to be confessing, I'll write it down. A little while ago, I had a brief fling with an Actor, arresting in looks and manner. He reminded me of Beardsley, but – on second thoughts – there was an even greater resemblance to Artaud. It was only after he upset me, following the Whistler performance, that I realised he reminded me of Artaud **after** *his incarceration. Some of his ideas* **were** *a little odd....*

One of the last times I came to this place I was with Anton. I'll tell you more when we meet. I'm looking forward to our meeting; we really do need those two days of talk. Anton's last visit was not a great success. He grumbled constantly about the cost of food and drink; we ate and drank sparingly. I felt a little nonplussed as (a) he has just inherited a sizeable fortune, and (b) we made a point of sharing all the costs. Everywhere we went, he pointed out things that weren't to his taste. Truckles and The Crusting Pipe were 'too trendy', too 'yuppified' – why should I 'stoop to go there'? The Lamb and Flag – or Bucket of Blood, where Dryden was attacked and left for dead – was dismissed as a gloomy dive; too small, nowhere to sit, and (inevitably) too expensive. Covent Garden was too busy, 'too cool'. I couldn't even get him to admire Thomas Arne's house, but that was a personal jibe. He claimed that I was too full of odd bits of information.... So!

I put my pen down.

No, it hadn't been a success but the next time I spoke to him – last week, in fact – was worse. I was sitting at home one evening, in a state of mellow abstraction, my perfumed candle burning low, the fading light filtering through the open windows and the sounds of Woburn Place impinging on my consciousness, when the phone rang: Anton.

To confirm the time and place of his imminent visit, I thought, but straight away I noticed that his voice sounded strained and his manner was oddly defensive.

'I can't make tomorrow,' he blurted out, just like that. 'Sorry, that's the way it is.'

'But Anton,' I protested. 'You promised. You promised ages ago. I thought you didn't let people down ... or perhaps it's only me you do that to?'

'It's my boss,' he explained, a conciliatory note in his voice. 'The one who sent me that memo accusing me of a lack of commitment, no seriousness. He offered me a lift – to and from the meeting in London. I feel I can't refuse. If I do, he will take it as confirmation of what he suspects. Do you imagine I would rather travel with him – exchanging small talk and pleasantries – than spend a day with you? You must be joking! He's really boring; it will be a strain but I've got to do it.'

'Anton,' I pleaded, 'what about my feelings? Surely you could accept his offer of a lift to London, but tell him that afterwards you'll be seeing friends and won't need a lift back. And thank him!'

'I can't do that.'

'Why not? It seems reasonable enough to me. You're not bound to the job 24 hours a day. The evening's yours, or it should be. We could meet as planned and you could still be in Bath late that night or early the next morning.'

'I'm not doing that. Sorry. Anyway, why don't you come down next weekend when Jenni's staying, and Layla – another friend – comes?'

'You know how I feel about that. When Jenni's around, *we can't talk*. I don't want a weekend of polite small talk. Please let's meet tomorrow. Please?'

'No.'

'Well, don't bother,' I snapped. And I slammed the phone down.

*

Sigma were playing The Arrival of the Queen of Sheba for the second time that morning. It seemed to be getting faster: À la Concorde, Tom, who was again leading, called it. As I sipped my Manzanilla I reflected on how lucky I'd been to avoid the

WEEKEND IN WOOLWICH

Layla weekend. Anton had sounded so sheepish.

For part of the time, Jenni had kept a low profile; Anton and Layla went to a restaurant. In the middle of the meal Layla leaned across the table, seized his hand and blurted out that she was getting on in years, the biological clock was ticking away, she wasn't particularly happy – despite her numerous suitors and overpaid job – doing, Anton said, very little – so why didn't they get married?

Feeble protests from Anton, followed by accusations from Layla that he was prepared to settle for a commonplace and suburban marriage, that he wanted someone dim and boring who neither presented a challenge nor stretched him; that he welcomed someone who looked up to him as to a god; who worshipped him with unquestioning and doglike devotion. Protests from Anton, followed by tears and histrionics from Layla; everyone in the restaurant listening, staring, and secretly enjoying the spectacle.

Later that evening they met Jenni; Layla by now silent and sullen, Jenni jealous, suspicious, watchful. They all went out and got drunk before retiring to Anton's flat, Layla sleeping on the sofa. Then Layla's half-hearted attempt to get into bed with them, followed by more accusations: 'prudery in your old age', 'small-mindedness', and so on. Layla dashed to the bathroom, threw up and passed out. All was relatively quiet until 4am when she – still drunk – got up noisily, declaring her intention to leave immediately and drive back to Sidcup. Somehow she was prevented and an uneasy truce reigned until 8.30am when she finally slammed out.

What a sordid business, I thought, enjoying my coffee. Until recently, I'd valued Anton's judgement, but there had been that other phone call ... one night at the beginning of May:

'You were right,' he announced, without further preamble.

'Right about what?'

'I couldn't bring myself to tell you before....'

'What are you talking about?'

'That I should beware "The Witching Day", 29 February; the "Extra Day". I'm sorry, I just couldn't tell you....'

'Christ!'

I was at the Moon & Sixpence with Jenni; the place in Shires Yard that you and I went to at Christmas, remember? Quite smart, quite expensive, lovely atmosphere, low-lit.... Jenni seemed nervous, edgy, as if she was waiting for something to happen. At the end of the meal she leaned towards me and asked me to marry her.'

'Oh no! What did you do? What did you say?'

'At first I dissembled, I dissimulated. What could I say?'

'You could have tried, "Look, this is a lovely, charming offer but, thank you, no!'

'Well, I talked, I reasoned. I argued that we already had an understanding; it went without saying. Why should she need a ring? It wasn't necessary. Anyway, it would be silly because I wouldn't be in a position to marry anyone for at least two years; I wanted to have the chance to sort out my own life, get the PhD out of the way, and the book published.'

'Go on.'

'Well, she started to look so hurt and upset that it ended

with me saying that if it meant so much to her – a mere scrap of metal – then I'd get her one. Mind you, it wouldn't be an engagement ring, or a promise to marry, and she wasn't to call me her fiancé or go around showing it off to everyone.'

'You're mad, Anton. You sound terribly confused. You've told me how you'd hoped that the relationship would drift apart ... and now you admit to this! You're not being fair to yourself or to her. It will get worse after you are married, not better. You're leading her on. No matter how loudly you protest, she will see that ring as an engagement ring. She's bound to.'

'I don't think so. I've told her it won't be.'

'Well, you delude yourself. From what I know of her, irrespective of what she claims, when she has that ring – no doubt chosen, with her usual impeccable taste, from Ratner's' – I added spitefully – 'she'll go to her family and friends, and to yours, and flash it in front of them. Both sets of parents will push for a date; she'll move things into your flat item by item, at first imperceptibly. It might be a furry toy or a dress "for tomorrow", but later a whole stuffed menagerie and her wardrobe will arrive. And much good it will do you.'

'You exaggerate.'

'I think not. Before long, she'll start suggesting little modifications to the décor. It will probably start with rag-rolled walls and ruffle blinds; something subtle, you understand. The books will – of course – have to go unless they're uniformly leather-bound, chosen for appearance rather than content.'

'You're spiteful. You've got a nasty tongue. No, a nasty mind!'

'I admit it, Anton, but I feel very strongly and I'm sure that what I say will come true, unless you get out now. Very soon you'll give her your keys. She might at first stay five days rather than just the weekend, but soon she'll be there all the time, and you will get swept along on a tidal wave of arrangements, invitations, wedding presents....'

'No, I don't think so.'

'I think you will. You don't have the nerve to be honest. Besides, it happened to me the first time, with Charlie, and when I realised what was happening, it was all too late and I couldn't bring myself to humiliate him at the altar.'

He hesitated: 'Perhaps you're right.'

'I'm sure I am,' I preached, 'but don't expect me to come to the wedding.'

I put the phone down, feeling disappointed and deflated.

*

LETTER TO ANTON

Shaw's Café Bar, London
Monday 25 May 1992

Well, here I am at one of my favourite haunts. Music blaring, the sound of the locals having corporate chit-chat over their cocktails, though it's beyond me why a cocktail bar should be named after a teetotaller. I'm sitting at my window seat. It's so hot today that I feel that I'm abroad or on holiday, which in a way I am. You tell me that you are to be married. What can I say? Congratulations?

WEEKEND IN WOOLWICH

You know my feelings already. You tell me that you want our relationship to continue as before, and there's the usual fine talk of Beauvoir and Sartre. No, no! I can't go on like that: I can't be so close. It has to be all or nothing now – so I think it's better to say goodbye for the moment – I need to get on with the rest of my life. Thanks for all the help and support you gave me when I moved to London, and I hope that I have helped with discussion/reviewing your PhD. I'm sorry that all this sounds so ungenerous. I wish you well, and for your sake, I do hope that I'm wrong about your relationship.

Prig! I thought, but I put the letter into an envelope and posted it at Russell Square Tube.

Then I went to The New Look, got out my pen, and continued my letter to Steve.

*

PART III

WEEKEND IN WOOLWICH

LONDON

JUNE 1992

L ANNE RUSSELL

THE INSTITUTION
TUESDAY 9 JUNE 1992

Judy brought in my post. There were requests for information and thank yous, references, queries and – as usual – lots of invitations. One in particular stood out: an exhibition of silk-screened monoprints by a young artist, to be launched that night with a Private View and Poetry Reading; an opportunity to see her colourful works and to hear the inspired words of the visionary poet. Quite an event, I thought, as I wrote it in my diary: *Wine: 6.30pm; Poetry: 7pm prompt.*

*

At the door I was given a glass of champagne. Then I saw The Cyclist across the room: tall, well-built, muscular, fit and confident-looking; a commanding presence.... He was wearing imaginative clothes: black Lycra tights which revealed his shapely legs, a black T-shirt with the emblazoned legend 'I'M ON MY WAY' and a pin-striped waistcoat. His blond hair was long and drifted about his shoulders. He had a nice face and a friendly expression. There was no doubt about it: he was attractive.

I stared at him; I smiled. I was sure that he had noticed me, so I started to minutely examine a picture. Suddenly he was at my side.

'Am I in your way?' I asked innocently.

'No, not at all,' he replied. 'Though I was looking at that picture, too. Wonderful colours! Have you worked out how she gets that effect? I *think it's ink* but it looks like a painting ... is it a painting?'

'No,' I said. 'But I only know that because I've already bought a couple of her works, on behalf of my employers, that is! Technically they're screenprints – that's what she calls them – but she prints them either as a one-off mono or a very limited edition; one of three, perhaps. She doesn't use stencils. She often throws as many as fifteen inks onto the screen where she mixes them, then squeegees them through to the paper. So, strictly speaking, they're paintings through a screen. It's an adventurous technique,' I went on as he looked interested, 'and it gives them great luminosity ... the inks are so thin, you see.'

'Do you know how long it takes her to work out a print?'

'She told me that some are done instantaneously, but then she will toy around with others for months, making sketch after sketch before committing anything to the screen.'

'They're good,' he smiled.

'I like her work, too, but I dislike some of the prurient imagery. The trout's-eye view of the woman striding across a stream is repellent. Why revel in so much pubic hair? She could easily have draped her!'

'But it's an inventive pose,' he countered.

'True, and there are precedents for such a viewpoint ... Apollo at the Palazzo del Te, and any number of dubious images commissioned for collectors and connoisseurs. Of course it would have been equally possible to drape them! The other thing I don't especially like is that there's something very narcissistic, self-indulgent, about her work; all the females look like her, with artistically perfected bodies. I suppose you could argue that many artists are self-indulgent....'

'Have you been to this gallery before?' he interrupted.

'Oh yes,' I said, 'several times. Though I generally give the Aboriginal shows a miss.'

'What do you do? Are you an artist?'

'No,' I laughed. 'People are always asking me that; I should stop wearing this stupid beret! Something far more prosaic: I work for The Institution and I look after everything artistic or historical. There's a large collection of modern works – second only to the Tate, it's said! – plus furniture, china, silver, tile panels, archives, research..... It's all very varied and interesting, no two days are the same; I learn new things all the time. What about you?'

'I'm an artist,' he said, as he looked at me curiously. 'Well, a sort of artist, but I'm not full-time. I've been trying to get a portfolio of things together, but I don't know, I'm not sure....'

'Perhaps all artists feel like that?'

'I don't know,' he repeated. 'I've taken photos of some of the things I've done; I set them all out in my flat one Sunday, but I could do with some advice. Perhaps you could have a look at them sometime?'

'I'm always pleased to look at new work.' I grinned.

'I write a bit, too,' he continued, 'but I suppose I'm really a musician.'

'What instrument?'

'You name it, I play it!'

This chap's multitalented, I smiled to myself.

I raised my (refilled) glass and asked: 'So, how do you make your living? As artist, writer, or musician?'

'None of those, unfortunately. I have a real job as well, full-time in computers, an IT manager. The trouble is that although I'm qualified, it's not very lucrative so I have to supplement it ...'

'Oh?'

' ... by riding twice a week for a cycle courier.'

'Hence the Lycra tights?' I exclaimed. 'Very fetching, I must say!'

Meanwhile thinking: *My God, what a thing to say! Whatever will he think? He'll think I'm kinky.*

'Yes,' he grinned. 'They're good, aren't they? You looked as though you might appreciate them.'

I noticed that the young blonde woman who'd previously been at his elbow was gesturing: 'Another glass of champagne?'

'I'm probably being dreadfully rude,' I said, 'monopolising your attention ... your friend over there, who you've not spoken to for the past twenty minutes, is wondering if you would like another drink. Hadn't you better go over? Shall we both go over?'

'Oh, that's Luba. She's not a girlfriend, she's a friend of a friend. Things haven't gone too well for her recently, so I suggested that she come along with me tonight. She's never been to anything like this before, you see. It's a real treat for her. I thought it might cheer her up ... though she seems to be OK for the moment!'

And indeed, a young man had just brought her a glass of champagne and engaged her in conversation.

'Let me get you another drink,' said The Cyclist. 'I told her I was going to talk to you. I told her,' he continued, giving me a significant look, 'that something was going to happen to me tonight.'

Ooooh! I thought.

He came back with two glasses. 'I'd like to take you to the cinema sometime,' he said.

'Thanks, I'd like that! You know that there's a Surreal Season at the ICA? My chance to catch up with all those films I ought to be familiar with: Dalí, Cocteau, Buñuel....'

'Oh, I don't usually go there, but I've seen surreal things, or at least things with a surreal connection. In Henry & June there's a scene where Anaïs goes to the cinema to meet Henry. He's watching Artaud in Jeanne d'Arc. At least I think it was Jeanne d'Arc. I didn't realise that Artaud had done any film!'

'I didn't until recently, when I read that he'd taken up acting to fund his drug-taking activities. Was it archival film?'

'Yes! I mean the Artaud bit was. Not Henry and Anaïs or Henry, June and Anaïs, unfortunately!'

We both sniggered rudely.

'Anyway, when Henry turns around, she sees that he's crying; tears are pouring down his face.'

'I wouldn't have minded seeing that if only for what they've made of her diaries,' I commented.

'Well, we can sometime, but I'd really like to see The Lawnmower Man.'

A sour note; my heart sank.

'I must admit that it's not one of my top priorities and the reviewers say that, apart from one or two – er! – *stunning sequences*, it has little to offer: bovine plot, dull pacing. Mind you, that's been said of Dr Faustus, and I've always hugely admired that; my top favourite play! So, yes, I'd be happy to see Lawnmower Man eventually, but a week on Saturday there's a screening of Last Year at Marienbad at the Tate. Now that's more my style! It's topical anyway; so many of the images are Magritte, and I've just been to the Hayward show.'

Suddenly I thought of my unspoken commitment to Steve.

We'd moved – at least in letters – beyond the 'penfriend stage' and but for a series of disasters, would have 'properly' met again last week. So, what was I doing setting up a date with this personable young man? Especially after that other little fling with The Actor (not to mention Jay). I brushed the thought aside.... How silly! What's the harm in it? Nothing's happened; I've only agreed to go to the cinema. I'm not going to leap into bed with him. Why shouldn't I see a film with a pleasant young man? Steve knows that I don't stay in waiting for phone calls; anyway, he wouldn't want me to lead a nun-like existence. Besides, I know nothing of his circumstances; he might be having it off with his wife – or mistress – every day....

The Cyclist meanwhile looked somewhat nonplussed. 'I'd like to try your film,' he said, tentatively.

'I think you'd enjoy it. I've seen it before, but I would love to see it again. Perhaps I should warn you that it's difficult to decide whether it's complete twaddle or high art. The critics are divided; I think it's wonderful. Resnais couldn't have failed with those images.'

He smiled: 'I don't know your name yet.'

'I'm Anna,' I said, extending my hand. 'And you?'

'Andrei.'

Nice! I thought. I gave him my phone number and wrote down his address. In Woolwich, I noted, with some surprise.

'That's funny,' I commented. 'Some weeks ago, I had dinner with an Army surgeon; he's in barracks there.'

'I can see that place out of my kitchen window.'

'You've no phone?'

'I don't need one. I don't really like them. Besides, if you need to contact me urgently, they can usually find me at work. Your number? That's somewhere in the centre? Bloomsbury! Isn't it expensive?'

'Yes,' I admitted. 'I can't pretend otherwise but, you see, the mortgage is cheaper than renting and I can tell myself that I'm making a sound investment.'

'Well, it must give you some security.'

'It does, it's nice; I've never owned my own home before. I've never really had my own place; it's just the way that things have worked out.'

We had another drink.

The end of the evening: 'I'll see you soon,' he said, and off he went with Luba; wheeling his bike with one hand, the other resting protectively on her shoulder. *What a nice man, I thought. How kind and considerate he seems....*

*

By the time the day of the screening had arrived, I'd almost regretted arranging to meet Andrei.

WEEKEND IN WOOLWICH

After all, I thought, as my alarm clock bleeped, my life's going along quite nicely. I want to see Steve; I don't want any complications. I don't know what I think about Andrei. He sounds a little doubtful, bewildered even, about some of my artistic tastes. He might not like the film; we might have a completely disastrous day.

'They' (the critics) say that it's one of the great films; all that repetition, for instance –

'Once again – I walk on, once again, down these corridors, through these halls, these galleries, in this structure – from another century, this enormous, luxurious, baroque, lugubrious hotel where endless corridors succeed silent – deserted corridors overloaded with a dim, cold, ornamentation of woodwork, stucco, mouldings, marbles, dark mirrors' – The Voice as incantation; the endless deserted corridors, the empty salons, the blurring of boundaries: dream versus reality; illusion versus dream. What does it mean?

Perhaps it won't be too bad seeing this with Andrei? It's intriguing, whichever way you look at it. *Is it a love story?* Did she really meet him 'last year' or does the idea *just take root*? Is it a metaphor for good versus evil? *Are they all dead, frozen?* It's fascinating, if overlong, but what will *he* make of it? I don't know. He might hate it. He might have 170-odd minutes of sheer boredom.

My reverie was interrupted by a dull thud, a letter landing on the 'magic carpet' in my hall. I smiled as I saw the distinctive hand: Steve.

'Dearest,' it began, but in place of the passionate and intimate tone I'd come to expect, a long and cautious missive:

how we should be trying to *understand* what was going on, how should we *analyse* our motives for embarking on a relationship: *Pairing? Security?* He'd been through all that and so had I, so what was happening? Then there was a suggestion that we engineer our meeting for ten years to the date of his very first postcard, sent when I'd known him in Manchester.

Damn! Cold feet! I thought. Just when I was beginning to feel more relaxed, more confident. What's happened?

I made some strong coffee and reached for my writing paper:

London
20 June 1992

Dearest Steve

I was dreadfully upset to receive your letter, but I can't quite account for my feelings. After all, you're being extremely logical, eminently sensible. Since Easter I've been trying to understand what's going on, but I am not sure that analysing the situation has helped.

You talk of meeting at **that Open Studio ten years to the day since your first postcard,** *and claim that it would be 'handy', a 'neat contrivance'. NO! No! I think that it's a rotten and ridiculous idea. I don't want our long-awaited, much-delayed meeting to be 'handy', 'neat' or 'a contrivance', and I certainly don't want to meet at a party. What about those first awkward moments? I might know dozens of people. I'm liable to be hailed, spirited* *away ... there's a lot to talk about and we won't be able to talk.*

*You suggest that I use my 'alter ego'. I can't do that. It's impossible; too many people know me. More importantly, if we were to meet 'ten years to the day' I would invest that meeting with all sorts of romantic notions and heady expectations. It would be too symbolic; like **The Last Night of the Proms**.... No! No! I couldn't bear it.*

*Perhaps I'm going over the top, but all this morning half-remembered words and phrases keep rattling around in my head: **'As proof of my love, I send you my tears'**.*

I sealed the letter and posted it; I had exactly thirty minutes to get to the Tate.

Andrei was on the stairs leading down to the Coffee Shop; he was all in white except for his pin-striped waistcoat; I was the "Golden Slave" in gold, pink and purple. He stepped forward as if to kiss me; I shook his hand.

'I've just been to check out the theatre,' he said.

'That's funny, so have I! We don't have to book seats, but we'll need to go in at least ten minutes before it starts.'

'Shall we have coffee?'

'Good idea,' I smiled. 'We've got time.'

In the Coffee Shop we sat side by side on the high stools overlooking the centre of the room.

'Last night I went out,' he continued, 'and I ran into an old friend, Vic. I hadn't seen him for ages: months and months ... so we ended up spending the evening together. There was a lot to talk about. I've invited him today; he might come with his girlfriend.'

I felt a bit deflated, but instead I replied – rather pompously – 'I hope that they enjoy the film, but I warn you if they want to talk during it, I'll probably glare at them! It's one of my top favourites; I don't want any distractions.... I want to submerge myself in the images.'

'So do I! Vic's OK. I've brought the car with me; I thought we could go to Hampstead Heath afterwards.'

'Let's see how things go. It's a nice idea, but I'd be equally happy to go to a wine bar. It would be good to just talk.'

Vic and Sandi were late. We were fifteen minutes into the film when they came in and flopped down noisily, putting – I noticed with distaste – their feet over the back of the next row of seats. Sandi started to translate in a stage whisper. I glared.

Much later, as we sat over coffee, Vic looked up and said: 'Someone's pulling my leg.'

'What about?' I asked.

'That film,' he said. 'It was crap. Absolute shit.'

'Very succinct! But it's claimed that *it is* one of *the* most important films since the war. It's inventive – the Robbe-Grillet/Resnais collaboration – all that about Magritte, the theories of Éluard, Breton and Dalí. Granted,' I babbled on, as he raised his eyebrows, 'it's impossible to work out what it means, but it's intriguing ... at the lowest estimate? Surely?'

'Nah! It was crap!' he yelled. 'CRAP!' And then – turning to Andrei and clapping his hands – 'Right, then, Hampstead everyone? Come on! In ten minutes? After another coffee?'

As he and Sandi went to the bar I said to Andrei: 'Look, count me out. I agreed to go out with you, not with your friends.

I'd like to talk and it's difficult to *really talk* in this crowd. I can't say that I'm wild about going to the Heath, and I'm certainly not keen to go with them, so I'll leave you to it. I'm off to The Dôme.'

He looked crestfallen, so I added as kindly as possible:

'Look, don't be upset. Please don't take it personally. I'll see you another time. *It's just that I don't feel like trooping off in a gang;* I don't feel comfortable, I don't know you very well. People behave differently in groups, and I'd feel uneasy. I'm not very good at this sort of thing.'

'But I want to see you, and I'd rather see you alone,' said Andrei. 'I don't really want to go to Hampstead Heath.'

'Why go, then? Vic's sweeping everyone alone in his wake. After all, it's your car and it was our date. But don't let me influence you. I can just as easily see you another time. We're both in London. I'm happy to entertain myself tonight.'

'No,' said Andrei. 'No. I'd much rather see you. It was just that when I bumped into Vic, we hadn't met for ages and he had this idea, a really good idea, he said – to go to the Heath in my car. Now I'm not sure it was such a good one, but it seemed like that at the time.'

'What are you two waiting for?' cried Vic, as he appeared with an empty mug. 'Come on, let's go!'

An uneasy silence....

'Sorry, Vic. I've changed my mind,' Andrei blurted out. 'Will you excuse us?'

Vic and Sandi looked annoyed and disappointed, disproportionately so, I thought.

'Andrei, you could give them a lift if they're so keen,' I suggested.

But they weren't interested. It 'wouldn't be the same,' they said. *'And that's the last time I'll do you any favours,'* Vic threw over his shoulder as they stormed off, *'so, fuck off!'*

'What an odd thing to say,' I remarked. 'What on earth is he talking about?'

'I don't know,' said Andrei. 'How should I know?'

We walked around the corner to Andrei's car. It was large, contrary to my expectations and his protestations of poverty, but the windscreen was pierced by a large 'bullseye', the cracks radiating outwards.

'A stone,' Andrei explained. 'It only happened the other day, and I haven't got round to fixing it yet. Sorry, it's a bit of a mess.'

The interior was covered with a tangle of wire and yellowing newspaper. Quite a surprise, given his neat appearance.... We parked in Lincoln's Inn and went to The Dôme, where we secured a table close to the open doors onto Wellington Street. We talked in a desultory fashion: Beauvoir, Sartre, Éluard, Breton, Genet, Artaud; the Theatre of the Absurd, the Theatre of Cruelty. We had a couple of drinks; we relaxed.

'I like café-bars,' Andrei commented approvingly, as he glanced around.

'So do I,' I agreed. 'Pubs tend to be male-dominated. I'd find it difficult to walk into one, order a drink and spread out my newspapers, as I do in this sort of place. In pubs, men tend to assume that a lone woman is "fair game", "a pickup", "she's short of company". Here, if I have any unwelcome guests, my pals throw them out.'

Andrei laughed, seized my hand and drew it to his lips.

A gallant! I thought.

'I like to watch people,' he said. 'It's so interesting. Do you do that?'

We ordered more drinks. I realised that I wasn't hungry although I hadn't eaten all day. As if guessing my thoughts, Andrei suddenly said: 'I'm not hungry at the moment, but now I look at this menu I don't think I can afford to eat here. I've been trying to cash a giro all day.'

An uneasy thought shot across my mind: I dismissed it.

'I'd rather go back to your place,' he suggested, 'perhaps we could have a picnic or something?'

'That's possible,' I agreed, 'but I'm a "rotten host". If you eat with me, you accept my "house rules"; I can cook, but I don't in Bloomsbury. That's partly because I don't have a kitchen – it's a bit too much like cooking in the library – and partly because I have better things to do. *So, you'll have to eat what I eat, and like it!* If that's OK, you're welcome!'

'Oh, that's OK. That's great!' said Andrei. 'We'd better get the bill.' He started to rummage in his pockets, a look of some panic on his face. 'Oh God!' he exclaimed. 'I haven't even got enough to buy you a drink.'

'Don't worry. I'll get it. You can buy me one next time.'

*

In my room, I opened the claret and made some coffee. We sat on the floor side by side. He kissed me gently; soon his arms were wrapped around me. I started to think about Steve and began to protest feebly:

'Andrei, there's something I have to tell you. I really don't think I want to do this.'

'Why not?' he asked. 'I only want you because of what I feel for you. I don't usually even *think* of going to bed with someone on the first date. But with you ... well, you're different. I've only known you a short time but you fascinate me. You're interesting, well read, articulate. You seem to have really made it in life. You've got things together; you know where you're going.' He pulled me towards him and kissed me again. 'I feel a lot for you already. I think I could really love you, and I would, you know. I would....'

He continued to kiss me. His body was pressed insistently against mine. He was naked under the Lycra tights, I noticed, and I could feel his hardness.

'Look, I have an unresolved situation on my hands,' I faltered. 'For months, I've been writing letters to someone. Someone I've become increasingly fond of.'

'Letters?' he interrupted. 'Have you seen him?'

'Not for ages. We knew each other vaguely years ago, and we met by chance before the exchange of letters, but I haven't seen him since.'

'That's silly, then!' he exclaimed. 'You don't really know him or anything about him.'

'But I do,' I insisted, 'I do. I've learned a great deal. You can tell a lot about someone from a letter. You can deduce things from their writing. He commits all sorts of things to paper, and he takes the time and trouble to write. Not many people would do that.'

But unfortunately Steve's cautious letter was at the front of my mind....

'Letter-writing's a form of commitment,' I continued, with less conviction. 'And I'd prefer to sort that out before we go any further.'

He kissed me again and my body began to melt; suddenly it was ridiculous to protest.

*

The following Monday Andrei rang me at work: 'I miss you,' he said. 'I miss you dreadfully.'

'But we're meeting tonight,' I laughed, 'and it's nearly lunchtime already. There's not long to go. Then there's next weekend – two and a half uninterrupted days – and a few evenings before then.'

'Can we meet for lunch?' he pleaded. 'Please? *Please?* I'm in Marylebone now. I could get on my bike and be with you in ten minutes. You could take me to that Archduke place you're always going on about.'

'I'm sorry, but I can't.' I smiled, feeling simultaneously flattered and alarmed. This had never happened before. Wasn't he feeling too dependent, too devoted? Wasn't this rather silly?' 'And I'm not always "going on about" The Archduke!'

I protested. 'Anyway, I've already agreed to meet one of my colleagues today. I'll see you in a few hours, as promised.'

'But that's a long time away. It's ages and ages.'

That evening he appeared at my Private View: Minimalist Works by a young artist. As he walked into the statue-lined entrance hall of The Institution, people turned to stare. *He was arresting, I thought with some pride.* 'You've got a good one there, girl!' my friend Gloria remarked. And so it seemed. He conversed intelligently; topics which we'd traded before, certainly – Beauvoir, Sartre, Genet, Artaud, his own professed love of words – but ones which he hadn't aired with my guests.

The exhibition had attracted all the usual Bloomsbury eccentrics; Marta, a scion of the Woolf family whose personal motto was *'Don't talk to me about my ex-husband, and please don't mention **that** family'*. Of course, she spoke, and most entertainingly, of little else. Then there was her friend 'The Pretty Strong Woman' who had once charmed George VI with her unusual prowess in bending nails; now rather weighty and not quite so pretty. There was also the 'Frustrated Russian', whose husband had been away for months. Her favourite cry, whenever she suspected that someone had been 'up to something' – and she *always* suspected me – was to throw her head back and bawl, at the top of her voice, irrespective of time, place or company, 'USE CONDOM!' Then there was the Cruel Clinical Psychologist, whose chief pleasure was to play – as per Who's Afraid of Virginia Woolf? – 'Get the Guests'. Fortunately, she was counterbalanced by the Charming Canadian, who often supplied the excellent wine. Andrei sparked in this moveable crowd. The Private View was a great success; three works were sold, my credibility was boosted and the artist's self-confidence restored.

Later, we walked to the Carnaby Street/Central Saint Martins Party at Alternative Arts, an organisation which commandeered empty shops and showrooms as gallery space for young artists. There were striking black and white photographs, wondrous fabrics and ceramics, powerful abstract oils, scale maps wittily imprisoned in ebonised cases, their impact slightly marred by our consumption of numerous tumblers of inferior red wine. One gallery had a window display of ceramic shoes, laid out in decreasing concentric circles. Inside, an arrow 'To the Changing Room' pointed down the stairs.

'Do you think that's left over from the dress shop?' I speculated. 'Perhaps not.'

The artist's two children appeared: 'We charge you to go down,' they chuckled, 'but it's worth it!'

'I'm glad you think so,' I said. 'Aren't you biased? Oh well, we'll try it!' and I handed them a few coins.

Downstairs a narrow corridor was strung across with half a dozen filmy white nets, overprinted with sizes and legends: 'Size 10 = tiny, beautiful; Size 12 = average; Size 16 = fat; Size 18 = huge, gross, ugly' ... and so on. We enjoyed the sensation of wandering through these, reading the accepted stereotypes. To the left, another arrow pointed to a recess. I walked through: a small, square room, the floor completely covered by a sea of new potatoes, carefully matched in colour, size and shape, with bathroom scales as stepping stones. I picked my way across gingerly, averting my eyes from the readings. Andrei was close behind me, laughing: 'Coward!' he shouted. 'I saw you! You didn't look.'

'No, I didn't,' I admitted. 'I weighed myself this morning, so I've got a pretty good idea of the damage. I'd have a fit if I'd put on several pounds today.'

'Have a look,' he said. 'Go on, have a look!'

'But I've got this bag,' I protested, 'and it's heavy!'

'I'll hold that. Just try them.'

I stepped onto one, and then another. What a relief: they were blank.

'Wonderful!' I said. 'A licence to eat!'

We hooted with laughter.

The next room was dominated by a distorting 'fun house' mirror, in which we looked alternately sylph-like and elephantine. There was a series of hangers marked 'Fat', 'Hugely Fat', 'Obese', with French translations appended; the pièce de résistance, a manipulated photograph of a chubby Princess Di with William, showing how – over a few days – the tabloids had elongated and slimmed her in accordance with her usual supermodel appearance. *Ha! Fat is a Feminist Issue, I thought.*

The artist's children ambushed us. 'We charge you to get out as well,' they chorused.

This artist has style, I noted privately, and she's passed it on to them. I wouldn't have dared say such a thing at their age.

'Alright!' I said, in mock despair. 'I'll swop you 50p for two glasses of wine, then we'll come out. Is it a deal? Otherwise we stay here! We're enjoying ourselves.'

'Yes!' they shrieked, and they scampered up the stairs clutching their coins.

Afterwards, as we stood outside in the failing light holding our stingy measures, Andrei turned to me and asked: 'Well, what did you make of that?'

I thought it was great! A challenge to all the stereotypes, an unashamed statement, a celebration. She's got panache ... it's inventive, thoughtful, amusing. I loved the sea of potatoes and the blank bathroom scales: an anorectic's dream! Imagine that in an institution or a clinic. It could make quite an impact. Favourable or otherwise, I'm not quite sure!'

'Will you borrow it?'

'I might.'

In my room we feasted on French bread, cheeses, salads, a bottle of rough red wine. Andrei wandered about, baguette in hand, scattering crumbs all over my spotless carpet.

Oh well, I thought. I'll sort that out later. The damage isn't permanent. It's not every day I have a guest.

*

By 24 June there was still no word from Steve. He's lost interest, I told myself; he's decided that it's all too much bother, it isn't worth it. It's far easier for him to retreat into his comfortable existence than it is to get to know me. So much for all that correspondence.

I went to the Tradescant Trust, the redundant, exquisitely peaceful church of St Mary-at-Lambeth, to write to him; an unpleasant letter, in which I put forward a justification for getting on with my own life, tying up the loose ends, and – by implication – putting everything into the new relationship. Not that I mentioned the new relationship. Buried somewhere in the opening paragraph was the accusation that he might be using me: after all, I said, I live close to Euston and King's Cross; very handy for all those exhibitions, parties and private views. I conveniently ignored the fact that all 'improper suggestions' had come from me. I posted it before I had time for second thoughts.

Andrei rang that afternoon. 'I want to meet you tonight,' he said.

'Great! I've got some free tickets to see John Malkovich in a new play. What do you think?'

'What do you?'

'I was fascinated by him in Liaisons Dangereuses – or I suppose that I should call it by its philistine title Dangerous Liaisons? – and transfixed by The Sheltering Sky, so I'd like to see him on the stage.'

'I don't mind,' said Andrei. 'Sounds OK to me.'

'Where shall we meet?'

He named some Holborn pub.

'Fine,' I agreed, but I was surprised at his choice of noisy, down-at-heel venue. I disliked pubs, especially that sort. Well, I thought, at least it's Victorian. I'll admire the décor and the tile panels. The drinks might be cheaper than usual. All this is costing me a fortune.

The play was all that I had feared. We left at the interval and retreated to my room. Andrei spread out my Cretan mat on the floor, and laid out the knives, forks, plates, glasses, French bread, and bottle of wine.

'Christ, not salad again!' he exclaimed. 'And there's pizza. That must have cost you at least £3. It's cheaper if you make it yourself.'

'I know that, Andrei, but I told you that if you eat here you eat what I eat. I've no wish to stay in all weekend, and I'm not going to waste time doing that now. I'm tired, we're both hungry; this is quick. Besides,' I went on, as he continued to stare at me, 'you've eaten quite handsomely at my expense for the past few days. You know that I don't like cooking in front of people. If I'm doing anything fancy, I shut myself in the kitchen, play loud music, make an unholy mess, really get into it. I can't do that here – no kitchen, no music; the smell hangs around for days.'

'You can do that at my place.'

'Well, I'm not going to,' I retorted. 'If I come to your flat, you cook or we picnic.'

To my shame, I burst into tears. A look of concern passed across his face.

'Why are you so darned sensitive?' he asked, sliding his arm around me.

'I've had a difficult year.'

'I'm sorry,' he said. 'Really I am.'

'Modern theatre's crap,' he suddenly announced.

'I don't agree. How did you arrive at that conclusion?'

'Via tonight.'

'That's silly. You can't possibly make such a sweeping generalisation. You're not exactly an expert. How much modern theatre have you seen? How much theatre have you seen? How many times have you been to the theatre recently?'

'Hang on, hand on,' he cut in, directing a cryptic glance at me. 'I've not seen that much. It's all right you talking like that ... I've not had money like some....'

'Our tickets were courtesy of the Staff Club,' I interrupted.

'Well, I've not been to much theatre and I've not been to much modern stuff. I know; I just know. The only other play I've seen recently was that thing at the National. That was shit, real shit! It proves my point that everything in the West End's poor.'

'Andrei,' I remonstrated. 'I saw it, too. I admit that it was poor; I couldn't have predicted it. The reviewers veered from the sycophantic to the ambiguous. I hated its swashbuckling, thigh-slapping vulgarity, and the Lego-constructed set was dreadful, but it still doesn't prove that the West End stinks. Anyway, it wasn't what I'd call modern theatre.'

'Prove that the West End doesn't stink.'

'It depends on whether you are talking about the geographical west end or West End, mainstream. There are far too many musicals, but I've seen some excellent fringe in the most unlikely places. The five-person fifty-minute Julius Caesar at Maison Bertaux was a triumph: sensitive and powerful, an essay on the philosophy of evil, and the two actresses in Intimacy gave it their all. You could almost *see* Sartre watching them with his toad's eyes from a café table. I don't think that you know what you're talking about. There's lots of good experimental theatre around, and it needn't cost a great deal to find it. All you need is Time Out and a bit of imagination.'

He seized the bottle and poured two more glasses.

*

On Friday morning I bustled about my room in some excitement. My bag was packed; in several hours I'd be with Andrei; the first of a series of long, relaxing, self-indulgent weekends, he said. Just what I needed. I'd only a half-day's work to get through, and a social gathering with my colleagues. As I locked my door The Caretaker, who was collecting the rubbish, hailed me:

"Ere! Come an' 'ave a look at this!'

Something in the tone of his voice suggested that whatever it was wasn't pleasant.

'I'm in a hurry,' I said.

'Aww! Come on!'

'Will I like it?' I asked, hesitantly.

'Nah.'

'Will it take long? I mustn't be late.'

'A minit, an' it's on yer way.' He grinned. He ushered me down the corridor. '103,' he announced.

'So, he's really gone?' I asked, surprised. 'It was only last night I heard him yelling out of the window, as usual.'

"Ee's gone alright,' replied The Caretaker. "Ee got out very late; I've 'ad t-job of clearing aat this lot. Staarted at five this morning.'

'I don't envy you that. I overheard some dispute about a settee.'

'Aar man wan't keen ter take it co's 'ee thought it'd be rank. Look!'

He threw open that door and gestured around the room. The frayed brown carpet was ankle-deep in cigarette ends, rotting food, debris; the walls were filthy, fingerprinted and scrawled with signs, ciphers, slogans; the mildest, just inside the door in shaky script: 'Five seconds is all you have. So, JUST FUCK OFF AND LEAVE ME ALONE!!' One spotlight was fixed to the ceiling; a long trail of loose cable dangled from the other socket. Power and water had been cut off long since with dire results in the 'kitchenette' and bathroom. As I looked, a huge cockroach scuttled for cover.

'Thev' been complainin' baat them thins next daar.'

'God above!' I shuddered. 'You'll have to get all the flats either side fumigated, otherwise we'll all get them. They'll just whip along the pipes until the coast's clear. How can anyone live like this? I thought that this place might be grim, but I'd no idea it was this bad.'

'Management'll tek it up, but place below's woss!'

'The solicitor's?'

'Yeah.'

'I'm not surprised. He might be highly qualified and well spoken, but he's permanently drunk or high. He's in decay....'

'103 spoke posh,' said The Caretaker. 'If yer spoke t'im ont' phone, yed think 'ee wo all there, doin' well, 'ad er good job. Mind yer, he wan't that easy ter speak to; not when 'ee wo drinkin' or tekin' drugs and somethin'. Most o' t'time 'ee wo sprawled in this doss aars.'

'Accent and education have nothing to do with it,' I commented. 'I've seen intelligent, educated, well-spoken people go to pieces. I don't understand how it happens. I'm horrified when I see it. What will become of the room? Is it being let?'

'Someuns baat it. Daart cheap ... they'll 'ave to staart agin. Rip ole lot aart, then it'll be right.'

'My God!' I exclaimed, with a feeling of rising nausea. 'I'd hate to be the next owner.'

*

That evening Andrei met me off the Woolwich train. I'd just come from my colleagues' gathering; we'd gone to a Mexican Bar for 'a cheap meal'. I should have noticed that the jugs of margarita were £25; we'd all spent a great deal more than we'd intended. I was carrying my backpack, containing casual clothes and smart things; my black work bag with my Filofax, notes, writing paper, and my ethnic bag from Neal Street East, today full of spice jars rather than the usual rolled-up newspapers. My entire collection; Andrei had promised to make a curry and had, he said, not a single spice. So why not use mine?

He was smiling delightedly, and he immediately started to apologise for the state of his flat. Woolwich wasn't a nice place, he said, which was why he'd come to meet me; he wouldn't dream of letting me wander around unaccompanied. His flat was a mess, so perhaps I might have some ideas on how to sort it out. He'd try to make the weekend more pleasant; we'd have a good meal, he'd show me his artwork, play some of his music, read to me. It would be relaxing, he said. He had a TV with numerous channels, including satellite. There were plenty of things to watch.

'But Andrei,' I protested. 'We've got lots to talk about. Why are you worrying? Aren't you getting paranoid over the state of your place? After all, my room is so ordered – some might say *so obsessively ordered* – that anything else might seem a tip by comparison. Don't worry about it!'

'Wait and see. You won't like it! You really won't, but remember I warned you first!'

We walked up a path which threaded its way through a colony of identical tower blocks set in imaginatively landscaped gardens. The area looked civilised enough, if a little boring. An odd thing: although it was a Friday night, there were no people in the streets and we met no one on the way to Hatley House. As we got closer its shabbiness become increasingly apparent. The porch was stained, its glass broken, the entryphone long gone; bare wires dangled from the wall. Many of the balconies served as rubbish dumps and harboured either an unlovely array of overstuffed black plastic bin bags, or bits of old furniture. It was a warm, airless night; washing hung limply from most windows. The surrounding area was littered with rags and discarded household equipment. Suddenly a bedhead whistled past us, and hit the ground where it smashed into two. We could hear the sound of a violent argument high above, and the sound of someone sobbing uncontrollably.

'The stupid buggers!' Andrei exclaimed. 'No wonder this place is such a dump. People are always ditching things out of windows: rubbish, used nappies, you name it. They won't use the rubbish chute and that's one of the few things that actually works! It's worse when people argue, and they do plenty of that here. Something about the place encourages it. Can you blame them if they give up trying to make their lives better, and turn their faces to the wall; become pigs like everyone else?'

I remonstrated mildly: wasn't he being harsh and cynical, surely people retained some pride, wasn't he exaggerating?

'But you don't understand,' he insisted. 'You can't understand. You live in a different world from this; quite different. Just look around you; look at the evidence. The trouble is that after a few years the atmosphere of the place gets to you, so you can't help living in a pigsty. You're lucky. You don't appreciate how lucky you are! Really, *it's all right for you....*'

Before I could summon up a reply he strode on ahead and pressed the button in the lift lobby.

The lift stank. The floor was covered with rubbish over which someone had half-heartedly sloshed some disinfectant and laid a soggy sheet of cardboard. We stopped on the seventh floor. His door was heavily boarded and distinguished from its neighbours by its ugliness and inelegance; the result, he said, of a break-in a couple of weeks ago when the burglars had taken his 'only valuable possession' – the compact CD system. He'd repaired the door himself because, he said, he couldn't afford to get it fixed properly. Despite its fortress appearance, people could peer through the open letter box and through the hole left by the missing Yale.

I wasn't prepared for what I saw inside.

There was an overpowering smell of cat. The hall was scruffy and dimly lit. On the left was what should have been the bedroom.

'We were jamming in there the other week,' Andrei explained, 'and I've not had time to sort it out yet.'

The floor was covered with an assortment of ragged carpet offcuts, salvaged from the tip or from the rejects slung out of the windows. They were piled willy-nilly; everywhere a tangle of wires. A broken television, hemmed in by some thirty carriers of empty beer bottles and six of old shoes, was propped against one wall. The bed, against the facing wall, was piled high with debris. Under the window – at right angles to the bed – was a small sideboard, its surface covered with electrical spares, a cardboard pyramid resplendent among the chaos. The most dominant object, displayed altar-style over the bed, was a massive framed and glazed jigsaw of Richard Dadd's Oberon and Titania, a work which Andrei revered.

'The wires are from jamming,' he repeated.

A day's jamming couldn't possibly have created this mess, I thought. It's more like the neglect of years....

The cat smell emanated from the meter cupboard on the right of the hall, a space the size of my tiny bathroom at home. The meter cupboard housed the brimming, lazily scratched litter tray, which rested on a mound of old newspapers and random assorted bike spares. The bathroom – next immediately right – was lit by a single red bulb to hide, he said, the peeling wallpaper. Its floor was stacked with empty cardboard boxes; the sink and bath so ringed with grime that I made a mental note to use them as little as possible. Two torn posters, Class and Wired for Sound, were tacked to the wall. Both, I noticed with dismay, were of stylised sex-object women, and gave the opposite effect to that presumably intended.

He ushered me into the main room. As we walked in, the cat shot under the settee.

'Babee,' he cooed at it, in an odd falsetto voice. I affected not to hear.

It was a large and well-lit space: some seventeen feet by twelve with a kitchen opening off one end, and a big, secluded balcony at the other.

'It's possible to sunbathe there starkers.' He grinned. He glanced around, a look of some satisfaction on his face: 'I've been tidying up. I've swept the floor.'

I would never have guessed it: every surface was covered with a white film of cat hair, the floor felt crunchy. Shabby pieces of furniture draped with blankets jostled for space around the walls: wing chairs, scratched down to their frames, settees sporting large cigarette burns. So, he thinks that the blankets make it look respectable? I speculated. He's kidding himself.

Tapes and records, in and out of their covers, were strewn about the floor. The computer table was a jumble of wires, spent Tiger Balm jars, pens, pencils, biros, and old paper; either, he explained – with a significant look – to recycle or to use for artwork. More paper spilled from cardboard boxes shoved between the furniture and under the single bookshelf. I was alarmed to see that the latter housed several New Ageist titles, rather than the serious literature that I had anticipated. There was much on aurae, the cosmos, 'alternative routes to ecstasy', and – the mark of a sick mind? I mused – assorted works by Aleister Crowley.

'A fine writer,' he commented.

Some incompetent drawings – the artwork! I thought with trepidation – were propped over the bookshelf or pinned to the wall. T-shirts and socks lay scattered about the furniture and over two woodwormed tree trunks 'rescued from the Thames'; pairs of leggings dangled from a string stretched across the room.

He waved airily at them: 'That's just washing. I'm into decay, you see ... really into it. This is progress. It took me years to get it like this.'

I began to feel uneasy.

The kitchen was worse. That anyone could cook there, eat and remain healthy seemed nothing short of miraculous. The floor was filthy, covered with crusts, crumbs, spent tea bags, and empty cat food tins, which had been aimed in the general direction of a plastic bag wedged between the sink and the cooker.

'I don't like bins,' he explained. 'They're ecologically unsound. I like to do my best for the planet.'

Dirty dishes putrefied in the sink and on the draining board. The fridge contained a gaping tin of cat food and a half-empty can of lager. I trod on something hard: cockroach or beetle? I daren't look.

WEEKEND IN WOOLWICH

The only nice touch, I thought in my naïveté, were some well-cared-for ferny plants flourishing in the strong light of the window.

I'd expected the place to be untidy, disorganised, I thought. But not like this! No, not like this! I hadn't anticipated unmitigated squalor.... How could I have known? How could I have predicted it? There was nothing in his appearance to suggest it. He looked so well organised, so clean, so presentable. He fitted into my room, bar one or two crumbs, beautifully. There he was tidy; he boasted that he was a good guest. I can't just turn around and go home. I promised to stay; I said that I would. If I go, I'll destroy his confidence. I decided to leave my best things packed in my backpack.

'Well, what do you think of the place?' asked Andrei, no trace of irony in his voice.

At first I dissimulated and then, because I suspected that my face betrayed my thoughts, took a deep breath and said:

'To be honest, I think that it's a shithouse, a doss heap. You told me that it left something to be desired. You said that it needed sorting out. You didn't tell me that it was filthy. It's like a squat, or what I'd imagine a squat to be. I'd no idea. How can you live like this? You always look so good.'

He looked stunned. 'It took me a long time to get it like this,' he said. 'I told you I'm into decay. It's a progression of ideas ... it's supposed to be like this. It's just that I wanted to take it to its greatest extreme; a scientific experiment. It's the yin and the yang, the black and the white, the id and the ego, the balance of life.... This place is like an energy field; it's all concentrated here. If I tidy up or clean I'll disperse it.'

'I can see that it's taken a long time,' I commented, 'but all your fine talk is so much flannel: "Like an energy field" ... what the hell's that supposed to mean? You're joking! You can't be serious? You surely don't think that I believe you? You're talking nonsense! You're making excuses ... yes, that's it! Making excuses ... because you're lazy about this place and you've given up!'

He blurted out: 'Well, all right, it started off seriously but it's gone too far now for me to do anything about it. It was in control; now it isn't.'

'Rubbish,' I replied. 'Really you might do a little housework. You could start by putting away the tapes, clearing the cat lit, hiding it where the smell doesn't hit you in the face; throwing out all the newspapers and cardboard, and getting rid of the old shoes. Why bother keeping them? I can't imagine what possible use they could be!'

A tear rolled down his face. I started to feel sorry for him; perhaps I'd been unkind?

'I thought I'd do something with them,' he protested. 'You've got no faith in me.'

'What exactly? They're all either odd ones or full of holes. You can't wear them. What could you do with them?'

'You're not an artist; I am. I'll build a construction.'

'What sort of construction?'

'A human figure. I'm not sure ... a sort of wicker man.'

'Well, perhaps that's one of your better ideas,' I said. 'You should get in touch with Nicholas Treadwell! And what's the cardboard pyramid for?'

'Go and look.'

I pulled down one of its sides. Inside, dead centre: a jam jar three-quarters full of water in which rested several razors with rusty blades.

'An experiment,' he announced, significantly, tapping his nose. 'Pyramid energy. I learned that the other day when I was reading. The blades sharpen themselves, you see. I save a lot of money that way.'

That's why he's always so stubbly, I concluded.

We shared a large mug of vinegary red wine. He gestured in the direction of his daubs. The two over the bookshelf, white impasto on black paper – apparently of the cat – were so ill drawn that it looked like a fox. There was a collage on the opposite wall made from bits of Sunday supplement: impossibly proportioned women with melon breasts, narrow waists and hips, dressed in leather or rubber; some sporting whips with long thongs.

'Why are they there?' I asked. 'It looks like a fetish wall.'

'Oh,' he explained, unconvincingly, 'it's because it's over the tape deck. It depends on what I'm playing.'

The collage partly obscured a twice life-size sketch of a woman's face: large doe eyes, tendril hair, diagrammatic mouth. A more successful effort, I thought, if you like that sort of thing.

'It was done after we were tripping one Sunday,' he said. 'There's nothing to do here except smoke and trip.'

'I'm surprised at you,' I said censoriously. 'No wonder you're always broke. Why don't you go out a bit? Go to Greenwich – see the Queen's House and the Observatory ... have a walk around the park, or you could read, write, do something creative. What's wrong with thinking? You could even try to improve your surroundings. You don't have to spend much money to do things.'

'You don't understand what it's like to be here!' he wailed. 'You just don't understand.'

We watched a film. We had another drink. Suddenly, it was late and I wanted to go to sleep.

In bed, he burst into tears. 'You've been here several hours,' he wept, 'and you haven't said anything about my artwork.'

I felt a momentary panic; the question I'd been most dreading. What could I say?

'I'm not on duty,' I replied, trying to sound convincing. 'I'm not working or evaluating now, I've been doing that all week. This is my weekend; I'm relaxing.'

I tried to stop my face saying:

Oh my God, I hope he doesn't guess what I really think. I haven't said anything because I wouldn't glorify his artwork with that name. It's a long time since I've seen such rubbish. He can't draw; he's got no grasp of form, little imagination, no points of reference and – bar one or two handy buzzwords – is art-historically ignorant. Mind you, that's not always important. The tragedy is that someone, either through misplaced kindness or lack of judgement, once told him that he's talented and now he believes it. But I'm a critic. I have to be honest; how could it be otherwise? I spend all my days examining and judging beautiful works. I can't praise these! It's not possible. They're crap!

I made some comforting sounds.

He put on an 'electronic noises' record, threw back his head and started to sob.

'Sometimes I put records on just to cry. It's good for you; it releases emotion.'

He pulled me closer. 'You're strong,' he continued. 'You're good, you're clever. With you I could be great; I could make something of my life. I want you to advise me; I want you to help me with my artwork and my writing. I want you to *reform* me. I want you to get me off this drugs habit.'

'Drugs habit?' I interrupted, horrified. 'But I thought that any habit you had was in the past, and....'

'Only dope,' he said.

'That's bad enough,' I protested, 'but I can't do that. I can't! You've got to do some things yourself. I'm not strong enough to carry you. Too much has happened; I've got a big enough job keeping myself sane. You can't expect me to sort you out, too. I can't do it!' His sobs grew louder. He held me closer; I felt him hard against me. 'What about me?' I continued. 'I've spent most of my life giving. I can't keep giving much more indefinitely – there's not enough left. *I've had enough!* I'm fed up with people feeding off my strength; it's time I got something back.'

Then suddenly he was on top of me.

*

Later he was calmer.

He started to talk about his past life; I listened with

increasing alarm. It was, at the lowest estimate, raffish. But then – I reasoned with myself – Henry Miller and Antonin Artaud led raffish lives, and it didn't cancel out their creativity. *I'm being prejudiced ... I must try to keep an open mind!* On the other hand, Artaud went mad ... completely lost the place ... that embarrassing performance for the BBC, for instance, when – for an hour or so – he bashed and banged gongs and screamed and yelled his guts out....

'There was that time I spent in a coma,' Andrei said, 'but I'll tell you about that later. I've done all sorts of things. I worked in a child rehabilitation unit. I decided to do it for a year because any longer would've been too much.'

'How could you make a decision like that?' I asked, 'Didn't you feel a sense of responsibility? What about your charges? Didn't they get attached to you? What about when you left?'

'I was in my early twenties,' he continued, ignoring me, 'so I wasn't much older than the Borstal kids. I got on well with them. I liked them; they liked me. I was sacked, you see, because I admitted I smoked dope; the boys did, of course, and so did the counsellors, but no one would admit it. It's just that I did. I suppose that that was pretty stupid; I should've kept my trap shut. But I was going to leave anyway, so it didn't matter. Afterwards I lived in a squat; it was good. It was cheap, it was relaxed. I made some good friends, but I couldn't sort myself out ... just couldn't get it together. I spent six months in Wormwood Scrubs....'

'Christ!' I exclaimed. 'How come?'

'Drugs charges.'

'*What?!*' I shouted.

'Only possession, but it wasn't my fault. *Really.* After the squat I moved to some chambers in Gray's Inn Road; the place Vic lives in now. Soon, I was completely broke. Some friends asked me if they could borrow the flat. They offered me a *huge* sum of money. It was a big temptation. I couldn't afford not to; I needed it ... I don't suppose you know what it's like,' he added aggressively.

'I do,' I protested. 'I know it doesn't look like it. Just because you think that I live in style doesn't mean to say that I have unlimited cash. I don't spend much; I walk everywhere; I skip meals more often than I'd like to. I don't have a car; I don't have enough clothes. I don't have a radio, stereo or a telly. I had to make the choice between paying the poll tax....'

'You pay it?' he interrupted.

'Yes.'

'That's what's wrong!' he shouted. 'That's it! You've subscribed to the capitalist system. First I learn that you own your own place, and now this!'

'I'm not sure that it means I've subscribed,' I reasoned, 'but I do have the remains of a social conscience. If I don't pay mine, everyone else will have to subsidise me and I'd hate that. Anyway, I was going to say that I had to make a choice between paying poll tax and paying for a travel card. So, I walk; I take on extra work: articles, exhibitions. You can't throw your accusations at me. That's not fair.'

He looked nonplussed.

'Do continue,' I said.

'In no time at all,' said Andrei, 'they'd installed steel doors and entryphones. It was like a fucking fortress. There were people coming and going at all hours, day and night. I went back to collect some things and it was then that we were busted. But I was innocent! I was set up! I wasn't even living there.' He broke off and stared into space: 'Six months inside! Does that worry you?'

'It's not an enviable record,' I replied, as kindly as possible. 'It's a great shame, but I'm glad that you have told me. I'm sorry; perhaps you can put that behind you.'

'You're gorgeous. I want you again.'

*

I fell into a fitful sleep. I awoke with a choking sensation to find the cat curled up on top of me.

'He's taken to you,' said Andrei. 'That doesn't often happen. He's very shy, very solitary.... I really love that cat, you know.'

Suddenly the doorbell rang and there was a great hammering and bashing. Someone started yelling through the letter box. Surely the postman's not so enthusiastic? I thought.

'Andrei!' I exclaimed, as I fumbled for my watch. 'It's early ... about eight, *and* a Saturday morning. You don't *have* to answer it, do you? You could be away.'

'But they can see,' he protested. 'They know I'm here.'

'They? Who are they?'

He ignored me and reached for a greying towel dressing gown, riddled with holes. I pulled on my clothes. He threw open the door.

It was Tracy, someone he'd spoken of. I'd not met her before and was surprised to see that she looked like a stereotypical tart: a stage tart. She wore a see-through lace top, buttoned at the back, a short, black satin skirt, clinging to and climbing up her fat buttocks; black fishnet tights, a gold ankle chain, and white, boat-shaped stilettos. On a leather thong around her neck, a small plaster skull with red eye sockets. She had greasy, bottle-blonde hair, a coarse accent and ingratiating manners, which contrasted oddly with the unpleasant looks she directed at me.

'You must be Anna,' she smirked.

'That's right.'

'How nice to meet you,' she replied, proffering the tips of her fingers.

'My! How cadaverous you look with that skull!' Andrei exclaimed. 'What brings you here so early?'

'Waiting for Andy. He's doing a deal round the corner so I thought I'd wait for him at your place. Unless' – she added archly – 'I'm interrupting anything.' She eyed Andrei sideways, put her can of Tizer on the table, crossed her legs and hitched up her skirt provocatively. He grinned lasciviously. *Charming, I thought. I bet he's had her.*

'Can I have a smoke?' she asked.

'I haven't got anything.'

'Oh well,' she replied with mock resignation, 'I'll have to have one of mine.' And she fished some greenish tobacco and a cigarette paper from her leather bumbag. I shut myself in the bathroom.

The doorbell rang again; again someone started hammering wildly. I opened the bathroom door and stuck my head out. Andrei wandered into the hall, his dressing gown gaping to reveal a pale flabby belly. How funny, I thought. I hadn't noticed that before. What a foul sight! He caught my grimace:

"S's not too good for a man to be too thin,' he said defensively. 'You've gorra 'ave somethin' to protect kidneys.'

Debatable, I thought, but why are you suddenly slurring your words ... why the lazy pronunciation? For Tracy's benefit?

Andy stood outside: a thin, weedy-looking, wimpish figure with baseball cap – worn backwards – tracksuit bottoms sliding off his hips, torn T-shirt, filthy trainers and incongruously heavy gold jewellery: an engraved identity bracelet, an engraved necklace, a fake Cartier watch. He was carrying a mobile phone and looked about fifteen. Twice that, Andrei later told me.

Tracy ran into the hall. 'Thank God!' she shrieked. 'Thank God you've come. I thought you'd been busted.'

'Bye!!' they both shouted, as they banged the door to.

'My God!' I thought. 'I've got to get out of this place!'

*

We had breakfast on the balcony; an otherwise pleasant space marred by the remains of two broken tables and another stinking cat lit tray. The view of the pond had been ruined by the collection of unsavoury items ringed around it; a bit of carpet dangled from one of the weeping willows. There was a cat hair on my toast. I flicked it away surreptitiously.

'Do you think I can make this place all right?' Andrei asked anxiously.

'Yes, I think so, with some work.'

'But I'm depressed,' he broke in, tears welling up in his eyes. 'I can't; I can't. I can't get going with anything. All I do comes to nothing.'

'Well, if you feel so bad you should get some professional help,' I suggested. 'I'm not the person to help, much as I'd like to. I'm not qualified. There's a limit to what I can do.'

'I hate this place,' he said. 'There's an unpleasant atmosphere. Too many ghosts, too many incubi ... too many succubae.... I can feel them. It's gone too far. It's beyond redemption!'

'Look, you're getting melodramatic. I can't deny that it's a mess; you mustn't get disheartened. It would take quite an effort to sort it out' – and fumigate it, I added mentally – 'but it would be worth it in the end. Anyway,' I asked, changing the subject, 'what brought you here? Why Woolwich?'

'When I was inside,' he said, 'I sent my old dog to a mate of mine who lived near here. So when I came out I followed the dog.'

'That's a pretty rum reason,' I observed. 'Like Julia in After Leaving Mr Mackenzie: "if a taxi hoots before I count to three, I'll go to London. If not, I won't". Of course one does and off she goes.... But that is a strange way to organise your life; pretty aimless. What happened to the dog?'

'It died.'

I suppressed a violent urge to laugh.

'Well, then, perhaps as there's now no good reason for you

to live here, you should cut your losses and move to Central London. There are loads of Peabody Trust places and it's not too much to rent one; lots of "my artists" do. There are some near Covent Garden. Imagine! I could make some enquiries. What do you think? Anyway, London's very stimulating; you'd have much more to do, and you might find' – and I said this without irony – 'that the move triggers off some new creative work. I can see what you mean about this place. I don't know what you could do here: it's stultifying.'

Andrei began to look more alert, more hopeful.

'I could clear up this place and let it,' he said. 'Though God knows, it was enough trouble to get it.'

He jumped up and started to rummage among the debris on the computer table. Finally he pulled out a crumpled piece of paper which he flourished triumphantly: 'Here's an ad I wrote ages ago to try and get people interested: "Wanted, students or similar for first-hand socio-economic experience of high-rise living in angst-ridden tower block. £40 all in".'

'Very witty. Did you get any replies?'

'No.'

'I'm surprised. I'd have thought it a dead cert for the wacky. And it's cheap, cheap ... almost derisory! Where did you advertise?'

'In the entrance hall.'

'That's silly,' I said. 'Anyone seeing it would already be here. You've limited your market to say the least. You should have tried Time Out, The Big Issue, Loot.'

'Dunno. Didn't think of that.'

WEEKEND IN WOOLWICH

Again the doorbell. This time the knocking was quieter.

'I thought you said that you weren't going to answer it,' I remarked, as he sprang up.

'I can't leave it,' he replied as he pulled his dressing gown to.

'But you're still not dressed and it's getting late,' I protested. 'And I've not put my make-up on. Are you sure that we're in to visitors?'

But he had already gone into the hall.

A thin, bedraggled, timid-looking person was standing outside. She had a curiously dead look about the eyes; her hair was short and unkempt, she was shabbily dressed.

'Hi!' said Andrei, smiling. 'Suzi! Are you coming in?'

'No,' she replied, catching sight of me. 'I'll be back later. You've got company,' and she turned on her heel.

'What was all that about?' I asked.

'How should I know? She lives in the flat opposite; I think she gets lonely. So, she comes round. She's done me some favours; like when I had the windows fixed. She kept the keys and let people in and out. But she's shy, you see. She wouldn't have come in because of you. You should've made yourself scarce.'

'Did she want something?' I asked, ignoring his last sentence.

'I suppose she wanted a smoke,' he said, in an offhand manner.

'Do you supply all of this block? I don't like the look of these dubious characters.'

'No. NO! You've got the wrong idea. Anyway, they're alright.

One night I was smoking; she came in, I gave her a joint. It seemed to please her. She's led a pretty awful life up to now....'

'And you thought that that would help?' I interrupted loftily. 'That's a joke. Retreat into mirth! Good God!'

'I don't fancy her if that's what you're thinking.'

'I'm not.'

'Well, after she smoked she sat on the bed. She was giving me the eye and I thought she fancied it.'

'You fancied *her?*' I asked incredulously.

'She's not that bad-looking.'

'Arguable,' I said, making a vain attempt to conceal my real thoughts: she looks like a stupid slut ... a stupid, diseased slut!

'I fancied *it,*' he insisted, 'and I thought I ought to make a pass at her.'

'Ought to? *Ought to?* What a strange thing to say.'

'Well, she's quite a nice shape and she was eyeing me up ... so I tried to kiss her. She bit me. She bit me hard on the lip. It hurt; it bled.'

'Serves you right,' I said contemptuously. 'Sex in exchange for dope.'

'Don't be silly,' he replied, but the rest of his words were drowned out by the doorbell.

This time, Suzi barged into the main room, threw herself onto the settee and kicked off her white stilettos. I noticed that there were holes in her tights and her fingernails were grimy; her feel smelt.

'This is Anna,' said Andrei.

'Hello,' she said, despondently, and then – ignoring me –

'Got some?'

'Nope. I had a quarter of an ounce on Thursday; now it's all gone.'

She sat in silence for another couple of minutes, then stood up abruptly: 'Well, you've still got company. I can see when I'm not wanted. I can take a hint, you know, even if you think I'm thick. I can't hang about all day. I'll have to be going, but I'll be back ... I'll see you later. Don't expect me to do you any more favours. You can sod off. You can't go on having it on a plate, you know.'

'Don't go,' said Andrei. 'Please don't! I'll still have company later.'

But she slammed down the hall and banged the door hard.

*

It was almost 4pm.

'We'll have to go down to the market,' Andrei said. 'You can pick up quite a lot of good stuff later on.'

'Hadn't you better get a wash, a bath, or something before we go?' I asked, uncomfortably aware that he hadn't washed for some days.

'No,' he declared. 'I'll just get dressed. I've no need to wash; it'll just remove all the natural oils. It's not good for you. How d'you think I keep my skin so nice? Anyway, there's the Kundalini energy' – he went on portentously. 'If I wash it'll all go down the drain. It's too valuable.'

'Kundalini energy,' I snorted. 'You're raving. I'm always

having baths and washing my hair and my skin's still in good condition. I'm not into all this New Ageist twaddle.'

He grabbed some black leggings from the string across the room and pulled them on over his bare skin; he slipped on his orange T-shirt and pin-striped waistcoat.

How is it that the general effect's so good? I thought. How come he looks so clean?

He rummaged in the cupboard under the sink and pulled out several plastic bags. A large beetle scurried from its hiding place.

As we walked towards Woolwich town centre, a car pulled up. The occupants, an Asian man in his fifties and a blonde, white, miniskirted, leather-booted girl, who looked no more than sixteen, hailed us. 'D'you know where the tattoo shop is?' they shouted. Andrei gave them precise directions. They drove off.

'Why should they ask us?' Andrei asked me.

'Several possibilities,' I mused. 'Perhaps we don't look like typical citizens of Woolwich ... you in your waistcoat, me in my jazz trousers. Some might think us outré, artistic? Perhaps we look as though we know our way around, or as if we're the proud owners of tattoos. I did think about getting one, as it happens; something small and discreet, on my left shoulder. What do you think?'

'A tattoo?' he said. 'I'm not sure. I don't think I'd fancy that. I'd rather you got one of those things we saw in the film last night....'

'In Masque of the Red Death?' – the scene sprang to mind – 'You mean a *brand*? That's awful! A dreadful idea!

I'm shocked.... Woman as farm animal, dumb, unspeaking, unfeeling; a mere chattel! Besides, it would be painful, at the time and afterwards. That's barbaric! Shame on you!'

But Andrei was visibly and spectacularly aroused.

'I'm sorry,' he muttered shiftily. 'I'll have to sit down for a moment. I didn't think this would happen; I should've worn underpants.'

I started laughing: 'God Almighty! What did I do?'

'You shouldn't have gone on about the brand.'

'I didn't go on about it. How should I know that you'd get off on that? It must be the association of ideas ... her blissful look when she becomes Bride of Satan. Either that, or you're kinkier than I thought. Well, I won't be getting one of those!'

'I'm not kinky. Anyway, what about you? You can't seem to get enough of it.'

'So you expect "nice women" to have no sexuality? We're all either whores or madonnas? I thought you a little more liberated.'

He demurred.

'Well, I'm not going to justify myself. It's been a while and so inevitably....'

But before I could finish, he interrupted: 'Anna, please. *Please, let's change the subject!* Otherwise I'll never be able to get to the market.'

I'd imagined that Andrei would go to those stalls just packing up, and barter for reduced goods. Instead he furtively surveyed the emptying square, bent down swiftly, grabbed a potato from a puddle and stuffed it into his carrier. He grubbed in the gutter for fruit which had just rolled off ... for the odd onion, stray carrot or squashed tomato.

'For God's sake!' I cried. 'Let's go to the supermarket.'

'But I haven't any money,' he said. 'Not a penny.'

'Andrei, I warn you! This is the *last* time that I'm going to finance you. You've stuffed yourself all week; I can't afford to go on feeding you. *And* I've paid for most of our wine and all of the pubs. You said that this weekend was your treat, but I'm not eating these ... these ... slops! We'll go to the supermarket – I'll pay by Access – but I'm only getting what we need for this meal. I'm not eating with you tomorrow!'

Back at the flat, he busied himself in the kitchen. The cat wandered in to join him and jumped onto the work surface. He stroked it and licked his fingers. By then, I was so hungry that I didn't care. After the meal he lit a briar pipe, and stared at the white wreaths of acrid smoke with some satisfaction.

'Good for mellowing out.' He sighed. 'Tomorrow's a practical day; I'm going to start sorting out this mess.'

'Good!' I said, but something in his tone made me doubt his sincerity. 'Doesn't it frustrate you? The lack of order, the fact that everything's everywhere. I know that I've got a thing about order, but I've never come across anything like this. I mean, *you can't find things!*'

'I can,' he said. 'That's unfair,' and to demonstrate his point he picked up six cassettes from the dozens strewn about the floor and half-heartedly put them into their boxes.

*

WEEKEND IN WOOLWICH

In bed he grabbed me roughly, without affection or passion.

I turned away, disturbed, surprised that he thought me still interested. My fault; I should have gone home, but I'd left it too late.

'I didn't mean to get upset the other night,' he murmured.

'But why were you? Look, take your hands off me!'

'You've been here over a whole day now, and you *still* haven't taken any notice of my artwork. I shouldn't have bothered doing it.'

That's true, I thought. It might have saved a good deal of pain and argument.

But instead I said: 'Andrei, surely you do it for yourself, for your own satisfaction, and not just for admiration? If it's admired and praised, then that's a bonus, but that shouldn't be its raison d'être.'

'You're not interested, are you?' he wailed. 'Call yourself an art historian? You're a fucking charlatan! A fake! You're here under false pretences. I wanted you to see my work and you said you would! I thought the mark of a real historian was to take an interest in artists' work. You're a joke! A bad joke!'

'I thought you asked me here because you wanted to see me; not because you wanted the services of a critic plus unlimited praise....'

Again he started to sob. There was no point in further discussion.

'And I thought you were interested in literature,' he went on. 'I offered to read you some of my work; I've really made an effort, but you don't want to know, do you? I may as well talk to thin air, turn my face to the wall ... like my fucking neighbours do! You can't blame them, can you? No! It's people like you who force them to! And you – you! – *you pretend you're intelligent!* Ha ha! If that's what university does for you then I'm glad I dropped out. It's all fucking elitism, snobbery. You're a cunt! A rotten, fucking cunt!'

My God! I thought, ignoring his obscene insults.... What should I say? What can I say? He thinks his scribblings are literature!

Last Thursday evening at some low-down, beer-bespattered, nicotine-stained Waterloo pub was still fresh in my mind. Why hadn't I heeded the warnings? Was I, as he claimed then, in love with him? How else could I account for my blinkered vision, my lack of judgement?

As I walked in he waved a small notebook in the air:

'I've been writing,' he announced. 'Yes! Look! I wrote three pages today while I was having lunch. I'm going to read them to you; you'll be the first to hear them. None of my other girlfriends have heard my work, so you're honoured. I mean it! That's because I worship and adore you. This is important.'

He opened the biro-splodged notebook. Instead of the beautiful italic hand I'd hoped for and expected, the pages were covered in an unpunctuated scrawl which meandered up and down wildly.

'Is this deliberate?' I asked. 'I don't wish to be pedantic, but what about punctuation?'

'Eh?'

'Well, surely it's considered the good manners of writing? It makes for a better understanding of the work. If I were to try to read it alone, I'd find it difficult.'

'I'll sort that out when I publish.' He grinned. 'Plenty of time for that; right now I'm too busy to bother about it. All that's elitist rubbish anyway; a stupid convention. Besides, this is good.'

'It's not "elitist rubbish," I said. 'You could punctuate as you go along. Isn't that easier?'

'Dunno. Don't think so. Don't see why I should. Anyway, I'm more worried about copyright. How do you copyright something? I mean – like – we're all living on the same planet, so I don't understand how you can. It doesn't make sense....'

'You've lost me there,' I replied. 'I don't understand what you're trying to say. I don't know why you're making so much fuss about copyright: once you've written it, it's yours. Anyway, there are stringent rules governing it and you can find out more when the time comes. Just write, get on with writing. If you don't plagiarise, don't worry. Worry about copyright when you publish.'

'Plagiarise?' he asked. 'How d'you mean? I'm interested in words. I'm a wordsmith, you know, but I don't know that one.'

'"What you copy, you steal, what you remember is your own", I quoted. 'I think that Burges – Cardiff Castle – said that, but it's rather good, isn't it?'

He ignored me. 'Let me read, let me read!' he shouted.

It was nonsensical, but despite the illiterate style, there were occasional and unexpected flashes of wit, odd acerbic observations. A nice line about 'self-satisfied bores' – and there were many holding forth in that pub – a few jibes about 'corporate sellouts'. For the most part, though, it was poor and I am sure that I looked puzzled.

'I'm really into writing, you see,' he added proudly. 'You can tell, can't you? I'm a natural, ain't I?' He broke off, gulped his beer, and nodded confidentially: 'And I've been trying to get into Automatism.'

Oh no! I thought.

'I didn't think that you could really try to get into that.' I said, in measured tones. 'Either it's there or it isn't. Surely the idea is that you go to a café, a bar, or a café-bar, and write down whatever surfaces. It mustn't be modified by analysis, convention, or reason. Just get it down. Don't analyse.'

'Oh, but I do! I do!' he claimed. 'Just look!' And he brandished some pages of hieroglyphics.

'You're joking! Very clever! This looks a bit self-conscious to me – a statement of style.... Can you really claim that these are your unconscious thoughts? Is your head really full of that? Come on, you're fooling yourself!'

'You're nasty!' he said, looking infuriated. 'You're unfair. You're not trying ... I'm an artist.'

I tried to change the subject but he picked up the book again and pointed out his sketch of three matchstick men around a pub table. I noticed with some misgivings that it was like a child's doodle.

Yes, I thought. A dreadful evening. I should have cancelled the weekend then.

He seized me again.

'Stop it!' I shouted.

'Even if you're not interested in my work, you're coming to my parents', aren't you?' he pleaded, his voice cracking, tears rolling down his face. 'You promised last week. *Don't, please don't, let me down.* I explained that they're getting old and need something to look forward to. I've started to call you my girlfriend, you see. I've had dozens of women, loads and loads, but I've never really had a proper, faithful girlfriend. They'd like me to have a family. I think they're worried about me. With a good woman, I could be different.'

'Andrei,' I said, 'it's getting late and I want some sleep. A lot has happened since Friday, and as for having a family ... isn't all that rather premature? I've not made any promises; I barely know you; I've not been seeing you long.'

'You don't know how important this is to me. I keep repeating it, but you don't listen; you hear the words but they don't really register! They've given up on me, but if you come it will give them grounds for hope.'

'That wouldn't be fair,' I objected. 'What about my feelings? I'm not your guardian angel. I'm not your saviour. I'm not a charity. I'm fed up of providing advice; why should I? Try to sort yourself out. That's your responsibility, not mine.'

He buried his head in the pillow, and my patience snapped: 'For God's sake, see a psychiatrist or a social worker!'

Again he wasn't listening.

'And you've forgotten about my sister, haven't you?' he cried. 'I told her we'd visit her Thursday. I'm not certain you'd like her.

You're such a snob you'll write her off as common. OK, she's got a loud, screeching voice, but her heart's in the right place. The kids are a bit unruly, too, but I've told her all about you.'

No! I thought, but I said wearily: 'Look, I've told you I'll meet your sister eventually, but I really don't want to discuss it now. It's long after midnight. I'm tired; let me sleep.'

'No!' he said. 'I can tell you've not done any tantric training. You wouldn't say that if you had because *you'd* be in control – not your body. It'd be mind over matter. Anyway, it doesn't matter – it's the weekend.'

'But it does,' I protested. 'I'll probably feel dreadful tomorrow, even if I have seven hours' sleep. My usual pattern has been disrupted. I've got a long day on Monday with loads of meetings. Right now, I'd rather listen to my body and get some rest.'

Again he started to weep.

'You've no time for me, have you?'

'What more do you want?' I snapped. 'I'm getting fed up with this. We've discussed your questionable theories; I've considered your point of view. Now it's your turn to consider mine. *I want to sleep!'*

'But you haven't said anything about my most important drawing.'

'Oh God! No! Please not again!'

The work he was referring to was a sketch self-portrait which I'd secretly titled The Artist as Computer Engineer/Master of the Universe. I'd noticed it earlier and had nothing to say. Now I'd had enough.

'You've pushed me into this!' I shouted. 'I think it's terrible. Ill drawn, messy, incompetent....'

He let out a loud groan and made as if to hit me.

'You bitch! It's not the drawing itself, it's the feelings behind it. I've given it years of my life.'

'I'm sorry. Your fervour's misplaced; you've invested it with something it doesn't have. It doesn't merit such attention. It's become puffed up in your imagination: a symbol, a cipher for something else. I don't think that others can easily see its worth.'

I dived off the bed as his fist smashed into my pillow.

*

SUNDAY 28 JUNE, 4.30AM

The early morning light was streaming in as I started to doze off. He shook me awake.

'Now what?' I demanded.

'I want you to come to Glastonbury with me and my friends. I've no money, but I'd really like to go. I could practise my tantras, I could mellow out or have an out-of-body experience.'

'NO! NO!' I protested. 'I don't want to go there, I certainly don't want to go in the company of your friends. I don't relish dossing or camping. I'm too old for that; I'd had enough of it twenty years ago. I don't want to – as you say – "mellow out". I don't want an out-of-body experience. And as for tantras ... forget it!'

'Cow! Stuck-up bag!' he shouted. 'You're narrow-minded; you haven't tried out any of these things. Just because my friends don't have a degree or sound posh like you, you've written them off. You think you're better than them. Well, let me tell you, you're not. At least they were supportive. They were great when I was in a coma.'

'I'm not narrow-minded! And anyway, just look at the mess that some of your "alternative training" has got you into. I could do without that. I'm not interested! I've nothing in common with these people; there's not the slightest reason I should find them interesting, except as head cases.' I started to laugh. 'And anyway, even if I wanted to go to Glastonbury, I couldn't afford to and I'm not subsidising you. I don't like your New Ageist ideas; I've had enough of that before. *Now let me get some sleep!*'

But he was trying to force himself on me.

'No! NO! That's enough!' I shouted. 'You're crazy if you think we're going to fuck again after all this. I don't want to. I'm not going to. Leave me alone.'

'There's something else I haven't told you,' he muttered petulantly.

'What? I can't stand much more.'

'The series of murders I did ... in the form of a pentangle,' he replied nonchalantly. For a moment something in his cold gaze unnerved me, and I almost believed him. Finally I said: 'That's not funny; I've read Hawksmoor, too.' And I turned aside.

I began to think – with mounting anxiety – of the past eight days; the contrast between his appearance and his flat, the number of times we'd made love. Correction: fucked, I thought. I've probably got every disease going now. I knew that, until I met him, there'd never been the slightest risk. Suppose, just suppose – and I began to feel sick – that he's laid addicts, prostitutes? What then? Part of me reasoned: don't be stupid. Prostitutes are generally sensible, more so than you. What are you talking about? He's attractive, if misguided. If he'd been injecting, I would have seen the marks. In any case, HIV isn't *so* contagious ... it's not *so* easy to get it.

I was just drifting off to sleep again when I awoke with a start: Well, I've really done it now. I wasn't to know; I really wasn't. But am I writing him off as 'infected' just because of his squalid lifestyle? Come on, come on, get a grip on yourself! You're being silly; you're prejudiced. We discussed all of that before we got into bed. All his relationships have, he claimed, been 'strictly safe'. He told me he'd only ever smoked, never mainlined.... but, I thought, I'm worried, I'm worried.

I woke up to find Andrei gazing at me tenderly. 'I'm sorry I was angry,' he said. 'Let's make love and forget it.'

I froze: 'I'm sorry, I can't. I feel as though I've been dragged through a hedge. I need time to think and consider; there are too many unanswered questions.'

'Like what?'

'Well, for a start, why did Vic react as he did when we told him we didn't want to go to the Heath?'

'Dunno.'

'Come on, Andrei, you must think me stupid.'

'Well, alright,' he signed. 'I'd got some dope in the car and we'd agreed to share it.'

'You should have told me; I'd have left you to it. I'm not into dope smoking; I don't find it as seductive as you do.'

He wept again; he hurled several cassettes out of the window.

'Very clever,' I commented. 'Anyway, I thought that today was going to be a practical one. You were going to start clearing out this shithole, and I was going to help you. I'll have to go home soon and you haven't even considered it.'

'I want to go with the flow,' he said. 'I can't do it just like that. Not after all these years.'

'Look, what you do with your place is up to you, but you asked for my advice. Now let's take some of those bottles to the tip.'

We loaded the car. Once there, Andrei lingered and started to poke about the skips.

'If you're going to go scavenging,' I put in, 'I'm not interested. I've got better things to do. You've got enough damned junk as it is; I'd rather go to The Dôme. I have had enough!'

*

At work the following day, the phone rang: Andrei.

'I'm missing you,' he said. 'I can't stand being away from you. You're so strong, so capable. Let's have lunch today; it's a long time till my sister's on Thursday.'

'Sorry, I really can't make it,' I replied.

I didn't have the courage to tell him that I didn't want to see him again.

WEEKEND IN WOOLWICH

In the evening, I went to The New Look. Home again! I thought, with some relief. It's good to be back. As usual, The Waiter, in his fetching little apron and black braces, was standing outside. He started to laugh as he saw me approach.

'What are you laughing at?' I called out. 'I don't see why you should find *me* so amusing. This is a *fine example* of "Notting Hill Angst": Sartre – the black beret, you see – and shades ... acquired in Brighton as it happens! I've even got a copy of Nausea in my pocket.'

'Anna, hello!' he shouted. And quieter: 'You look slightly dazed. Did you have a good weekend?'

'I'm not sure,' I replied rather doubtfully. 'I can't quite decide how I feel. It was rather like "The Curate's Egg" – "excellent in parts"! I'm indebted to my assistant Will for that gem,' I added.

'I thought that you had a date.'

'That's just the trouble, I did: Andrei – the Lycra-clad cyclist – the one I brought in here the other night.'

'Not that boring Army surgeon?'

'NO! For God's sake, no! "Mr *I'm On My Way* T-shirt". Anyway, I couldn't have predicted what he or his place would be like. It was a dump, a squat; quite beyond my experience. It said a lot about him, things I hadn't picked up on before. He looked so presentable, he sounded so knowledgeable; at first, anyway. I think that he was good at name-dropping and at latching onto bits of information – nodding vigorously at the mention of Existentialism – that sort of thing. I'm not sure that he really *understood* anything. He called on me to praise his artwork and writing. I couldn't! I couldn't.'

'Why not?

'They were rubbish, dreadful! He hadn't the slightest talent.'

'He didn't hurt you?' asked The Waiter, with a look of some concern.

'Physically no; emotionally yes. What really upset me was his wish that I should reform him ... I haven't the strength. But there are two awful things: I'm dreading Thursday because I'm supposed to be meeting him at his sister's, and I have to finish with him....'

'Anna, Anna,' The Waiter interrupted. *'Don't be silly. You can't see him; there's no point!* Ring him, write to him, but, for God's sake, don't see him! It will just be worse. He sounds unstable to me.'

'But it seems more honest, kinder, to tell him to his face. To ring him or write a letter might seem to him to be the coward's way out.'

'I can understand why you might feel like that. Anyone with a modicum of compassion would. *But don't see him!* You've done the hard bit, you've made the decision; there's nothing more to be said. Anyway, what's the other awful thing?'

'Oh, it's worse, far worse. Remember my letter-writing friend? The one I write to when I'm here? Well, I sent him a really horrible letter. I regret it. I was supposed to be seeing him soon.'

'You want to see him?'

'Yes!' I exclaimed. 'Good God, yes! It would have been our first real meeting in years. And now I've blown it. I've completely blown it.'

'Surely not.' The Waiter smiled. 'Have you spoken to him; have you written? Have you ever tried phoning? I believe you to be a resourceful woman. I wouldn't be at all surprised if the next time you come here, he's with you.'

'I hope you're right.'

'Now,' he grinned. 'Let me get you a drink. I can offer you the table near the gents' loo.'

'Charmed,' I said. 'But I'm not moving even if a crowd of seven come in!'

The Waiter, still smiling, brought me my kir.

I picked up my pen. Steve, I thought, I could scarcely blame you if you never wanted to speak to me again.

*

Monday 29 June 1992
London

Dearest

I'm sorry.

This sounds inadequate; how can I apologise for that horrible letter? If there was something I could do to wipe it out, I would. Can you forgive me? I can explain how and why it happened, but it would be easier across a café table than in a letter. For now, all I can say is that 'I blew my fuses'. The cautious letter arrived at an unfortunate time; I thought that you had had second thoughts, that it was all too much bother. You might have, of course; how should I know? Well, anyway, it coincided with meeting someone who made a pass at – and flattered – me. He said nice things; he paid me attention, made declarations. I began to think that I should put everything into whatever was going on. But now I need to speak to you. You once said that you thought me 'unusually caring and supportive'. All those who have taken the trouble to find out say that this is true. I hope that I might still be.

I signed it 'with much love' and ran across the road to post it. The Waiter, haggling with a large crowd, grinned.

On Tuesday, I was at my desk at 8am. At 9.30, feeling slightly queasy, I dialled Andrei's number. 'How are you?' I asked uneasily.

'Anna, I'm missing you,' he gasped.

'Andrei,' I blurted out, 'I'm sorry, you're not going to like this. I won't be coming to your sister's, and I don't want to see you again.'

'What?!' he shouted, sounding stunned.

'I'd rather not have had to phone you at work, but I couldn't see any sensible alternative. I'm sorry. The weekend was just too much.'

'Oh.' There was a catch in his voice.

'Goodbye,' I said quickly.

'Oh, so it's like that, is it?'

I put the phone down.

At noon, as soon as I decently could, I decamped to The Archduke, a haven of peace and quiet, tucked away in Concert Hall Approach under the arches of the Hungerford Bridge. Lush hanging plants, prominent green pipework, tables covered with jolly red and green oilcloths; the classical music occasionally interrupted by the low rumble of an overhead train. I ordered an orange juice and a large glass of house white. Now, Andrei – what can I say?

Dear Andrei

I'm returning the book that you gave me; perhaps you should save it for someone else. I'm sorry that I had to ring you today, but I couldn't see any other way. You ask me why. I just don't want to go on; I haven't the strength or the inclination for it. I have already explained that I've spent too much of my life giving and caring; there's not much left – I need something in return. I believe that each person is responsible for their own welfare, their goals, their directions. I'm disturbed by your demand that I advise, direct, reform you. I can't do that. Why should I? It's up to you. I don't find your dubious friends attractive, nor do I like the DSS subculture you and they move in. It's not my world, nor do I want it to be. I don't think you're the person for me. To spin matters out would only be more unpleasant for both of us.

I signed it 'yours', and put it and The Middle Eastern Route to Ecstasy into a jiffy bag. I dropped it into the postbox on my way back to the office. When I unlocked my door that night, though, the first thing I saw was a long, white envelope on my magic carpet. From Steve. Our letters had crossed. 'Damn!' I thought. I read it with mounting unease:

I only checked the post the other day to see if there was a letter from you. There was, and what a letter! It begins with a casual greeting and ends with goodbye. At first I felt shocked, but that passed quickly enough; now I feel sad at what might have been; sad that we might have misunderstood each other.

As I read, my eyes filled with tears. In comparison with my dismissive letter, it was kind, generous, understanding. I'd hurt and offended him; after all, he remarked, why should he have gone to so much trouble if he'd just wanted to set up an affair? If that was all he was interested in, why bother to write? He written more to me in a few months than to anyone else in years.

Although I can't agree with your reasons, I accept that your decision is sound. You're probably more hurt than you sound in the letter, but it would be pointless to argue with you. Love (no irony intended)....

Well, that's really that, I thought. What a shame. And I won't be able to contact him until tomorrow, *and* he might refuse to speak to me. I turned the page over. There was another line penned, it seemed, as an afterthought:

I'm incurable, you know. Quite incurable! I checked my pigeonhole this morning just to see if there was a letter from you. There wasn't, of course, but I couldn't help wondering.

Perhaps there's still hope? I thought.

*

On Wednesday morning I was woken by the metallic clink of the letter box opening. Eight pages from Andrei, three of them blank. Automatic writing? I wondered. It was a very odd letter, certainly: hand-delivered, misspelled, unpunctuated, deranged in its tone:

Look, I'm confusd when we parted on Sunday we paretd on the best of terms and then in the phone call u ask me how i am is this some kind a joke, a bad joke? a bad joke would be typical of you because you are a bad joke so I went to my sisters Tuesday instead and at 3 in the morning the kids kelly and cindy woke up and woke me up and they woke her up too but i took them downstairs and put on a video while I dozed on the settee but they kept jumping on me when k wanted apples slicing and c wanted oranges peeling, but what the hells that got to do with it anyway? you let me down, cow! me the first world war hero me who was shot down in a plane and who timed his re-entry to coincide with the DNA helix in the 1950s.

HOW DARE YOU YOU BITCH! I knew u would do this when you cryed off my sisters but i can already see its useless and thats the way its going to be so bugger off too. why should i trust love when it consistently lets you down i dont expect you to reply to this – [I won't I thought] – *because this is a new ventur for me and im writing this as much for me as for u but you know i can write anyway but i was in such a state the other night that i locked myself out and i had to go and stay with Vic we tripped we tripped all night* – [at this point writing took an unsteady lurch up the page] – *and we had a jolly good chin-wag. but you you bitch you cant be bothered with people can you? cunt thats all your good for* – [the writing now barely legible] – *you don't care about the likes of me youve got it made cos you only like your fucking buildings and pictures. So bugger off.*

Much followed in this vein with pages 5, 6 and 7 blank.

On page 8, a skull and crossbones, and then the real point: *Look you've been warned off me because of my drugs habit real, imagined and/or actual* followed by a *'quote from death row'*, and what I took to be blank verse: *'u can fly thro the window u can break your leg'*. The final line veered off the page altogether, but it seemed to imply: 'I've been written up and filed away, so I'm not needed'. True, Andrei, I thought. If you've written this to endear yourself to me, forget it. It won't work. I entered into everything openly and with hope, but that's it; any feeling I had has gone.

Later, at The Institution, I went for a blood test and spent an anxious morning awaiting the result and hoping that I wouldn't be recognised in the corridor.

'Negative,' said the doctor. 'A positive result would have been highly unlikely – in view of what you have told me – but have another in a few weeks just to make sure. In the meantime, don't worry too much.'

Perhaps Andrei told the truth about things that really matter? I thought. I'm certain that he's not all bad....

Back at my office I played my answerphone messages. There were two, both from Steve. I rang him immediately.

'Anna ... your letter.... Are you sure, really sure that you want to meet?' he asked. His voice sounded warm and welcoming, as though he were smiling.

'Yes! Oh, yes!' I said. 'I'd love to see you; I need to talk to you.'

'What about tomorrow? Would it be too short notice? I need to sort out one or two things here.'

'That would be perfect,' I said. 'Absolutely perfect.'

THE END